LOST

SECRETS

BERNARD GRISONI

ISBN: 978-1-7180-6626-7

To Lauralan,
Wife and partner,
Eternal love

CONTENTS

PREFACE

Otzi is the most famous mummy of Neolithic times, a man who lived in Europe 5,300 years ago. The study of the Otzi mummy provided a unique window of insight into day-to-day life during the Neolithic time—through his attire, what he ate for his last meal, his osteoarthritic disease, the cause of his death, and so on. However, no one knows the beliefs of the people during Neolithic times. Archaeologists have found intricate stone carvings from that period but no trace of written records. The places of worship they left behind provide the most information about their belief system. Celestial orientation of these monuments leads researchers to believe that the sun and the moon had a crucial role in their worship rituals. Of the countless monuments they erected, Stonehenge is the most famous. However, many other sacred places, such as Newgrange and Ggantija, demonstrate that very large populations labored on these constructions for generations. Silbury Hill, a man-made mound near Avebury was built five hundred years before the ancient Egyptian pyramids, and it was already as big as one of them. Still, archaeologists cannot comprehend how these laborers transported enormous stones to build their sacred places before the invention of the wheel. For instance, how did they transport the Dolmen of Menga's capstone thought to be the largest stone ever moved by Man in Europe weighing approximately 180 tons? Even with today's technology, it would take an amazing amount of effort and equipment to achieve such a daunting task.

Somehow, we assume that Stone Age people were simple farmers, but their technological prowess seems to indicate that they may have lived in more sophisticated societies that we currently accept.

As previously stated, it is still unclear what faith motivated the Neolithic people to invest so much time and resources into building these monuments. We are left in conjecture.

You are to enter the world of Tesimo, a young shepherd who lived in these Neolithic times. Based on archaeological findings, all the monuments he visits were either being built or already in use at the time.

ACKNOWLEDGMENTS

I want to thank my wife and children for their support and help during this long project. Many thanks to David for his advice and guidance as I was working on my manuscript. Also, I would like to thank my beta readers and editors: Elise, Gabrielle, Lauralan, David, John, Chris, Bob, Richard, Elton, and Emily. Their input was very helpful in the consecutive editions of the book. Thanks to Wikipedia and Google Earth for providing free information on this topic. Thanks to the Great Spirit for inspiration.

CHAPTER 1

SEPTEMBER 22, 1991
LATE EVENING

Night had long since fallen by the time Professor Alexander Zelinger left his office. Streetlights were reflected in the puddles of rain that covered the deserted streets and walkways. Zelinger was not concerned about the rain. Whatever the weather, he always walked from his house to work. His office was about twenty minutes from his house on Peter-Mayr Strasse, where he had been living alone since the death of his wife and the weddings of his two daughters. He enjoyed the walk, especially the quietness of Fritz Pregl Strasse, which ran along the picturesque West Cemetery for a couple of blocks. He saw his daily strolls as therapeutic, not just for the health benefits of walking but also to help clear his mind of the day's issues.

Zelinger was a large, burly man. Honest and decent, he was a scholar dedicated to his students. In his glory days, he had been a great field archaeologist who made important discoveries in the ancient ruins of Hazor in Israel. As much as he loved the fieldwork with all the travel and discovery, he now enjoyed teaching and mentoring aspiring archaeologists.

Guiding students and seeking out their potential was keeping him alert, engaged.

Tonight, however, Professor Zelinger was not enjoying his nightly stroll. His mind was preoccupied by the events of the week. He had just returned to town from a three-day time-consuming meeting that he viewed as a waste of time with the bean counters of the Education Ministry in Vienna. They went over his department budget and the inevitable budget cuts that were imposed by the administration. He had fought valiantly to preserve most of the funds allocated to his department, but he was forced to eliminate a position. On his way back to Innsbruck, he had decided that he would have to let his assistant professor go.

Even though it was past five in the evening when he arrived in town, Professor Zelinger went directly to his office to pick up the assignments he had given to his students earlier. He was surprised to find his assistant professor still at his desk, working on the recent discovery of a mummy. Because he was still preoccupied with the Education Ministry directives, Professor Zelinger made the mistake of immediately telling his assistant the unfortunate news. Zelinger simply wanted the faculty member to know that he had no choice and that the assistant professor's position was the only one he could eliminate. However, his assistant did not understand. He snapped at the news, yelling insults and storming out the door. The outburst surprised the professor; his assistant had always struck him as a levelheaded man. Nevertheless, tomorrow Zelinger would fill out the paperwork and give his assistant the official two-month notice of termination.

He was still shocked at the altercation and consumed by these thoughts when he crossed Freisingstrasse. He shook his head at the car with no warning lights on that was double-parked in the road. He couldn't see the inconsiderate driver.

When Zelinger was in the center of the road, the car suddenly sped forward, hitting him squarely on his side. The impact sent Zelinger flying through the air, and his body slammed against the pavement ten feet away. As he lay in the street, he opened his eyes. The car that hit him had stopped ahead on the road, its rear lights still dark. He was wondering whether he could move any limbs when he saw the car moving backward toward him. Zelinger lost consciousness; in that moment everything went black.

Bernard Grisoni

CHAPTER 2

DAY 1
VOREP

This village was not the first one that Thyssa had ever burned. It was routine to kill the fighting males, rape the women, and take new slaves. But today, he wanted to destroy everything, kill everyone. Thyssa was enraged, and this village was going to suffer for it. He had lost three more warriors in an ambush set up by these worthless peasants armed with long spears. He was sure that the men he was pursuing had instructed the peasants on how to stop Thyssa's horsemen.

Thyssa was the nephew of Urheimat, an important tribal leader who was rearing his herds of horses and cattle a few hundred miles east of this mountain village. Thyssa and twelve of the best riders were sent by his uncle to scout the western plains. Four days before, he had spotted a troop of walking warriors led by a man dressed in strange blue and red clothing. Thyssa had never seen blue clothes before. Certain that these were important men, he wanted to prove his worth to his uncle by capturing them and presenting them to him as a gift. A battle occurred when his riders confronted the warriors in an open field. Thyssa and his men were surprised by the warriors' fierceness. When he thought he had them cornered, the colorful leader and a few others escaped by jumping in a raging river bordering the battlefield. Thyssa and his men could not follow the men down the rapids with their horses and metal armor. They had to find a place to cross the river.

They paused first to mend wounds and count the dead. Thyssa's troop had killed nine of the pursued warriors, and he had lost six of his own men and five stallions. Thyssa was shaken when he found his firstborn son among the dead. What began as a quest to prove himself to his uncle had become one of vengeance. His heart was filled with hatred, and his blood boiled with fury.

Going from house to house, his warriors found the dead body of one of the men they were pursuing. That meant they had come here, and they were now gone. Thyssa was infuriated that his prey had escaped him once again and decided the village that took part would be destroyed. The remaining peasants fought a lost cause with their wooden clubs and spears. Their houses were burning, and the occupants were killed as they fled the flames. Thyssa was on a mission to raze this village—to burn it to the ground and kill every living thing he found.

He crashed open the doors of a barn, looking for hiding villagers or animals. The barn was empty, except for a haystack and a ladder leading to the attic. As he climbed it, he heard a man calling his name. He abandoned his search of the barn in hopes of more promising violence, lighting the hay on fire with his torch as he ran toward the voice.

One of his warriors pointed over the deep ravine separating the village from the other side of the mountain. Even from this distance, Thyssa could see the colorful clothes of his target. He rallied his remaining men, ordering them to jump on their horses. In a flurry of hooves, they all galloped in pursuit, leaving the burning village behind.

CHAPTER 3

SEPTEMBER 22, 1991
MORNING

S ophia Bruckner was looking through the window while the computer was loading the satellite picture she'd requested. She could hardly believe that she had been living in Innsbruck for one and a half years and had little to show for it. Other than her church activities, her social life had been pretty much empty. For one, she had realized that the older she became, the harder it was to make friends, especially when she knew from the start that her tenure in the city was temporary. That, combined with the experience she'd had with her last boyfriend, took away any motivation to put herself out there and meet new people.

Sophia was almost twenty-three years old. She was a slender, attractive woman of medium height, with black hair and blue-green eyes. She had spent her youth on the family farm near Linz in upper Austria. After high school, she went to college in Vienna to study anthropology. During her junior year, Sophia met a charming sociology major in her church choir. They dated for more than a year, and Sophia thought she might have found the man with whom she would spend her life.

After graduation, she decided to follow her dreams and get a master's degree in archaeology. It had been a difficult decision. Although the best program in the country was at Innsbruck University, her boyfriend needed to stay in Vienna, where he had a part-time internship while completing his own studies. They were to spend all possible weekends and vacations together, but less than six months later, she discovered that he was cheating on her while she was away. She was deeply hurt by his betrayal, and they had a painful breakup. This experience made her jaded. Since she dedicated most of her time to her studies, she was ahead in her classes. She was planning to complete her thesis and graduate within the next six months. However, if she didn't find a job by then, she would have to move back to Linz, back to the family farm.

Sophia did not like the stress of large cities, so Innsbruck, a lovely college town surrounded by beautiful tall mountains, suited her well. The Inns River, meandering slowly through the old city, gave her a sense of tranquility. As the capital of Tyrol, an Austrian province wedged between Germany and Italy, Innsbruck was the cultural and economic center of western Austria. The prestigious Innsbruck University was founded in 1669 and was now one of the largest universities in Austria. The archaeology department was located in Universitas Leopodino Franciscea, one of the oldest buildings on the campus, built in 1826 by Emperor Franz I. The four-story building with a severe neoclassic façade was alongside Innrain Strasse, with the back side facing the green waters of the Inn River.

Her thesis adviser was Professor Alexander Zelinger, the head of the archaeology department. She liked Professor Zelinger because he was an honest, fun-loving, and generous man. She learned that just before she joined, he had negotiated with the administration to restore—on his dime, no less—the attics above the department. The growing archaeology department had a small corner of the fourth floor and had become overcrowded. In order to increase working space for his graduate students, Professor Zelinger thought to expand his department into the attic above. When the authorization was given, he personally renovated it with the help of his students. The attic was connected with stairs that led up from what used to be the department's study room.

She even liked how Professor Zelinger had decorated his office. He didn't care for the government-issued furniture that furnished the other professors' offices. Since that was where he was spending most of his time these days—writing papers, going over his class notes, grading exams—he had brought his own antique furniture made of cherry, ash, and oak woods. He had stocked one of his cabinets with a bottle of scotch, which he liked to drink while smoking his afternoon cigar or for occasional celebrations. His office felt more like a private study than a room in a public building.

Knowing her tight financial situation, Professor Zelinger had given Sophia the job of lab assistant, providing her with a small but much-needed salary. Her job was to maintain the institute's artifact collection and display them to students doing lab work. A perk of her job was to have a tiny personal office on the fourth floor. For a graduate student, it was prime real estate and even came with its own window overlooking the river winding its way through town. She also had free access to the department's computer system, which she used for her studies. Her research was focused on Malta's Neolithic culture and more specifically on the interactions and influences Malta's culture had with the other prehistoric peoples of Europe.

Malta was a small archipelago in the Mediterranean Sea, fifty miles south of Sicily and two hundred miles north of Libya. The Maltese archipelago consisted of two main islands: Malta Island and Gozo Island. The islands were very small, with a combined landmass covering only 122 square miles, about the size of a square measuring eleven miles by eleven miles, making Malta one of the smallest countries in the world. Regardless of the islands' small size, Malta's earliest temples were some of the oldest freestanding stone structures in the world. They were witness to one of the most sophisticated cultures in the ancient world. Sophia would have loved to visit these temples and perform actual fieldwork for her research, but budget restrictions precluded any such hope. Thus, her research was mainly theoretical, based on published literature and historical documents.

Sophia learned that hunters or farmers coming from Sicily had settled in Malta approximately eight thousand years ago. For two thousand years they lived in caves and huts, and then, suddenly, about 5,600 years ago, they started building magnificent temples. The first built was Ggantija,[1] located on Gozo. Ggantija is one of the oldest known megalithic temples in the world, five hundred years older than Egypt's pyramids. Several of the stones used to build Ggantija's walls weigh more than fifty tons, making them some of the heaviest stones moved by prehistoric people. Some of the temple's thresholds were carved from a single stone slab weighing more than forty tons, the portal opening hollowed out of the slab's center. These enormous stones fit each other perfectly, an amazing achievement considering that Malta's inhabitants only had stone tools available for the work. Sophia could hardly imagine the incredible amount of time and resources it took to build this temple, as well as the close to fifty others known on the bigger sister island of the

Maltese archipelago. The temples' construction and orientations proved that these ancient architects had sophisticated mathematical, engineering and organizational skills far beyond what would be expected from simple farmers. Sophia had no doubt that it took millions and millions of working hours to build these temples, and she wondered about the beliefs and motivations of these people who had dedicated so many resources to this effort.

Malta and its temples prospered for two thousand years. Then, forty-five hundred years ago, the settlers vanished, and the temples were abandoned. The predominant theory is that the island inhabitants depleted the resources of these tiny islands and migrated back to Sicily, their mainland.

Despite all that she learned, there were still many mysteries surrounding these temples. For one, the temples were constructed on these desolate islands without any architectural antecedent. The cloverleaf architecture of these temples was completely unique to Malta. Prior to Ggantija, no buildings of this kind had been found in the region or in any other part of the world. There was not even a trace of any substantial wood structures on the island prior to the stone temples. These gigantic temples, with their unique architecture, seemed to have sprung up from nowhere yet were complete in every way. And what surprised Sophia the most was that the ancient builders started their construction with Ggantija, the largest and most remote of all of Malta's temples.

Sophia also often wondered why such a small archipelago like Malta needed so many temples. It was doubtful that Malta had the resources to support more than ten thousand people during that period in time. [2] She wondered how Malta found the resources to feed the generations of workers who built these megalithic temples.

She was also curious to understand how such minuscule islands could support the great numbers of worshippers expected to visit these temples. Food and supplies must have been brought in from neighboring lands. This led Sophia to believe that Malta had a strong influence on a much larger territory than conventional theories allowed.

Sophia had searched through countless publications hoping to understand why people from Sicily went to the trouble of sending workers to build Ggantija on the tiny rocky island of Gozo, instead of building it on their much larger island, where a workforce and supplies were more readily available. What was so special about Malta's islands for these people to go through this enormous effort? What specifically happened in Malta that caused these people to commit so much of their livelihood to building and maintaining these enormous structures? These puzzles were the driving questions behind Sophia's research.

Neolithic people made no written records, so it was impossible to know with certainty their motivation and worship rituals. Statuettes found on site suggested that these ancient Maltese worshiped a goddess—a matriarch or mother figure. Based on physical evidence found on site, Sophia learned that at one point in their history, Malta's worshippers practiced some sort of animal sacrifice.

Sophia first researched Malta's influence on the neighboring lands of Sicily or Italy, but none could be clearly found. She then studied all the other major European Neolithic monuments from that time period, including Stonehenge [3] in England, Brodgar [4] in Scotland, and Newgrange[5] in Ireland. Since these buildings were different in size and architectural style, it was accepted that each of these monuments was the result of local, independent cultures, with little or no interaction with each other. Most experts assumed that local farmers built them, and there had never been any Neolithic megalithic civilization across Europe. Surprisingly, she had to go as far as Ireland and Scotland to find the closest use of architectural elements similar to those employed in Malta, much farther than she would have expected.

She had noticed striking similarities between decorative spiral motifs found on Malta's temples and those found on the main front stone of the Irish temple of Newgrange. However, even though spiral engravings at both sites were intriguing, they could be coincidental and provided very little evidence to support any serious cultural interactions. In addition, those were the only similarities she could find. Newgrange was a monumental man-made mound of dirt and boulders, with a small chamber in its center, while Malta's temples were built of dressed stones, with large clover-shaped ceremonial rooms. And most important, these two places were located at least a thousand miles away from each other. She knew that artistic similarities between Newgrange and Malta were too weak to help her research, but still, she found herself often contemplating a possible long-range connection.

The night before, Sophia wondered how long it would take a messenger to walk from Malta to Newgrange. Within the research literature she had in her apartment, she was not able to find any information about the actual distance between these two places. This morning, she woke up early, and to satisfy her curiosity she decided to measure this distance using satellite imagery from the lab computer.

The satellite picture finally displayed on her monitor screen. She entered the coordinates of both locations. Using the computer software, she measured 1,576 miles from the center of Newgrange mount to the center of Ggantija temple.

One thousand five hundred seventy-six miles was certainly a great distance for Neolithic people to travel, especially considering crossing seas, rivers, oceans, and mountains. Sophia wondered how long it would take for information to travel that distance, if it were carried by messengers traveling mainly by foot.

Let's take as a first assumption that it was only flat land, she reasoned. *Walking at three miles per hour, ten hours per day, a messenger could travel the distance of 1,576 miles in 526 hours, or about fifty-three days. Assuming it would take twice as long to forge the rivers, climb mountains,* and cross the seas, it would take 106 days. What's that? Three and a half months. That's not so long after all. Even adding extra time for finding food on the way, it seems plausible that someone could go from one of these places to the other in just a few months. It might have been be possible for Malta and Newgrange to exchange information.

When she zoomed back on the Newgrange mount on the computer interface, what she saw made her jaw drop.

At that precise moment, Aton Schmidt barged into the office and asked, "Have you seen Gregory?"

Aton was assistant professor for the department, and since Professor Zelinger was in Vienna for administrative reasons, Aton was in charge of the department. Gregory was one of the students working under Aton's advisory. "I need Gregory's help! Where is he? I can't find him!" Then in a snap he added, "Since you are the only one here, I need you to come and help me. Bring your gear; we have to make a field visit. Also, grab a jacket because it is cold where we are going. This takes priority on anything you are working on. Let's go; people are waiting for us."

Sophia was stunned by his arrogance. *What a jerk! Luckily, I didn't have other plans for today,* she thought. She stood up and took her jacket and followed him.

Walking in the parking lot, Aton explained, "The Austrian police called because a frozen body was found a couple of days ago on a ridge of the Fineilspitze Mountain in the Otztal Alps, near the Italian border. The body was half buried in ice when hikers discovered it. They thought it was the body of a recently deceased alpinist, presumably the victim of some climbing accident. They alerted the police, who came the next day, and those *idiots* tried to extract the body from the ice using pneumatic drills and ice picks. As they uncovered the remains, they realized that the body was mummified and possibly much older than they'd thought, possibly hundreds of years old. They stopped the recovery at once, and the coroner's office called our institute to evaluate the age of the body and to decide whether it should be transferred to the morgue or to the university. The body is now half exposed, so they asked us to come quickly before it becomes damaged by animals, souvenir seekers, or weather conditions."

Sophia did not like Aton very much. She thought he was a haughty windbag and preferred to have as little interaction with him as possible. Shortly after she joined the institute, Aton invited her to his house for dinner, as it was customary for new researchers to be welcomed by the faculty members. He was single and lived alone in the house left to him by his deceased parents. His career had not been going very well, and he had not published any significant papers for several years. At first, she thought he was just cold and disinterested, but soon she sensed arrogance under his monotone voice. He seemed to enjoy ridiculing his students whenever he could. The few classes Sophia had with him did not leave her with good memories.

They climbed in Aton's gray Volkswagen Polo and hit the road. Today, Aton seemed unusually animated and talked continuously while driving. He went over and over the recovery protocol and methodology that they would have to follow with the police when they arrived. After ninety minutes of winding their way through the mountain, they finally saw the four-by-four emergency vehicle that was waiting for them in a parking area on the side of the road. They parked their car and climbed into the sturdy vehicle. They drove uphill on a dirt path for more than half an hour until they reached the edge of the snowpack. There, they were provided with snowshoes in preparation for a lengthy hike. A little more than one hour and two miles later, they arrived at the rocky outcrop where the body had been discovered. Near the body, another police officer and a couple of hikers were having an animated conversation. At their feet, Sophia could see a desiccated body half buried in the ice, along with straw and leather clothes and ancient artifacts.

It was immediately obvious that the mummified body was extremely old. As they assessed the best way to free the man from the ice, they recovered some of his loose clothes and gear as well. He was still wearing his left boot, which was made of what seemed to be multiple layers of rope, straw, and leather. The man had been dressed for cold weather; he had a thick woven-grass cloak, as well as a coat, a belt, leggings, and a loincloth, all made of leather. A broken arrow shaft was protruding from his back.

Aton carefully extracted the man's weapons, which were in remarkably good condition. More than the man's bow, Sophia's attention was drawn by his flint knife and copper ax. These suggested the end of the Neolithic era and the beginning of the Copper Age. A copper axe in this part of the world at that time period would have been the mark of wealth and power. Sophia guessed this man must have been some kind of an ancient chieftain.

Following a long-standing tradition, Aton named the mummified man the "Man of the Otztal," from the discovery's location.[6] They took notes on the location and preservation state of the mummy and its artifacts. While Aton was discussing the last details with local authorities regarding the safe removal and transportation of the mummy, Sophia stopped to observe the beautiful surrounding mountains. Mount Eisskugel was on her right and Mount Similaun on her left. Down the steep slope of the mountain, in a deep valley between her and Mount Mastaunspitze on the Italian side, the turquoise waters of Lago Di Vernago reflected the midday sun. The snow covering shimmered against the gray slate of the mountains. A burst of wind made her shiver. She had not planned for a mountain excursion, and her coat was not sufficient for the climate.

Losing herself in contemplation, she wondered what this man—she'd already nicknamed him Otzi—was doing on this isolated ridge, eleven thousand feet up the mountain. *And why would someone have shot him in the back in this desolate place?*

Sophia could not know that the last thing Otzi's now-mummified eyes saw before dying was the face of his son, yelling to him, "Father! Behind you!"

CHAPTER 4

DAY 4
THE RIDGE

Tesimo's scream came too late; an arrow pierced his father's back. Lightning fast, Tesimo grabbed an arrow from his quiver and let it fly. Tesimo's arrow stuck Thyssa above his right eye, stopping him in his charge, making him topple dead in the snow. On Tesimo's right side, Zuoz and Hryatan were charging the three other Yamna attacking them. Hryatan was holding a sword made of a shiny metal that Tesimo had never seen before. In a few deft moves, Hryatan reduced the spears of the two closest men into kindling. In one fluid movement, he hit one man's face and the other man's thigh. At the same moment, Zuoz's arrow stopped the third man dead. In an instant, all assailants were dead, their blood staining the fresh snow from the last storm. A great calm followed the echoes of the fight on this remote mountain ridge. When it was clear that there were no more attackers, Zuoz and Hryatan returned to where

Tesimo's father lay. Tesimo's cousin Druso, who had been frozen in fear during the whole attack, regained control of himself, dropped his bag from his shoulders, and ran toward the wounded chieftain. Tesimo was already at his father's side, assessing the severity of the injury. He was lying face down, bleeding profusely from his arrow wound. Tesimo could see that blood was also bubbling at his mouth. Through the gagging breaths of the dying man, Tesimo heard his father say, "Tesimo, lead these men to the pass." And after a few more incomprehensible words, Tesimo's father was gone.

Just like that, Tesimo lost his father. He started to cry, shocked that he would never be able to speak to his father again. Quietly, Zuoz placed a hand on Tesimo's shoulder.

"Tesimo, I am sorry for the loss of your father. It is clear that the Yamna are after us and I am afraid there may be more coming. We have to keep going!".

Hryatan tried to remove the arrow protruding from Tesimo's father's back, but the shaft broke, leaving the arrowhead inside his body. Since they could not bury him in this rocky ridge or carry him with them, they moved the body to a rocky recess and hid him under the snow. As was the tradition, they buried him with his belongings, including his beloved and invaluable copper ax. Zuoz and Hryatan then asked Tesimo and Druso to rearrange their packs to carry any provisions that were in Tesimo's father's bag. Meanwhile, they went to the dead Yamna to recover any weapons they could salvage.

From the edge of this frozen ridge, still sobbing, Tesimo looked at the lake down in the valley. He had never imagined his father would die so young. Death in his village was not uncommon, but he was not expecting his father to die anytime soon. Tesimo had always thought his father was in remarkably good health. He still had most of his teeth and was walking so much better since his last visit to the healer, who relieved pains from his back and knees. Now he was gone so suddenly, and Tesimo felt alone, lost. His heart was broken, and he didn't know what he should do now. As he redistributed the provisions in his pack, choking back tears, Tesimo replayed in his head the events of the last four days.

***

Tesimo was hunting wild goats with Druso when they saw the group of strangers approaching Vorep, their village. They ran to the village and told Tesimo's father, the village chieftain, that two men carrying a wounded warrior were coming. All the village men went to meet the strangers. Two were dressed with materials Tesimo had never seen before, neither animal skin nor the woven grass that all his kin wore but some kind of soft colored material unknown to him. One stranger had a brown cloak, a blue tunic, and pants made of soft brown fabrics. He had a long bow across his shoulder and a walking stick in his hand. The other man had darker skin. He wore a black cape over an orange tunic and carried on his side a sword nested in a sheath. The wounded warrior had a stab wound above the knee. Looking at his pale skin, Tesimo understood that the man had lost a lot of blood.

One of the oddly dressed men spoke to them in a strong, unfamiliar accent. "My name is Zuoz. I have a message for the high king. The lord of this valley, the Lord of Baden,[78] has given us safe passage and sent an escort of twelve of his bravest men to help us cross his lands quickly. On our way, we were attacked and lost most of our men. We left the royal road to escape our foe. We need your help to cross the mountains and continue our mission."

Tesimo's father immediately recognized the wounded man by his red tunic and bonnet as one of the men of the Lord of Baden. Tesimo had heard of them, but this was the first time he had ever seen a man from Baden. His father welcomed the strangers and took them to his house to offer them hospitality and any comfort he could provide.

From stories he had heard around the fireplace during the long winter nights, Tesimo knew that the Lord of Baden was the man who ruled over this mountain and the valley below. The Lord of Baden was the man who gave his father his beloved copper ax during a ceremony in Baden's grand hall, when Tesimo was still an infant. The ax represented his authority as chieftain and protector of the village. Tesimo's village was small and poor, and no one else in Vorep possessed such a beautiful thing.

Goat jerky, ground einkorn, and goat cheese were brought to the strangers. The village healer came and started to attend to the wounded man. Zuoz explained that he and his companion, Hryatan, were going north on the east side of the mountains. They stopped in Baden, where they learned that the Yamna,[9] horse-riding savages, were roaming the eastern countryside. So far, they had not attacked Baden's territories, but to be on the safe side, the Lord of Baden provided them with an escort to safely cross his lands. Unfortunately, two days ago a band of Yamna ambushed them. He and Hryatan would be dead without the sacrifice of Baden's warriors, who covered their escape through the woods and the river. They had not seen the Yamna since and assumed they had lost them in the mountains.

He thanked Tesimo's father for his hospitality and promised him they would leave by first light the next morning so they could cross the mountain as fast as possible to complete their mission to the high king.

Tesimo, who knew very little of what lay beyond his village, could not make sense of what this man said. He wondered, *Who is the high king? What is a horse?* While the strangers were getting some rest, Tesimo's father gathered the village's men in the largest barn. He relayed what the strangers had told him and added that he would go with the strangers tomorrow to guide them safely to the mountain pass. During his absence, his brother Ronolo, would be in charge of the village. He asked for two volunteers to go with him. Tesimo immediately stepped forward, and soon after, Druso, his cousin, volunteered as well. His father smiled at the two young volunteers and told them to make arrangements for a ten-day march.

After the meal, Hryatan instructed the villagers to arm themselves. "Get your spears, and I will show you how to fight the Yamna if they come," he said. As they were getting ready for their trip, the wounded warrior succumbed to his wound and died.

Later that night, Tesimo stepped away from the preparation and went to find Elena to bid her farewell. Elena was a beautiful, strong young girl he had loved all his life. They had been promised to each other, and their union was planned to be only a few moons away. They loved each other and had already stolen some private moments together, which only served to fuel Tesimo's desire for their first true night together. He found her waiting for him outside the meeting room.

"Tesimo, promise me that you will come back," she said to him, crying softly.

"I will. I promise. I'm going because I have to take care of my father. It should not take more than ten or twelve suns. I will be back. You too promise that you will take care of yourself! Will you?"

"I will be here when you come back. Be careful!"

They held each other in a tight embrace for a while. Then, reluctantly, they let each other go to rejoin their own families.

The travel party left the next morning before the sun broke the horizon. The only way to cross the narrow ravine that separated the village from the next mountain was a long uphill path that led to an overpass. From there, the path wound around the mountain toward a narrow valley and ultimately on to the main pass of the mountain ridges.

As the sun rose to light their way, they reached the canyon ridge opposite the village. They were horrified when they saw that the huts of their village were burning. With dismay, they could see silhouettes of warriors riding monstrous beasts, rampaging through the village. They watched as the villagers were mercilessly struck down as they ran out of their burning huts. The horrible beasts and their riders trampled some who tried to escape. Arrows pierced the backs of others before they reached safe ground.

Tesimo and Druso wanted to run back to the village to save what friends and family they could, but Tesimo's father stopped them. "Tesimo! Druso! Don't go there! You will be running to your own death. Look—they have seen us! They are coming after us!" On the other side of the canyon, the Yamna abandoned Vorep's burning ruins and rode north, following the path the travelers had taken that morning toward the canyon crossing. "We have to move forward—for our own lives and to lure them away from the village."

They decided to continue following the ridge they were on. Tesimo's father led them over the narrow rocky path, hoping that the riders would not be able to follow. They walked all day, but as the sun lowered over the mountains, they were forced to stop. The path was too steep and impossible to travel safely in the dark.

After a sleepless night in the rocky slopes, they resumed their journey at daybreak. They moved as fast as they could, fearing the warriors were still on their trail. They finally reached the deep canyon, making their walk easier. The following day, thinking they were safe from the pursuing horde, they slowed to a more bearable pace. Suddenly, as if from nowhere, a group of terrifying horse-riding warriors wearing shiny pointed helmets appeared over a ridge and rode straight at them at an unbelievably fast speed. They fled the canyon, scaling the steep rocky mountain's face to escape the riding warriors. After hours of vigorous climbing, they reached the snowpack.

They could no longer see the warriors or hear the beat of hooves. At nightfall, they hid behind large rocks, where they would spend the night, hoping they had escaped the bloodthirsty killers. The next day, Tesimo's father led them on a climb through the frozen landscape, back to the path of the mountain pass. They thought the Yamna threat was over, but they had underestimated the tenacity of the Yamna warriors, who never stopped searching for them.

Now, Tesimo stood on the desolate mountainside. His father was dead, his village destroyed, his friends and family killed, and he was running away from bloodthirsty Yamna in the company of strangers on a mission for the high king. He had no choice but to obey his father's dying wish and guide Zuoz and Hryatan across the mountains.

CHAPTER 5

SEPTEMBER 22, 1991
EARLY AFTERNOON

Aton could hardly wait to have the mummy brought back to Innsbruck, but he needed the proper equipment to extract the body from the ice and transport it to the lab. The complex operation needed to be organized, and Aton wanted to return to the institute as soon as possible to begin the preparations. Since it was still technically a crime scene until the proper paperwork was filed, they were not able to retrieve the mummy's belongings. After urgently pleading with the police, Aton was able to take a sample of the straw from the mummy's shoe for carbon dating. The police enlisted the help of the keeper of the nearby Similaunhütte to guard the mummy against curious onlookers, animals, and the elements.

Making arrangements with the police on the freezing ridge took about an hour. The mummy was covered with a tarp, and Sophia and Aton hiked back to the four-wheel-drive vehicle that was still waiting for them. They finally returned to Aton's car and made their way down the valley. It was well past noon, and Sophia was starving, but Aton did not want to stop for food. He kept dictating notes to Sophia, listing in detail the necessary equipment for the mummy retrieval. Aton's attitude made it very clear he was not interested in Sophia's input or opinion but considered her only as a second pair of hands. Aton told Sophia to go to the Institute for Experimental Physics of Innsbruck and have the straw carbon-dated. He needed the results urgently to estimate the mummy's age for the police report.

After a while, Aton finally grew quiet, concentrating on his driving and thoughts. Sophia tried to wrap her mind around the incredible events of the day. Earlier in the day, she'd made a potentially significant discovery regarding Neolithic Newgrange, and with no time to consider the ramifications, she'd ended up on top of a mountain, face-to-face with what could be a Neolithic mummy.

That is just crazy, she thought. She would love to be part of the team that would take on the investigation once the police handed it over, but she knew it was Aton's bone to pick, and he was not the type to share opportunities, least of all with mere graduate candidates. Besides, what she found this morning could be a breakthrough on its own. If her observations were correct, it would keep her busy for the next few months. She couldn't wait to show her personal discovery to Professor Zelinger when he returned from Vienna.

It was midafternoon when Aton parked his car in his usual spot in the faculty parking lot of the university. Before disappearing from view, Aton reminded Sophia to go directly to the physics department and start organizing the analysis of the straw sample while he organized the transportation of the mummy to the university labs.

Sophia took a bus to the physics department, which was on the west side of the Inn River. The department was renowned for its contributions in physics, particularly in quantum mechanics, spectroscopy, and solid-state physics. Such hard science was not at all her specialty, but she appreciated having some of the top minds in the field only a short bus ride away. The bus left her on Technickerstraße, just a block away from the institute, which was housed in a modern ten-story concrete-and-glass building, just on the edge of the campus' park. She enjoyed the short walk; the weather in the valley was warm, a relief from the recent mountain chill. Students were relaxing on the lawns, enjoying the sunshine and playing pickup ball games.

Wanting to get Aton's errand over with as soon as possible, Sophia hurried on to the fifth floor of the building to the spectroscopy department, where carbon dating studies were performed. The reception area was empty, and she wasn't sure which office was which. She was just about to leave when a student peeked out of a side office to ask if she needed some help.

"I need to speak to the head of the physic department. I have an important carbon dating test order from the archaeology department. It's quite urgent." She smiled at the student and figured she'd give him a hint. "Freshly found mummy, possibly Neolithic."

The student explained to her that the department head was at a symposium in England, and he was not expected back in the lab for at least a week.

"Is there someone else in the department who could perform the test? It's very important that we have this test done as soon as possible."

"I would be happy to help you. I'm Erwin, the lab assistant. And you are?"

"I'm Sophia Bruckner, a graduate student from the archaeology department. The mummy was discovered in the Otztal Mountains, and we were asked by the police to help assess the approximate age of the remains for their report. We went there this morning, and I have here a sample of straw taken from the mummy's clothing that needs to be dated."

"I guess I can do that for you. I know how to operate the equipment," said Erwin.

"When can you start?" asked Sophia.

"Well, I can't do it today. I can't stop the experiment I've started, and it will take another two hours before it's over. I can start tomorrow if you're ready. I would not mind taking a break from my research and analyze that for you. Anyway, it seems more exciting than what I am currently doing."

"Thanks—that would be great. Would it be possible to start first thing in the morning? I have the sample right here. What else do we need to get started?" asked Sophia.

"I don't know about first thing in the morning. We need first to determine the analysis protocol and sample preparation."

"Can we do it now?" inquired Sophia.

"I told you; I can't do it right away," replied Erwin as he looked at his watch. "I should be able to wrap up my work here around six, so what about meeting after six this evening?"

"That would be fine! Where do you want to meet?"

"I skipped lunch today; I'm hungry," answered Erwin. "What would you say about grabbing a bite together while we organize tomorrow's workday?"

"Um, let me see." Sophia was also starving, but she didn't really want to go to dinner with this guy, although he seemed nice and was kind of cute. She thought she couldn't just refuse a work dinner, especially with a colleague who just agreed to set aside his own work on her behalf. Somewhat hesitantly, she accepted.

"Great!" Erwin said. "What about going to Branger Brau? Have ever been there?"

"I know where it is, but I've never been there," answered Sophia.

"You've never been there? Then that's decided; we're definitely going to Branger Brau tonight. You'll love the place. What about meeting there around six thirty?"

"Okay. Thanks for your help. See you tonight," said Sophia as she left the lab.

It was close to five when she finally got back to her office. All day she had been eager to get back to the lab's computer to verify this morning's discovery. As she pulled up the satellite pictures she had looked at earlier, she wondered if it had just been her imagination. Again, she carefully plotted the line from the center of Malta's Ggantija temple to the center of Newgrange. It was undeniable. Right there, in front of her eyes, was something that she had never read about anywhere before: the Newgrange chamber was perfectly oriented toward Malta, located more than a

thousand miles away.

Is it possible? she wondered. *Could this have been done intentionally? Could this support that there was more connection between Newgrange and Malta than currently thought possible?* Sophia knew that Newgrange was built at approximately the same time period as the Maltese temples, starting about 5,300 years ago. But what made Newgrange different was its size.

Newgrange's mound was the largest tumulus in the world, made of an enormous number of boulders—250,000 metric tons, piled over five hundred large stone slabs that were used for the construction of a vaulted inner chamber and as outside peripheral decoration. Each boulder was a foot or more in diameter and was brought from several miles away. The larger stone slabs were six to twelve feet tall and weighed many tons each. They somehow were transported, largely uphill, from a rocky formation called Dundalk Bay, located twelve miles away. The domed chamber was nearly twenty feet high with three side alcoves. The chamber could be reached through a sixty-three-foot-long narrow corridor. The mound was covered evenly with soil several yards thick. It long had been established that the corridor was oriented toward the direction of the winter solstice sunrise. In addition, the length of the corridor was sloped and curved in such a way that only a narrow beam of sunlight would pass through, illuminating only the chamber's floor once a year for seventeen minutes, during the winter solstice. The whole façade of the building was adorned around the corridor entrance with large white quartz rocks. It was estimated that it would have taken a minimum of thirty years to complete the Newgrange tumulus.

Sophia wondered how many men would have worked to build the mound. She took out a pad and did some quick math.

Two hundred fifty thousand tons of piled boulders come to about five hundred million pounds. Assuming the boulders have an average weight of fifty pounds each, that means that there are about ten million boulders on the mound. The boulders were brought from deposits located four to ten miles away. So let's reasonably assume that each worker would have been able to carry only two boulders per day over such a distance. At this rate, it would have taken five million working days just to transport the boulders to the site. For a thousand men, it would take five thousand days to pile up these stones. That comes to fourteen years working every single day. If we account for rainy days or other weather conditions preventing the work, thirty years seems a reasonable estimate. But if a thousand men were working year round on the project, there must have been an army of people providing food and other needs for the workers. And that's just for the boulders! What about the five hundred large stones weighing five tons each and the yards of soil on top of that? That construction must have been of monumental importance for the surrounding populations to support such a difficult project over so many years.

This immense man-made mound was one of the greatest cathedrals of the Neolithic Age. Sophia couldn't help but be amazed at the incredible achievement of people whose technology didn't even include the wheel. Why and how they made these monuments was anyone's guess, since not one written record has been found from the time when Newgrange and Ggantija were built. Sophia knew from her archaeological studies that these temples were built at about the same time, and they were maintained for more than fifteen hundred years before being abandoned. The purpose of this type of construction was not really known. They were assumed to be a mortuary sanctuary; these tumuli also were called passage tombs.

Newgrange and the other tumuli of the region showed that the Neolithic people from Ireland had sophisticated knowledge of architecture, engineering, and astronomy. The monuments suggested a highly organized, settled society with complex rituals concerning the treatment of the dead and contact with the ancestors, requiring permanent sanctuaries. Archaeologists believed that Newgrange, alongside hundreds of other passage tombs built in Ireland during the Neolithic era, was evidence of a religion that venerated the dead as one of its core principles. They also believed that this "cult of the dead" was just one particular form of European Neolithic religions, as other megalithic monuments displayed evidence for different regional religious beliefs, many of them centered around solar worship.

It was clear that the whole structure was designed around its center chamber with the chamber's corridor oriented toward the winter solstice sunrise, but for Sophia it seemed more like a temple of life than a temple of death. For Sophia, capturing the first rays of the sun during the winter solstice was marking the regeneration, the rejuvenation of earth for the new year, the victory of light over darkness, life over death.

Sophia was stunned by the perfect alignment of the corridor toward Malta she had just discovered. Did it mean that there was much more to know about Newgrange than she had already learned in school? She realized that a person sitting in the chamber, looking through the entrance opening, would be facing Malta at any time of the year. Her mind was racing with the possibilities. *Religious monuments were often oriented in a direction that was significant for the worshippers, like early churches facing the Holy Land or the mosques facing Mecca. Is it possible that Newgrange was built in such a way? But how could it be that Newgrange's orientation toward Malta could also be the orientation with the winter solstice sunrise?*

This discovery, along with the similar spiral engravings, suggested that Newgrange and Malta could be much more closely connected than currently was accepted. Feeling dizzy with the implications, Sophia was preparing to leave her office to meet Erwin when she overheard Aton having a heated argument with Professor Zelinger. Apparently, the professor was back from Vienna, and she had been so engrossed in her research that she had not heard him entering the office. Sophia quietly approached the professor's door to get the gist of the argument.

It seemed to be a dispute about budget cuts and layoffs. "I'm sorry, but your position will be eliminated," she heard Professor Zelinger saying.

"That's not possible. You are not going to take the mummy away from me," barked Aton.

"There's nothing I can do, Aton. We don't even have the funds to study the mummy. It will be brought to the university and stored here until we have additional resources to study it," Professor Zelinger responded

After a pause, the professor explained in a calm voice that over the past few years Schmidt's performance had not been stellar, and in light of the budget cuts, he could not justify keeping him over others. The decision was made, he would file the paperwork, and tomorrow Aton would officially get his two-months' notice.

Sophia hesitated at the door as Aton became more and more heated, insulting Professor Zelinger and the ministry. The professor seemed to remain calm in the face of Aton's insults and said, "I'm sorry, but my decision is made. If you don't want to understand, you can pack your things and go."

Fearing she'd be caught eavesdropping, Sophia retreated to her office, flicked her light off, and stood in the corner out of sight. She heard the professor's door slam shut. From the shadows of her office, she saw Aton Schmidt storm down the hall and slam the main door as he left the department. He looked furious. Sophia was glad she had hid in time. Aton looked like he had completely snapped. Sophia looked at her watch and realized she had to go, or she would be late for her meeting with Erwin. She decided her talk with Professor Zelinger could wait until tomorrow. She ran down the stairs and rode her bike over to Branger Brau.

Erwin was waiting for Sophia when she arrived at the restaurant. As they waited for the server, they talked about themselves and their aspirations. She learned that Erwin was twenty-seven years old and had been born and raised in Vienna. He was the youngest child of the family and had a brother and a sister. His parents were proud of his achievements and always encouraged him in his studies as an applied science engineer. It also happened that Erwin was good in mathematics, holding a degree in material science engineering with merits. With an industrial grant, he was pursuing physical engineering research through the PhD program at the Innsbruck Physics Institute. He had moved to Innsbruck about three years ago and was planning to graduate by year's end.

As he talked, Sophia couldn't help but notice Erwin's dark blond hair and hazel-blue eyes. Without his lab coat to disguise his shape, Erwin looked quite fit, with muscular arms and shoulders. She liked how he expressed himself, confident but without arrogance.

As they were finishing their entrées, a couple leaving the restaurant passed by their table and waved hello to Sophia. "Members of my church," she explained to Erwin. "They were the first people I met when I moved to Innsbruck." Like most Austrians, Sophia had been raised Catholic, and she found a great deal of peace and comfort in her faith. She told Erwin that she enjoyed going to church because it was the one place where she always felt welcome, especially after moving to a new city like Innsbruck.

"What about you, Erwin? Do you go to church?" asked Sophia.

"No, not right now."

"I see. You're welcome to come to my church if you're ever interested."

"Thank you. I'll think about it. Just for you to know, I think of myself as a Christian, but I am not limited to Christianity."

"I beg your pardon?"

"It's a long story. You see, like everybody else in Austria, I have a Christian education. But after I learned about the history of the church and its abuses of the past, from the Inquisition to slavery, I lost my faith and became an atheist. Later, quantum physics stretched my conception of reality, and it made me think more deeply about my inner self."

"In what way?" wondered Sophia.

"You see, quantum physics is telling you that the particles constituting your body are not really here. They can be anywhere in the universe at any moment in time. It's just that you have more chance to find them where you body is, but nobody knows where they are at any specific moment in time. Actually, they are even not little beads but waves of probability coexisting with the whole universe. So for me, it became difficult to accept that my mind, my identity, and my thoughts were the result of random particle interactions. They had to be the construct of a greater order.

"I started to study teaching and practiced all the main religions, but I was not able to fully commit to a particular one. A few books cannot capture the immensity of God. This introspection brought me back to faith. I ended up believing that there is only one God, and that all religions are different facets of the same divinity."

"How did you come to that conclusion? Do you think that Yahweh is the same as Vishnu? Or Jesus the same as Buddha?"

"Not exactly. I think in the end, they all represent the same God. There is only one earth. We are all from the same Creator. I have friends from all horizons—Christian, Jewish, Muslim, Hindu, atheist. They are good people, and I love them very much. I am pretty sure that if there is a life after death, if there is a paradise, my friends will go to paradise. And I hope that I too will go to paradise one day. I cannot imagine that I would be separated from my friends in the afterlife. I think we are all going to be in the same paradise, regardless of the religion we practiced while we were alive. So if there is only one paradise, does it mean that there is only one God? What do you think?"

"I don't know," answered Sophia "Maybe it's a little simplistic. Do you mean that all religions are wrong?"

"No, not at all. What I meant to say is that I think that all religions have a common core that I would call the true faith. The true faith includes the belief that there is life after death, that each soul will be judged at death, and that our daily actions on earth affect how we will spend the afterlife. The true faith is telling you to treat others as you wish to be treated and not to hurt humans in the name of God. It doesn't mean that people should not defend themselves, but people should not attack others in the name of faith. That's why I think that no matter what religion one is practicing, everyone respecting the true faith will go to the same paradise."

After a pause, Erwin added, "To me, the differences between religions only reflect the understanding that peoples had at different times and places in history. For cultural and traditional reasons, most people practice a specific religion not by choice but because they are born into it. I think that in the end, we are like bees landing on a light box made of colored glass. Some bees see the light blue, some see yellow, some red, and so on. But in the end, there is only one light inside the light box. "

"Interesting. So you are telling me that it doesn't matter which aspect of the divinity you worship."

"Correct. Faith is greater than God's name. As long as your heart is in the right place, we all believe in the same God. In the end, all religions lead to the same God."

Sophia wondered where they were going with this discussion. "I'm not sure I can follow you that far," she answered. "I agree that there may be some commonalities between religions, but there are also major differences. Look—I too studied religions in anthropology classes, and I know that what is holy for some is blasphemy for others. I respect other religions, but I am comfortable with my own faith. It brings me hope and peace."

"I understand," said Erwin. "I am not trying to convert anyone one way or another. I just wish that the world's spiritual leaders could be more focused on religions' common aims and values, rather than on their differences.

You see, I am concerned about the critical issues that affect our world, like overpopulation and the exhaustion of natural resources. Humanity can address these problems only if we all work together. We need the world religions to unify all of us in solving the world's issues. Or maybe we just need a new global faith in better accord with today's scientific knowledge, and that could bring people together."

"You don't think it is bad to mix science and religion?"

"I am not proposing to mix them. Science is not an act of faith. It is established on verifiable proofs. Science cannot prove or disprove the existence of God, but it can help us to understand God's creation, as well as what God is not. I mean, people used to see diseases or storms as acts of God. We now know how diseases arise and how to cure many of them. We now know that storms are weather patterns, and that human activity may actually affect the climate.

"Scientific theory also tells us that our universe is expanding and that everything in it is destined to annihilation and randomness. However, in that flow of chaos, we can see creation of temporary order. In each living creature is a force that assembles and organizes particles to form a physical body. And we can see that over the last 3.5 billion years on earth, evolution has brought more and more complex organisms from the elementary forms that initially appeared. To me, science is actually showing us how God works, the deep reach of His hand in the fabric of the universe, and His infinite patience in creating the human species."

"Looks like these questions have tormented you often."

"Yes, I guess. It's more like a curse. I'm sorry I took the conversation so far off track. I just meant to say that it's not because I currently don't go to church that I don't have a spiritual life. Sorry it took so long to say so little."

"It's okay. It's always interesting to learn people's thoughts. I must say that I will have to think a little more about our discussion before I give you my response. That's a lot to digest."

"Again, I'm sorry. We still have to plan tomorrow's workday if we want to start first thing in the morning"

Wow. This guy is definitely different! thought Sophia.

They quickly went over the protocol they would use to perform the carbon-dating analysis of the mummy. Sophia took many notes for her report as they worked on the details for another half hour. As they left the restaurant, Sophia thanked Erwin for an excellent dinner. After deciding to meet at the Physics Institute the next morning at eight o'clock, they went their separate ways.

Sophia was feeling tired as she bicycled back to her apartment. It had certainly been a long day, and she could scarcely believe all that had happened so quickly. She pondered if she liked Erwin or not. She didn't expect to have such a deep discussion about humanity and religious beliefs with someone she had just met. Even though she didn't agree with him on many points, she had to admit that his views had their own logic, and after all, they were harmless and well intended. Actually, it was courageous of him to take head-on the fundamental questions of life. Indeed, it had been refreshing to talk to someone about something other than the trivialities of life. And she also thought his cuteness was a bonus. She enjoyed an evening with an attractive academic acquaintance. Handsome and a little bit crazy, which was appealing in its own way. *It is a shame we didn't meet earlier*, she thought, bitterly remembering that Erwin would be leaving Innsbruck in a couple of months. *It might have been fun to date a guy like that.* Past memories of her last catastrophic long-distance relationship were surging back, repressing the pulsing feelings she started to have for Erwin.

As she locked her bike on the rack in front of her building, she heard a police siren wailing in the night but thought little of it at the time.

CHAPTER 6

Day 5
The Lake Village

Though he was only fourteen, Tesimo was well built, tall, and strong for his age. He had black curly hair, brown eyes, and a wide smile. He was quick, curious, and daring. His skin was deeply tanned by the sun. His right leg bore a gnarled scar from when he fell while climbing the rocky slopes around their village. Tesimo was always the one leading Druso to explore the other side of the mountains that surrounded them.

Druso was the same age as his cousin Tesimo, with the same curly hair and skin complexion, but his frame was a little broader and of shorter stature. They had been best friends since they were crawling. They spent their days hunting and herding wild goats and exploring the mountains. Tesimo, being clever and skilled with his hands, always invented new traps for the rabbits and small game. Druso was better with animals and had a treasured dog companion that accompanied them hunting and herding that he had now assumed was lost after Vorep's destruction. Both had made their own bows of ash wood and goat guts, as well as the twenty or so arrows fabricated using sharp flint stones and straight three-foot shafts of dogwood held in the quivers they were wearing around their shoulders. Tesimo's bow was known in the village to be the most accurate. Tesimo could kill a wild goat from more than one hundred feet away.

Both cousins wore heavy jackets and pants made of woolen goat and rabbit skins and underclothes made of soft goatskin. On top, they wore parkas made of thick long grasses woven together and coated with animal grease to repel the rain. Their shoes consisted of straw held around their feet by a woven straw net and protected by a thick goat leather outer layer. They carried flint daggers on their belts and food provisions in their backpacks. Their backpacks were attached with ropes on a frame made with a tree branch bent backward and secured with lashes, like an overstressed bow. Their meager foodstuffs consisted mainly of dried goat meat, dried berries, and mushrooms. Tesimo's pack also contained a small bag with a flint and dark stones that sparked their nightly fire. He had flint blades, a small bucket made of birch bark, and a couple of copper blades taken from the Yamna. In a small bag, Tesimo carried a concoction of dried plants his healer had given him to treat wounds.

Tesimo was destined to replace his father to lead the village into the next generation. He had never expected that his life would be turned upside down so rapidly. He could not believe that Elena and his father, mother, brothers, relatives, and friends were all gone. Everyone he had known was now only a memory. All his worldly belongings were in the bag he was carrying on his back. He was left with only Druso and the strangers he was guiding to the main pass. After that, he was not sure what the future held.

Shortly after the encounter with the Yamna, a snowstorm commenced, and the small party traveled through freezing winds as quickly as they could for most of the daylight, with Tesimo as their reluctant leader. Tesimo only knew about the pass from a day when he had adventured with his father in this part of the mountain. He remembered his father pointing at certain faraway mountaintops and telling him that between them was a pass that led to the other side of the mountain.

Tesimo's strength was dwindling; he had never hiked so far or so fast. At night, instinct set in, and the group huddled together in a heap to keep warm. Finally, after two more days of excruciating effort, the group reached the main pass.

Covered with snow and with icicles in their beards and eyebrows, they stopped to rest for a while.

Zuoz placed a hand on Tesimo's shoulder and told him, "We have made it to the pass. Thank you from both of us for your valiant services. You are free to do what you want now, but you should both stay with Hryatan and me. You will die if you try to go back to your village in this weather."

Shivering in the cold, Tesimo and Druso looked at each other and moved away from the strangers to speak privately.

"We've fulfilled our promise," Tesimo said to Druso. "It's time to go back to the village. Do you think we can make it back alone in this storm?"

"I don't think so," answered Druso, his face dusted with snow. "This is a bad storm. Moreover, our village is seven suns away, and we barely have more than three suns of foodstuff with us."

"It's my fault, Druso," said Tesimo. "I made a wrong turn in the storm, and it took us much longer than planned to reach the pass. I made us waste two suns."

"It doesn't matter right now. Our chances to survive are better if we keep going ahead," Druso said reluctantly. "Your father told us that there are valleys on the east side down the mountain, four suns away from the pass."

"What about our village? What about all of them?"

"Tesimo, it hurts my heart to say it, but nobody in our village survived the attack. They are gone! All of them! You saw the village burning, as I did. No one could have survived the slaughter. And if anybody survived, by the time we get back they would already be in Baden for safety. The village is gone. Dying trying to get back now through the storm or waiting for better weather would not make any difference. If we follow Zuoz and Hryatan, we may find another village that will shelter us and where we can wait for better weather to go back to Vorep."

"Druso, I need to go back. I gave my word."

"Yes, we will go back, when it's safe to cross the mountains."

Tesimo told Zuoz and Hryatan their decision. They all agreed they needed to proceed quickly before their provisions were completely depleted. So they continued forward over the pass, further and further away from all that Tesimo knew. They climbed mountain after mountain and crossed passes Tesimo never knew existed. Their reserves of food were exhausted, and they were nearly starved when, three days later, they finally reached lower and warmer lands. The snow-packed mountains disappeared, and the landscape changed from rocky hills to pine forests on gentler slopes. Behind them, the mountain summits were still covered with dark clouds.

At the edge of the woods, Tesimo spotted a deer. He immediately drew an arrow and shot the animal. As they carefully approached the wounded animal, Zuoz grabbed the arrow shaft protruding from its side, softly pronounced a few words that Tesimo could not understand, and pulled the arrow from the mortally wounded animal. Druso and Tesimo quickly gutted the deer as Hryatan and Zuoz made a fire. As they were eating, Tesimo asked Zuoz what he said when he removed the arrow from the animal's flank.

"We are all one," Zuoz answered.

"What does it mean?"

"It means that we are all related. You, me, other people, animals, birds, insects, trees and plants, and even rocks, rivers, mountains, and valleys. We are all related; we are all parts of earth. We are all one."

Tesimo was intrigued by the thought. He was raised to believe that spirits animated the world. The people of his village used magic, spells, enchantments, and talismans that could entice the good spirits to protect them from the malevolent spirits. He believed the plants, animals, mountains, water, sun, and lightning were all spirits but each independent, each with its own will. He never imagined that they all could be united into one being.

The next day, as they reached the summit of a hill, they could see from the heights the next valley widening into a large plain that stretched to the horizon. After another day, they left the mountains behind and came to a valley with pine trees taller than any trees Tesimo had ever seen before. The air became warmer, and the last of the snow-patched slope behind them melted away to green under their feet.

They followed the course of a creek that led them to a marsh on the edge of the plain. On the marsh's edge, they saw a group of women and children collecting mushrooms where the woods met the water. The women and children saw the company approaching, and the children ran quickly into the shadow of the woods. It was not long before a dozen men emerged from the woods bearing spears and running toward them. Druso and Tesimo were tense and prepared their bows, but Zuoz told them to be quiet.

Before they knew it, armed men who questioned them in a strange language surrounded the companions. To the cousins' surprise, Zuoz started to speak to the warriors in their language. The men listened and cautiously lowered their spears. Tesimo relaxed his weapon as well and took in the strange appearance of these men. They were the same build as the men of his village but were wearing leather pants and woven tunics decorated with stitched patterns. Tesimo could see that the women hiding behind the warriors were wearing long soft leather dresses also decorated with stitched patterns. They all wore necklaces and plug earrings made of colorful shiny stones. Tesimo found the bright and polished surfaces of their stone weapons and jewelry remarkable. The effect was absolutely stunning.

The strangers led Tesimo's party to a nearby village nestled between the river and the woods. The cousins were amazed as they approach the village; it was built over water. The houses were built on platforms supported by pylons. The platforms were made of a latticework of tree trunks and small branches that were linked to each other with wooden passageways. As Tesimo's team was led to the village's center platform, women, children, and elders watched the companions and their escorts make their way through the maze of passageways. From what Tesimo could see, the houses were one- or two-roomed wooden huts with beaten clay floors, furnished with wooden benches and tables. From his counting, Tesimo estimated that there were at least thirty-five pile houses in the village.

A large man, who was clearly the village chief, welcomed them into his house, the largest of the village. The villagers offered them fish, meat, and wild fruits served in beautiful clay vessels, decorated with patterns unknown to Tesimo. The cousins had only ever known roughly carved wooden bowls and the clay bowls felt heavy and strange in their hands. Nevertheless, they all devoured the food that was offered to them. All the villagers gathered around the chief's house straining to see the strangers and hoping to meet them. At the end of the dinner, they were shown a place to sleep on a bed made of fresh straw and animal fur. Exhausted, they fell asleep as soon as they lay down, too exhausted to be haunted by thoughts of their destroyed village.

When they woke up the next morning, Zuoz suggested that they rest in the village for a day to recover from the brutal hike through the mountains. While they were eating the morning meal, Zuoz told the cousins that the village was called Inn's Bridge. It was named for the bridge built at the end of the lake, to cross the river Inn down the valley.

"We have now entered the kingdom. All the lands you can see," said Zuoz, looking north, using his arm to make a circle from west to east, "all these lands belong to the kingdom."

"Do they belong to the high king?" asked Tesimo.

"Yes. The high king takes care of these lands, and he takes care of us, the Dwelling People. The king often journeys throughout the kingdom to listen to the people. He had paths built that connect all the villages for his messengers to travel easily, bringing him news of his people. Every village has the duty to shelter and protect the high king's messengers. That is why these villagers welcomed us when we explained that we are the high king's messengers."

While the cousins were trying to understand what was being said, Zuoz continued. "Hryatan and I are both on our way to deliver a message to the high king. The High Priestess of Malta sent me after she heard whispers that whole villages had been abandoned in the Krpy[10] region, north of here. We heard that these villages were left with no trace of the men, women, and children who once lived there. Only elders were found dead, half eaten by animals. The high priestess sent me to report our worries about these people to the high king. During Ostara, the spring equinox, the high king resides in the town of Sarup[11] on the island of Funen, much farther north away from here. Since my road is taking me near Krpy, I was asked to investigate and directly report my findings to the high king."

"Is Hryatan your guard?" asked Druso.

"No," Zuoz answered. "Hryatan is a different messenger. He is a monk-warrior from the kingdom of Akkad. I understand that he is bringing with him a secret art to help defend the kingdom. Hryatan and I met on the road a few days before we reached Baden. We both have to leave tomorrow. You are free to stay here or try to go back to your village. If you decide to try returning to your village, I am sure that the villagers will offer hospitality until you regain enough strength for the crossing, as well as provide you with food supplies for your journey.

"But even if you do find your way back and survive the mountain crossing again, I doubt that there is anything left to return to. We saw your village burned. I am sorry to say, but there is nothing left alive there. On the other hand, you are welcome to come with us on our mission to the high king. This will be a perilous journey, but you have proven yourselves to be worthy travel companions. We would be happy if you chose to come with us. If you want, you could become messengers and serve the kingdom like we do. As I said, we have to leave early tomorrow morning. Make your decision by day's end so you can be ready when we leave."

The villagers offered the travelers a change of clothes with new shoes made of soft leather. Once dressed with new leather pants and a fiber cloth shirt, they looked like the other men of the village.

The cousins stepped outside on the house's platform, where women bustled to and fro, looking after the small children, drying fish or meat, and tanning hides. Looking around them, they could see women and children chatting and laughing as they performed the household's chores on the other platforms of the village. Tesimo's was still amazed by the sight of these houses. A village built over water seemed unreal to him. It was so different from his now-destroyed village, composed of small stone houses with thatched roofs dotting the side of his beloved mountain.

The cousins decided to explore their surroundings and walked to dry land through the maze of passageways. By the edge of the river, they found men of all ages polishing stone blades and axes against large flat stones that banked the river. The wet flat stones had been used for so long that deep grooves were engraved on their surfaces. They were amazed by the workmanship of these men, slowly transforming rough stones into smooth and shiny objects. Through Tesimo's eyes, the stone axes and daggers these men were making were far more beautiful than his cherished stone knife he'd made a long time ago with a chipped flint stone. One of the men addressed them in a language the cousins could not comprehend. Luckily, Zuoz came up behind them and was able to translate what the man was saying. With pride, the man told Tesimo that his village was famous throughout the kingdom for their green polished ceremonial axes. The green stone could only be found on the slopes of the sacred White Mountain. He explained that the White Mountain was the highest mountain of the kingdom, the place where earth met sky. These green axes were sought throughout the kingdom for the magic power they received from the sacred mountain.[12] Every year they sent their most beautiful green axes to the high king as gifts.

Further along the riverbank, women were making clay pots, decorating them with beautiful imprint patterns made by pressing clam shells into the soft clay. Tesimo had never seen shells before. He asked Zuoz what they were and how they came to be such a shape. Zuoz told him that they came from the Blue Sea, the sea of the South.

"The sea? What's it like?" wondered Tesimo.

"It's an immense body of water, larger than any river or lake you have ever seen, expanding farther than the horizon, the most water you can imagine in one place," answered Zuoz, spreading his arms wide. Both cousins nodded, but they couldn't imagine that water could stretch farther than the horizon.

Compared to the plain wooden bowls they had in their village, the cousins thought that these clay bowls were the most beautiful things they had ever seen.

As they strolled farther down the riverbank, the cousins watched strong men fishing with spears. A man harpooned a fish and tossed it on the riverbank. There were no fish in the creeks around Tesimo's village, and the sight of the shining animal flip-flopping across the ground fascinated both cousins. The fishermen laughed at the cousins' wonder and their wide-eyed amazement. One man spoke, and Zuoz translated. "He is wondering where you come from that you do not know what a fish is." Tesimo replied by pointing back toward the faraway mountains. Smiling, the man led them into shallow water and demonstrated spearing. Druso and Tesimo were given spears to try catching these bright creatures darting to and fro under the water. They quickly gave up after much struggling in the water without success, to the joyful entertainment of the men assembled on the bank.

"It's harder than it looks," commented Tesimo.

Druso muttered, "The villagers jeering laughter likely scared the fish away anyway."

Around midday, the men who had left before sunrise to hunt returned with their prey. They surprised the cousins with more strange animals they had never seen before, with names like beaver, otter, duck, goose, and boar. Groups of women also returned from the forest, carrying baskets on their heads full of berries and herbs. They were walking in line, singing songs that Tesimo couldn't understand but with melodies that delighted him.

It was just midday, and while the village prepared for a communal meal, Zuoz pulled the cousins aside. He told them he was going to determine the best path for the next leg of his journey. Zuoz planted his walking stick in the flat ground, and then tilted the staff, making the shadow grow in front of their eyes. When the shadow was at its longest, he made a slash mark in the dirt at the far end of the shadow. Tesimo had noticed Zuoz's walking staff, made of very hard birch wood, had engraved lines at even distances the whole length down. Then Zuoz used his staff to measure the distance between the slash mark and the depression made when he planted his staff in the ground. He then pulled a strange loop made of strings from his bag. From the loop radiated strings of all different lengths, each tied with knots. Zuoz held his string loop in one hand, while his other hand ran along one knotted string to the next. Finally, he raised his head and said, "We are about two hundred fifteen miles south of Krpy. If we are as far east as I think we are, it will take us at least fifteen suns to reach Krpy. We should be there by the end of this moon."

"How did a net of strings tell you the distance?"

"These are talking knots," answered Zuoz. "The bundle is called a khipu." He held it out for Tesimo to examine. It was a rope circle from which hung many secondary cords and various tertiary cords attached to the secondary ones. Zuoz explained that knots made on the cords represented units—twelves and sixties in kingdom counting. "The cords are different colors to designate the different concerns of the kingdom. Khipus are used for keeping all kinds of records—the high king's life and achievements, village tributes, land limits, religious ceremonies, celestial events. Judges, priestesses, astronomers, village leaders, and heads of families all record events using khipus. The kingdom's khipus are kept in large storage places; the largest one is in Brodgar, far away in the northwest. The khipu in my hand keeps the records of the sun's position for every day of the year along this direction across the sun's path. My staff is a kingdom's yard, divided in three feet of twelve thumbs each. The longest shadow at noon is measured when the stick is square with the sun. Once you understand how to measure it, the shadow length tells you the height of the sun in the sky. Using this khipu, I can measure how far north we are. If I also knew what the kingdom time was, I could also tell you where we are in the east/west direction. But this village is too small to have a time counter."

The cousins turned to each other, baffled. They were completely lost in Zuoz's explanation and didn't dare ask for further description.

After the meal, the cousins helped carry supplies for some villagers who were building a new platform. Workers had already used fire to burn one end of a wooden pylon into a sharp point and were bringing it close to a dozen other pylons erected in the marsh. Standing on top of the standing pylons, men placed the pylon, pointed end down, and drove it deep into the mud using heavy stone hammers, while others prepared the next post to be planted.

As they observed the villagers and moved among them, the cousins argued about their future plans. They were still debating as the day grew dark and the time to make a decision was drawing near. They were torn by the choice in front of them. Their hearts ached to go back to their village, where they belonged, where their roots were, where they understood how to survive. However, they doubted they would survive the mountain crossing by themselves, without the warm bodies of other travelers to prevent them from freezing through the bitter-cold nights. Even assuming they could find their way back to the village through the snow and ice, they knew that there would be nothing there waiting for them.

The image of their village burning to the ground and their friends and families slaughtered was forever etched in their memories. They knew that Zuoz was right; nothing could have survived the fire, and if, by some chance, any had, they would either be dead or gone by the time they returned. As much as they longed for home, they would only find a torched and abandoned village, no longer a home.

Their only real options were to stay in this strange but beautiful riverside village or go on with Zuoz and Hryatan, assisting the messengers in their mission to the high king, and become part of this new wider world they had just discovered. By nighttime, with heavy hearts, the cousins had decided to follow the messengers and see where the path ahead would take them.

Zuoz and Hryatan were pleased with their decision. Zuoz told them to prepare for a long journey. He told them to keep their fur coats in their pack, because it would be cold where they were going.

"First we must go to Olkam,[13] a large village close to the crossing of a large river, east of here," Zuoz explained. "It will be an easier walk, now that we're on the king's paths. We should be able to reach Olkam within seven to nine suns and then Krpy about another nine suns north of Olkam. Now it is time to get some rest. We leave as soon as the sun lights our way."

The village chief's house was packed with people eating their evening meal, the last they would have in this village. The villagers told stories the cousins could not understand, and they looked at each other with surprise every time the crowd erupted in laughter. Finally, the companions were left to their much-needed rest.

In his bed, Tesimo's mind churned with everything they had learned that day, everything the cousins had decided. There was a whole different world only a few days from the mountain's pass, and he had never known it. In his old world, there were only mountains and people like him and Druso, living the life of their parents and ancestors. LA life centered around their kin, the mountains, and the wild goats they hunted or herded. Now he rested in a wooden house suspended above water—water deeper than he had ever imagined. He was in a new world full of animals he had never heard of, even in the stories told around the hearth at night. Before finally drifting to sleep, Tesimo thought about each of the familiar faces of his slain friends and family and a vision of Elena's smile that tore at his heart. He whispered goodbye to each of them in the night and asked for protection for his coming journey.

Early the next morning, the companions took the sacks of provisions the villagers gave them and secured them to the wooden frames they carried on their backs. Zuoz told the cousins that there would be messenger shelters along the way, but he could not guarantee they would all contain food. They would need all their strength, for they would be walking as long as they had daylight and maybe into the night. The companions thanked their hosts and left the village behind, following a well-maintained path heading eastward.

Zuoz led the group, setting a quick marching pace. Zuoz's demeanor and strength impressed Tesimo. He was just over twenty years, well built, a fist taller than Tesimo. Dark curly hair framed a pleasant face, with brown eyes set deep in his skull, giving him an intense gaze. His black beard trimmed squarely gave him a dark look. Zuoz so impressed Tesimo that he could not imagine what the king that this man followed must look like.

As they walked, Zuoz immediately began to teach the cousins the kingdom's language. He started with basic words, building up to long discussions in both languages, going back and forth between languages to help the cousins learn as quickly as possible. Zuoz described the place where he was born, a small but beautiful island much farther south. The cousins had no word for "island." Zuoz described his island in detail for the cousins, but the cousins struggled to imagine it. They wondered if an island was land floating on water or coming out of the water like a mountain. The cousins were also baffled by Zuoz's claim that the edges of the world too were like those of an island, all surrounded by water.

They walked the whole day through a thick pine forest,

and the night was falling when they reached a hut built on the side of the road. Zuoz told the cousins that it was a messenger's relay, a shelter to keep messengers safe at night. The walls were made of thick branches joined together with ropes, and it had a grass roof. The company entered the relay, where they found resting benches, a hearth, and firewood. In a corner, there was a pantry with a door locked by a wooden pin. To the liking of the travelers, the pantry contained dried meat hanging on ropes.

Zuoz smiled at the filled store. "The nearby villagers have well fulfilled their duties to the messengers. We may not always be so lucky."

After unburdening themselves of their bags, the voyagers refreshed themselves with the water of a nearby small brook. They ate and rested, sitting on the floor around a fire, which kept them warm for the rest of the night. Before going to sleep, both Zuoz and Hryatan told the cousins that they had to perform their ritual of thanksgiving. They went outside to a clearing in the woods, and then, facing the moon, they recited words unknown to Tesimo. They then came back to the hut to rest for the night.

The next day, Zuoz and Hryatan went to a small pond near the stream for bathing and ablutions. Both encouraged the cousins to join them in the water. "It is too cold," Tesimo protested. "How do you not lose feeling in your legs?"

"This is not a mountain stream, Tesimo," Zuoz informed him. "It will not chill you."

Reluctantly, they immersed themselves in the clear water. They soon discovered they truly enjoyed the feeling. During their ablutions, Tesimo noticed that Zuoz had a tattoo on his chest, similar to the cross-shaped pendant on a leather strap tied around his neck. Hryatan, too, had shapes tattooed on his back and shoulder, taking appearances of strange animals when he was moving his body. Before seeing his companions' beautiful, intricate tattoos, Tesimo had only seen the small ones on his father. The tattoos were made by the village's healer to relieve his father from pain in his back and knee, and they were simple little lines.

After bathing, Zuoz and Hryatan combed their hair with combs made of carved bone. When they were ready to go and before harnessing their luggage, they walked back to the same place as the night before. There, facing the sun, they uttered words incomprehensible to Tesimo. They stayed still for a while, listening to the birds interrupt the silence of the forest. Then the companions gathered their belongings and left the relay. It was still early in the morning when the companions resumed their journey. On the road, Zuoz continued his teaching of the kingdom's main tongue, reviewing what the cousins had learned the day before while adding new words to their vocabulary. They walked at a steady pace for most of the morning. Around midday, they met some neighboring residents, who were waiting for them on the side of the road with fresh water and food supplies.

"How did they know to expect us this sun? Surely they don't wait here every sun?" Tesimo asked.

"A runner brought the news, naturally," Zuoz explained.

"A runner? From where?"

"Messengers like Hryatan and me walk from relay to relay, preserving our strength with an even pace so we can travel across the kingdom. The runners rarely go past the next village but can travel very quickly, like wind across a wide-open space. The village behind us sent a runner ahead of us, and he may be home by night. An urgent message can be sent by runners going from village to village. Runners usually carry only simple messages, like warnings about predators, requests for help for large undertakings, or any urgent needs. Anything more complex must be carried by long-distance messengers such as Hryatan or me. Otherwise, the message will be altered over too many transfers from one mouth to another. You will see more runners as we reach the main road."

CHAPTER 7

SEPTEMBER 23, 1991
MORNING

Before going to the Physics Institute, Sophia went to her office early in the morning to pick up the straw sample she'd left in the fridge and to make copies of the log sheet she had prepared. Waiting for the copy machine to warm up, she looked through the window at the trees turning their fall colors. From her fifth-floor window, she could see Aton Schmidt climb out of a cab a block from the university entrance. She wondered how Aton was feeling today, after the argument he had last night with Professor Zelinger. *I guess he is still going to the mountain to bring back Otzi.* The main office's door opened, and Gregory stepped inside, on his way to the attic expansion.

"Gregory, where have you been? Aton looked for you everywhere yesterday."

"Me? Why?"

"You didn't hear that we went to see a mummy stuck in a melting ice pack in the Otztal Mountains?"

"What? No!"

"It should have been you! Since Professor Zelinger was out of the office, Aton had to go there to decide what to do about the body in collaboration with the police and the coroner's office. He wanted you to go with him, but you were nowhere to be found. And guess what? He found me instead. Where were you yesterday?"

"I was in the library. I found an incredible map showing why the first gothic cathedrals were built on the locations they are. I had to verify that by myself with the library computer. I didn't have time for Aton."

"Too bad; you missed quite a lot!"

"So what was it? One of Napoleon's legionnaires?"

"Much older than that. From his clothing and artifacts, my guess is that he is a beautiful specimen of a late Neolithic man. Incredible, isn't it?"

"Whoa, not too bad! I'm sure I'll see that mummy pretty soon. It was not worth spending the day with Aton."

Gregory had the misfortune to have Aton as his lazy thesis adviser. Aton was treating Gregory like his personal servant, asking him to do anything he did not want to do himself.

"I understand what you mean. Anyhow, I was glad to have a chance to see that mummy encased in ice. And by the way, Aton may be gone soon."

"What do you mean?"

"Last night, I heard a heated conversation between Aton and Professor Zelinger, and I think Aton may be let go."

"That would not be a big loss. Let me show you what I found."

"Gregory, if you're still avoiding Aton, I suggest we continue this somewhere else. I just saw him getting out of a cab, and he'll be here in a minute."

Sophia grabbed her copies, and they both walked over to the library, a few doors away. They ducked into a study room in time to avoid unwanted interaction with the unpleasant department assistant.

Gregory started his education in architecture and then fell in love with gothic cathedrals. So he decided to pursue a master's in archaeology. His thesis work was centered on finding the safety coefficient of these monumental, enormous structures. The ancient constructors determined the sizing and placement of building elements, like the gigantic columns supporting 130-foot ceilings, by drawing large geometric figures, like circles, triangles, and squares, directly on the construction site's floor. The ratios of each dimension to the others followed ancient geometrical proportions.

Gregory was amazed that these ancient builders, with primitive tools and without any real knowledge of resistance of materials, were able to specify colossal structures that had resisted the stress of their own monumental weight for more than eight hundred years.

Gregory started his study with Notre Dame of Chartres, [14] the most mystic of all the French gothic cathedrals. Using modern data and computer modeling, he was trying to calculate the minimum dimensions of these architectural elements for the cathedral to stand on its own. The intent was to determine the structure's safety coefficient by comparing the calculated minimum dimensions to the actual dimensions in order to assess how much excess material the ancient builders used in their construction; the less excess material, the smaller the safety coefficient.

In the library, Gregory couldn't wait to show Sophia the source of his excitement. He grabbed some papers from his briefcase and explained that two days ago he'd found a book about Chartres Cathedral from a French author, Louis

Charpentier.[15] The book discussed the construction and locations of the first gothic cathedrals. The ancient gothic builders seemed to have a master plan from the start. Charpentier showed that these first cathedrals, which were consecrated to the Virgin Mary, were built in specific locations in order to project the Virgo constellation on the French territories. Gregory took a map of the Virgo constellation printed on a transparency sheet and placed the transparency upside down on the table.

"That's how the stars of Virgo would look if they were projected on the ground," he explained. Then he took a piece of paper out of his files, placed it beside the first one and said, "This is an overlay of the cathedrals' locations I made from a map of France. Look at that, their locations correspond to the stars of the Virgo constellation."

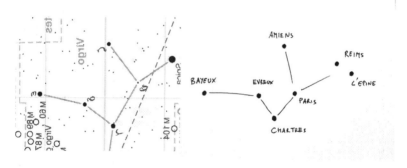

Gregory kept going. "I know. The cathedrals are not exactly where they should be. But at the same time, it is understandable that the actual locations selected by the builders had to make the most sense on the ground, like fertile lands near major river crossings."

"You know," argued Sophia, "there are so many gothic monuments in France that you could probably find an alignment to fit any constellation you chose."

"You're right; it's possible," agreed Gregory, "but in this case there is compelling evidence that it is not a coincidence. To start with, these cathedrals were the first gothic cathedrals built. Furthermore, they were all dedicated to Notre Dame—the Virgin Mary, the Mother of God in Christian tradition. I don't know if you are aware, but there are not that many gothic cathedrals in France dedicated to Notre Dame. Next, we aren't talking about just any French cathedrals but the most prestigious ones like those of Paris, Chartres, Bayeux, and Reims.

"Finally, confirming the master builders' plans, the fourteenth century Notre Dame de l'Epine was built on the location corresponding to Spica, the brightest star of the Virgo constellation, also known as Epis de la Vierge in French." Gregory put extra emphasis on the first three letters when pronouncing the French names of both the cathedral and the star. "The French *epis* means 'ear of grain,' retaining antique symbolism to Virgo, the goddess of harvest. You see, I've always wondered why this enormous Notre Dame de l'Epine was built there. L'Epine is a small village of about six hundred inhabitants in the middle of nowhere. The village has always been so small that its entire population could not fill such a sanctuary, let alone pay for the construction of the monument. It would make sense to built such a cathedral there, if the gothic masters wanted to more closely mirror the Virgo constellation on the grounds of France, consecrating it to Mary, Mother of God."

Sophia was interested, but she was becoming eager to get on her way to the Physic Institute.

"But you should know everything about Chartres, right?" added Gregory.

"Why do you say that?" asked Sophia, coming out of her distracted reverie.

"I thought your thesis was about Neolithic religions."

"Not quite. My thesis is less about Neolithic religions than about the regional influence of Malta's culture and religion on the neighboring territories during the Neolithic period."

"I see ... I thought you knew about Chartres because it was discussed in my European Neolithic class. Chartres has been the most holy place in the region since the beginning of time, well before the region became Christian. The name Chartres originates from the name of an ancient people called 'Carnutes,'[16] which means 'Keepers of the Stone.' It is said that more than five thousand years ago a large clearing was created in the middle of the immense European oak forest, and a huge dolmen was erected in its center, overlooking the Eure River. It is believed that the first Chartres cathedral, built in the fourth century, was placed directly on top of the dolmen. The current gothic cathedral is the last of at least five cathedrals successively built on this dolmen. And that's why Chartres Cathedral is not oriented toward east like most other cathedrals but northeast, following the orientation of this exact dolmen."

"A dolmen?" asked Sophia. "One of those monuments built with two or more upright stones supporting a horizontal stone slab?"

"Yes. Dolmens were very popular in this part of the world over five thousand years ago. During these times, the region of Chartres brought dolmen construction to its apex. Take a look at these pictures of the Dolmen de la Bajouliere and the Dolmen of Bagneux to appreciate the size of these constructions." Gregory pulled out a pair of photographs from a file he had in his briefcase. The constructions were impressive.

"These dolmens are made of huge two-foot-thick granite slabs, with squared-off edges and corners. The stones making the sides are ten feet tall and twenty-five feet long, weighing close to one hundred tons each. On top are twenty feet by twenty-five feet squared stones weighing more than one hundred tons each. These are probably some of the largest dolmens in the world. And they did all of that without any metal tools. It's still a mystery how they managed to move these enormous stones without the luxury of a wheel. Imagine how many years and how many workers it took to cut these immense stones, as well as a multitude of farmers to feed and shelter them."

Sophia took the photos politely and gave them a cursory look. "These are amazing. I was just about to be on my—"

"My guess is that the dolmen under Chartres Cathedral must be enormous," Gregory interrupted, "the largest of all. When the cathedral was built, the dolmen was completely encased to form the core of the crypt. Based on the encasement dimensions, the dolmen could be as big as thirty feet wide by a hundred feet long. But of course that is just an estimate, as the crypt core has never been excavated."

"That's a shame. I really should—"

"You know what is ironic?"

"No, what?" Sophia said automatically and then bit her tongue, realizing she'd fallen into Gregory's trap.

"You can find many preachers teaching about Jesus and the Saints, but very few preach about Mary, even though, the greatest gothic cathedrals ever built rose here in France in the name of Mary.

"You see, Mary has very little relevance in the Gospel's message, other than Jesus's miraculous birth. The few times she appears in the Gospel, she is treated quite rudely by her son, both at the wedding at Cana, and Jesus's preaching in Capernaum's synagogue where he denied his affiliation. The fathers of the church initially condemned Mary's worshippers as idolaters and persecuted them for centuries. It's not until the fifth century that the persecutions stop, after an ecumenical council decided to recognize Mary as Theotokos, the Mother of God.

Sophia was interested, but it was not the time. She had an appointment with Erwin to run Aton's errands and tons of homework due soon.

"We know that from time immemorial, peoples from this part of the world worshiped a great goddess-mother on the site where the cathedral now stands," Gregory kept going. It is likely that Christianity was so quickly accepted there, because these peoples assimilated their great goddess, the virgin who birthed the world, to Mary the Virgin, Jesus's mother, the mother of God.

"Chartres Cathedral enshrined one of the few Black Virgins of Christendom. They were colored black symbolizing that when the virgin was pregnant of God, she contained everything in the universe, including the light itself. [17]"

The deluge of information overwhelmed Sophia. She had to go. She was going to excuse herself when Gregory continued excitedly, "Don't you think the whole thing is very odd? It looks like the cult of Mary, centered around Chartres, was the renewal of the goddess-mother worship practiced thousands of years earlier near this dolmen, still buried under the cathedral. From that place, an immense movement started that spread cathedrals over hundreds of miles, all dedicated to the Mother of God, all located on a projection of the Virgo constellation across the French countryside."

Sophia nodded, considering all that he told her. When it looked like Gregory might fill the silence with more information, she quickly interjected, "While this is fascinating to consider, I must be off to the institute. I have someone waiting to perform carbon dating for me. You may want to stay here for a while if you don't want to see Aton. If he is still working here, he will soon be on his way to recover the mummy we saw yesterday. I have to go. Good luck!"

Sophia left Gregory with his research and went back to her office to get Otzi's straw sample that was still in the office's refrigerator. Aton's door was open, and she heard shuffling noises in his office. She didn't want to see him and quietly headed toward the door. She thought she was home free, but before she could reach the office's main door, she heard Aton's voice behind her, asking, "Sophia, have you seen Gregory?"

Sophia turned around and answered evasively, "I saw him earlier, but I am not sure where he is now."

Aton frowned and said, "Darn! And what about you? Have you made any progress yet on the sample date?"

"Last night I went to the Physics Institute and arranged the analysis for this morning. I was on my way to the lab when you stopped me."

"Good! Place the results on my desk when you get them. I'm leaving shortly. A driver and a refrigerated truck are waiting to pick up the mummy and bring it back to the lab. I may call on the way this afternoon to check on your progress. I hope you will be at your desk."

"I will let you know as soon as possible. What about your car? Is it okay?"

"What do you mean about my car?"

Sophia jumped at the harsh tone in his voice. "Oh, I don't know. I noticed that you took a cab this morning. Is something wrong with your car?"

"My car is fine. I must have left the lights on—the battery was dead this morning. Just get to the lab and get the carbon dating done."

Sophia was happy to leave him. Climbing down the stairs, she shook her head. *This guy is crazy,* she thought. *What was the deal with the professor last night? Is he or is he not on his way out? Anyway, Aton must be in over his head with the mummy extraction, especially if he wants to impress the professor and keep his job.* She reached the main floor and exited the building on Innrain Strasse, where her bicycle was attached to a rack. Her old gooseneck bicycle was a hand-me-down from her mother. The black paint was chipped, and rust was showing here and there, but it was functional and that was all that mattered to her. She looked at the gray sky above her head and wondered if she should take the bus to the Physics Institute. The weather was rather warm for the season, and it was not supposed to rain until the next day. She decided to take her chances since the bicycle ride would be faster than using bus transportation. She unlocked her bicycle and sped off down the street toward the Physics Institute, eager to be moving the analysis forward and happy to see Erwin again.

CHAPTER 8

DAY 15
OLKAM

 For the first few days, the messengers marched east through a dense pine forest. The two cousins had made new walking sticks they modeled after Zuoz's stick in length and size. They found that walking sticks were helpful for them to reach and push from places otherwise inaccessible. Sticks also helped keep away the snakes they met once in a while on the track, sunbathing in the patches of sun piercing the forest canopy. Slowly, the mountains receded, and they entered wide plains covered by more sparse oak forests. Each night they were either hosted in small villages near lakes or rivers, or they slept in relay huts along the king's roads.

Beside each village they passed were circular enclosures where the dead were buried. As they arrived in one village, they came upon villagers performing a burial ceremony. Their corpses were painted red and placed in a crouched position inside a hole dug in the ground. Zuoz explained the hole in the ground represented the womb of Gaia, Mother Earth. It was for the dead to exit the world the way they entered it. Friends and family of the deceased were singing a song that sounded melancholic to Tesimo. The body was then covered with dirt. In Tesimo's village, the dead were buried under a pile of rocks outside the hamlet. Though the customs were different, this burial custom felt familiar to Tesimo, just as the mournful song reminded him of his own grief.

His thoughts wandered to Elena. She would have turned thirteen in a couple of moons. Dark questions tormented him every time he thought of his love. *What happened to her? Is she dead, her bones scattered by scavengers? Was she taken as a slave? Could I have done anything to save her? What about the promise I made to come back to her?* It was a sore reminder of how, in an instant, all that he was and had been—his youth, his life, his hopes and dreams—had been shattered forever.

Shortly after they entered a new forest, the companions realized a young starving female dog was following them. She was smaller than a wolf and had brown fur. This dog reminded Druso of his dog, now lost. Using dry meat, Druso befriended the animal, and the dog started to trail along behind them. Two days later, the dog started to look much better. Druso decided to call her Garkan, which meant "dancer" in his own tongue. Her tail was no longer tucked under, and she had newfound energy, frolicking back and forth in front of the travelers as they walked, leading them.

Druso and Garkan became inseparable. The dog was very intelligent and quickly learned to obey Druso's commands. Although Garkan added to the burden of food required throughout the journey, she had proven herself a valuable companion for the travelers, alerting them to arriving voyagers or wild animals before they encountered them on the trail.

Every passing day, Zuoz taught the cousins more of the kingdom's language and traditions. As they were passing fields of tall grass, Zuoz spoke to the cousins:

"This is flax. Flax is very much loved in the kingdom. We can eat its seeds and make clothes out of the stems."

"Are you speaking of different clothes than the ones we are wearing?"

"No, not at all. The clothes you are wearing are made of flax. Flax stems are brushed into fibers, and the fibers spooled together into strings. With the strings, we make clothes, as well as rope, fishnets, and many other things."

"Why are some clothes colored red or green?"

"The colors are added by dipping the fibers into slurry made of water and plants, like bog berries for deep blue, goldenrod for yellow, oak bark for orange, snake weed for light yellow, red onion skin for deep green. Certain ground powder can also be used to color fibers."

"What about the blue color of the clothes you wore when we met?"

"That blue is made with a blue flower not found in these lands. That's why blue clothes are not found in this part of the kingdom."

"And how do they make these beautiful patterns of lines and animal figures?"

"It's the way they make the fabrics. The strings are woven on a loom. I am sure you will soon see a loom. The weaver uses uncolored strings to make the bulk of the fabric and colored ones to form the patterns you see on some of the clothes."

"I like flax fabric," commented Druso. "It feels better than goat leather. It's soft, warm, and keeps you dry."

As they drew closer to Olkam, they emerged from the forest and entered the grassy countryside. The track widened to a road, and more and more often they encountered people. One night, they came within view of a village near a river. To Tesimo's surprise, the village was surrounded by a wooden enclosure made of tree trunks planted in the ground, side by side. Zuoz explained that the fence was there to protect the villagers and their livestock from beasts like wolves and bears that prowled the countryside. The cousins also noticed that around the village patches of land were covered with plants that grew in neat, even rows.

"Why are those plants growing like that?"

"Because they were planted that way," Zuoz explained. "The rows you see are best to keep the soil healthy with water and to promote bountiful harvests. The plants produce seeds that are collected when the time is right. These seeds contain life; they are a gift from Gaia. We eat some, we plant some, and a new harvest is offered. Each type of seed has its own cycle known by the region's priestess and astronomer, who instructs the villagers when to plant and when to harvest."

The entrance to the village was flanked by totem poles. The cousins marveled at the painted animal figures carved in these large tree trunks. Zuoz explained that the animals carved in some of the poles represented the animal spirits that protected the village. Other totem poles related stories and accomplishments of the villagers' ancestors.

Alerted by the watchers, a delegation of the village's council had gathered for them as they entered the gate. The village was composed of two dozen longhouses, about twenty feet wide by sixty feet long, clustered around a main plaza, where other totems had been erected. With walls made of large timbers and dried mud, and pitched roofs made of dry grass, the rectangular houses seemed massive compared to the relay huts or even the lake dwellers' homes. The houses' entrances were on the small end, facing southeast. On the northwest side of each house, animals that Tesimo had never seen before were kept in enclosures, some looking like wild boars, others like hornless goats. Tesimo also saw wooden cages containing birds with brown, blue, and orange feathers.

The people were dressed differently than the lake dwellers. Men wore long pants made of soft fabrics, and the women wore long dresses with decorated patterns. Some of the dresses had stitches made of threads colored a red so deep Tesimo wondered at first if they had been soaked in blood. Their dark hair was long and ran straight down their backs. Some of village's leaders wore beautiful jewelry around their necks and decorations made of elongated shells.

The companions were guided to a house in the center of the village. This house was the largest of all, close to twenty-four feet wide by one hundred feet long. The village leader was standing with notables on the open porch by the house entrance. He invited the travelers to enter and offered them hospitality. In the first room, they passed some storage areas and a room where two women were weaving fabric on a loom. The loom consisted of a five-foot-tall frame, and from the top horizontal bar, a multitude of vertical strings were tied to weights, keeping them in tension. Tesimo later learned the vertical strings were called warps. Horizontal threads of different colors, called wefts, were threaded through the warps to make decorative patterns. Beside them, two more women were seated, spinning flax fibers into strings using stone spindle whorls.

They reached the central hall, where an extended family of around thirty people were already gathered, men and women sitting side by side. In the center of the large meeting room were benches and tables spaced between the timbers that held the wide roof. Farther away, Tesimo could see a passageway leading to the sleeping areas, close to the livestock stalls and grain storage areas. The sleeping quarter was partitioned into living spaces with heavy cloth for each closely related family.

On one side of the hall was a large communal kitchen. After being seated at one of the long tables, they were offered water in beautifully decorated clay cups. The companions were then given soft bread, a food that both Tesimo and Druso had never experienced. In their village, they were accustomed to eating coarsely ground wheat einkorn, usually in a broth that softened the hard kernels of grain. They had a difficult time comprehending how something as soft and delicious as bread could be made.

With Zuoz translating, Tesimo learned that bread could be made from different types of grains. The bread he was eating was made of wheat, but it could be made of flax, rye, or barley, plants that Tesimo had never even heard of. In one corner of the kitchen, two women were grinding grains between two stones into a thin white powder that, when mixed with water, formed a dough. The cousins learned that the dough was left to rise and then baked in an oven to form this delicious bread.

Under Tesimo's questioning, the villagers were happy to tell him how they were planting, growing, and harvesting wheat, barley, peas, lentils, squash, and beetroots with the rhythm of the seasons. After harvest, grains and beans were kept dry and stored in silos or woven baskets and eaten later, during the rest of the year.

More villagers came and joined the group at the table. Like their host, they wore bangles, bracelets, and belt buckles made with elongated shells. Tesimo learned that these elongated shells were called tooth shells. The shells had a central hole that allowed for their attachment to fabric. Most of the tooth shells were white, but a rare few were dark. The dark ones were used to create decorative patterns in their necklaces, belts, and bracelets. Since dark shells were less abundant, they were more sought after, and consequently one dark shell was worth two white shells. Tesimo understood that these shells were also used to trade in livestock and grain baskets. A sheep was worth twelve black shells; a bag of wheat was worth six.

More food was brought—scrambled eggs and mushrooms, smoked meat, nuts, and peas. The assembly was joyful, and everybody was talking over everybody else. The villagers started to share stories that everybody listened to with attention. Tesimo was impressed by the many stories these people knew. They seemed to have stories for everything. Tesimo quickly learned about the kingdom's rules and history, about ancient heroes and their accomplishments, and about the daily life in the village. They also had funny stories that made them laugh about the ways life can be tricky. Some stories were so well known that it was just sufficient to call them by name to make points in conversations. Tesimo tried to remember the stories he knew from his village, but he remembered very few. As the evening came to an end, the villagers withdrew to their quarters, and the guests were left to sleep in the banquet room.

The following morning, after thanking the villagers for their hospitality, the company left for Olkam. On the way,

Tesimo observed the farmers along the road, herding the multitude of animals or attending fields, seeding and harvesting fields of orange and dark green produce. They were using long wooden tools to churn the dirt. Tesimo marveled at the channels the farmers had built to bring water to their fields.

Along the way, Zuoz had explained to the cousins that all the kingdom's villages had a chief, supported by a council. The chief could be a man or a woman, usually a descendant of the village founder or someone known for his valor. The men and women who formed the council included the village's elders, the healer, and, in large villages, the astronomer and the priestess. The larger the village, the larger the council. Tesimo understood that the women were the deciders, and the men were the organizers, both having equal importance on the council. He also understood that one-twelfth of the harvest was set aside as an offering to Gaia, and the rest was equally divided among all villagers, whether or not they worked in the field. The priestess and the priests took care of the offerings given to Gaia. They stored them and distributed them to those who had hardships in the village, the region, or in other parts of the kingdom.

The more he learned, the more Tesimo realized that he had entered a completely new world. The abundance of food was something unimaginable for a person who had spent all of his life in an isolated mountain hamlet, relying all year round on goats and wild plants for survival. These people lived in apparent harmony with routines and order that made their lives so much easier and safer than his had been in the mountains. Tesimo felt that the people were happy, enjoying life with one other. He noticed that when the children were released from their chores of helping their parents, they played together. Not once had Tesimo seen an adult reprimand a child. When an order was given, it was delivered with a soft voice. Tesimo would have expected the children to be spoiled from the leisure time, but he was always amazed to see how likable, outgoing, and intelligent these children were. Peace was reflected in the way the people interacted with each other. Hunting, planting, and harvesting were all enjoyable occasions when the community worked together. As they divided meat and goods among themselves, the villagers gathered in kinship, enjoying the time together with no squabbling over the equal share of goods. They all helped each other because they knew the favor would be returned if they ever found themselves in need.

These people were also filled with a great sense of honor, which was a central part of kingdom life. Breaking a promise was the greatest taboo, bringing shame on ancestors and family. If individuals offended the community gravely or too often, they were temporarily expelled from the village, and all their possessions were destroyed. At the end of this time of exclusion, the offenders were recalled and welcomed back by the villagers with gifts and assistance, allowing them to start a new life in the community. Tesimo admired these people so much that he found himself resolving to live his own life with such peace and honor.

Along the way, Tesimo met more and more travelers, either walking in groups or alone, leading their herds. Once in a while they encountered runners going from one village to another. Many other travelers were carrying baskets full of goods, either on their shoulders or with the help of travois, triangular frames made of two long poles lashed together on one end, with a wooden platform or netting stretched across the other end. Goods were loaded on the platform and the frame was dragged with the sharply pointed end forward, either by hand or with shoulder harnesses.

The cousins were amazed by the diversity of goods these people were carrying. Some travois were loaded with sacks or baskets of grains of all kinds—wheat, barley, lentils, beans. Others were packed with hides or with painted potteries, woven baskets, leather shoes, colored cloth, white or gray stones, clam shells, bags of raw flint, or finished stone tools, such as daggers, awls, chisels, and axes. At least once a day, the companions met runners from the surrounding villages, either crossing their route or passing them on their way.

Zuoz explained to the cousins, "Goods are traded everywhere in the kingdom. Some parts of the kingdom are better than others at making certain items, or they have unique resources, like the green stone from the first lake village we visited. They trade their goods for things they don't have. Here, the people have salt that is mined in the nearby Hallein Mountains. People come from very far away to exchange their goods for salt to take back to their villages."

Tesimo recalled the first time he tasted salt and the heightened flavor of the meal he was served that night. He'd been surprised to see villagers grinding a piece of a white rock and pouring the resulting powder onto their vegetables. He remembered how much he enjoyed the flavor it added to the food, and since then he used salt whenever it was available.

At one pit stop, youth who were camping nearby by asked Tesimo where he was from. At that point, Tesimo realized that he, himself, was now the one who was the stranger. Tesimo had not seen many strangers in his lifetime.

Before Zuoz and Hryatan came to his village, he had only twice seen strangers coming from Baden. He was now the one in foreign lands, following this road like a dead leaf floating on the current of a river. He was now homeless, without any roots or anyone waiting for him. It took him a while to remove these sad thoughts from his mind.

Tesimo had noticed that when they spent their nights in relays and the company rested around the campfire after dinner, Zuoz sometimes drew figures with a finger on the dirt floor. These drawings were shaped like entangled spirals, circles, rectangles, and triangles. Then Zuoz stared at the drawings, transfixed in concentration for a while, before erasing them with the palm of his hand. One night, after Zuoz came out of his trance, Tesimo dared to ask him about the figures on the floor.

"These drawings are the paths of the souls," Zuoz answered.

"Paths for the souls in the otherworld?" inquired Tesimo.

"No, the path of the souls in our inner world. The paths our souls can take to reach unity with God. I will explain more about the kingdom's faith but not tonight. We have to rest."

Tesimo knew nothing of "soul" or "faith," and he sensed it was more than the simple struggle to learn the new language of the kingdom. He wanted very much for Zuoz to explain, but he understood that it was not the right time. He too was exhausted and was willing to wait.

It did not take long. Only a few days later, Tesimo got a new opportunity to learn more about the kingdom's faith. As they were progressing through the plains, the companions came within view of large stones placed in a circle a little distance from the road. They had already seen several of these stone structures along their path. The stones were always in remote places along the road, away from villages. Some of the stones were so large that Tesimo thought only giants could have erected them. As they passed the stone circle, the travelers saw a crowd of people by the stones, performing a ceremony that Tesimo did not understand.

"What are these people doing?" questioned Tesimo.

"They worship Gaia, the mother goddess," responded Zuoz

"Tell me more about Gaia," Tesimo said.

"Gaia is earth, the mother of all. Wise men from the past showed us that Gaia has two sides. On one side, she is the one who birthed the world, the essence of life, the dispenser of harvests. On the other side, she is the refuge from death, the caring mother who receives the souls of the dead. Gaia's life force flows from the deepest places of this world."

"How can she be one?"

"Tesimo, Gaia is everything you can see on earth, but she is not alone. Gaia is in unity with Sky, her companion and partner. When the light of Sky first met the night of Earth, their union conceived the Child, the Great Spirit. The Great Spirit is what animates all things. Each living being, plant or animal, has its own spirit, a sliver of the Great Spirit."

After pondering on it for a moment, Tesimo asked: "Zuoz, where do the first people come from?"

"Our first ancestors emerged from the revered cave of Lourdes, Gaia's womb, the cave of the original birth, farther west from here. From there, they multiplied and populated these lands."

Thinking further, Tesimo enquired: "Zuoz, where do

the souls come from?"

"The souls are sent to earth by the living being's spirit heads. Ancient astronomers saw where each of them resides in the sky, and they gave to constellations the names of the hosted beings' spirits. Man's spirit is from the constellation of Orion. After their time on earth, the souls are welcomed by Gaia in the otherworld."

Then Zuoz added, "You see, Tesimo, the union of sky and Gaia also created the two guardians of the world, sun and moon, to rule over the days and the nights. The sun oversees the living, and the moon oversees of the dead."

Tesimo looked up at the sun as he walked and listened to Zuoz. The sun was bright, warming his face and stinging his eyes. He concentrated, trying to understand all he was being told. "Guardian sun gives beings life and subsistence. After death, their souls migrate to the guardian moon. There, the souls are weighed for their transgressions. The honorable souls are given a place in the night sky, the land of the ancestors, where they reside with the stars. Those who have transgressed but repented are sent back to the sun, where they are given another chance at life. Those who have willfully transgressed without remorse will die forever."

After a pause, Zuoz added, "You see, Tesimo, death in this world is nothing; it's natural. But death in the otherworld is an abominable death, a death that rips a soul apart, spitting it into nothingness. These souls obtain no peace in this death, and the darkness does not bring calm to their eyes. It is a death consumed with fear, even more powerful than the fears we feel inside us walking unknown paths of a strange land in darkness. Death in the otherworld is also felt among the living. You see, Tesimo, we are all one in the Great Spirit. Man spirit, animal spirits, plant spirits—we are all one, before and after life. For those who feel all souls, the death of a soul in the otherworld brings deep sorrow and suffering to the spirit of living men."

Hearing Zuoz's description of the souls' fate, Tesimo immediately averted his eyes from the sun, suddenly afraid he could be violating an unknown taboo.

"Zuoz, what does transgressing mean?"

"Gaia gave our ancestors life's commands. Transgressing happens when you ignore or break Gaia's commands."

"What are Gaia's commands?"

"The first command is 'Respect your parents and ancestors, for they are wise with experience.' The second command is 'Treat others as you want to be treated.' The third is 'Never hurt a child, a human, or an animal for pleasure, for unnecessary suffering is pure wickedness.' The fourth is 'Help the needy around you, for you may be in need one day.' The fifth is 'Respect the authority of the high king and his lords, for order is good.' The sixth is 'Stay pure, for purity is honor,' and the last is 'Give your due to Gaia, for she is your earth mother, and she holds your soul in her hands.' Killing a human being is a transgression. It happens that we have to kill to protect ourselves, but our basic premise is 'do not hurt innocents; have mercy.'"

"Zuoz, how do you repent?" Druso, who had been listening to the conversation, suddenly asked.

"Repentance takes time, Druso. Repentance starts with the recognition of one's transgressions and admission of guilt. Guilt is the feeling you have when you realize that what you have done is wrong, and you wish you had never done it. To repent, you have to agree to change yourself in order to not transgress again. You also pray and offer sacrifices to the goddess."

Zuoz let some time pass for Druso to absorb what he

just said. Tesimo broke the silence, asking, "How do you pray?"

"Praying is a simple act. We all pray in the kingdom— sometimes by asking, sometimes to praise. Tesimo, know that most of us failed at one point or another. So we pray to Gaia, simply saying, 'Holy goddess, mother of all, care for us poor transgressors from now until the time of our death.' If we are sincere, it's possible that our repentance washes our transgressions and guardian moon allows us to become stars, like our faultless ancestors."

As they walked, Zuoz continued explaining the practices and rituals of the kingdom's religion and beliefs.

"For us, life is a succession of cycles, like suns after suns, seasons after seasons, years after years, death in one world and rebirth in the next world. Everything we do in our life is to honor Gaia. At the center of all is Gaia, the source of life. The first surrounding layer is the feminine area, the area of peace and prosperity represented by the guardian moon. The second layer is the masculine area, providing protection and security, represented by the guardian sun. Everything in the kingdom is made in accordance to these truths."

Tesimo learned that giving back as sacrifice is the most important thing people do to develop their true lives.

"We believe that the greater the sacrifice to Gaia, the greater reward in love we get in return," explained Zuoz. "Our people learn this at an early age. When they come of age, our youth spend one sun cycle with priests and priestesses, who instruct them in faith, service, and community. This is called the year of passage or year of sacrifice. During that sun cycle, youth are engaged in communal works and practice service to others. They learn to empty themselves of selfishness, to become empty vessels able to receive the Great Spirit's wisdom."

Tesimo and Druso gave each other puzzled looks as they listened to Zuoz's explanations. The sun and the moon were two of many spirits they had always wondered about, along with rain, thunder, and animal spirits. But these spirits were personal to them and each family of their village. Tesimo thought that the closest thing he had experienced to the religion he was learning was the taboos he had to follow in and around his village, as well as watching the village's healer perform marvels with herbs and incantations. They had heard many stories by the hearth during the long winter nights but nothing like the organized rituals and ceremonies these people performed. Later, Tesimo and Druso argued in vain the merits of their own beliefs as compared to what they were learning about the faith of the kingdom.

One evening, after the companions stopped for the night at a relay, Tesimo went for a walk alone in the surrounding woods. He considered the events that led him to enter this fantastic world in front of him. Why did the spirits of the mountain allow the destruction of his village? Was Mother Earth interested in his destiny? He realized that all the new things he had learned over the past days were helping to relieve his spirit from the pain he still experienced about the loss of Elena and his family. He was curious about all that was out in the world, waiting to be discovered. Looking at the myriad stars, he wondered what else he, a simple goat shepherd, would discover by following Zuoz on his way to meet the mighty king of this world.

During their long marches, Tesimo was hesitant to talk directly to Hryatan because his stature and demeanor impressed him. Hryatan was tall, almost two fists taller than Tesimo, and had broad shoulders. He wore a trimmed thick black beard. The contrast of his honey-colored eyes with his dark tan skin was striking, giving him a deep, penetrating gaze. He was quiet and only seldom talked. However, from the multiple discussions Zuoz generated to teach the cousins the kingdom's tongue, Tesimo learned fascinating stories about Hryatan's land and people.

Hryatan came from a very faraway place, in the direction of the sunrise. He was from a very large village called Hamoukar.[18] The houses of his town were made of stones or bricks, with plastered walls, decorated with paintings. The entrances to their homes had portals in the rooftops. He explained that his people told ancient stories that described how they tamed the animals many generations ago and learned agriculture from the great goddess. When some of his people moved west, they brought with them wisdom about plowing, planting, and raising livestock. The Hamoukar people were very skilled at working copper that they formerly received from the north. But now, the Yamna had invaded the northern territories and cut the northern supply route. They now received copper from the south, along with many other goods from other distant places by way of long donkey caravans.

Hryatan was a monk-warrior, skilled in fighting to combat aggression from eastern tribes. Monk-warriors also kept the roads safe and often assisted judges of law in the application of sentences. Nowadays, because of the Yamna threat, most of the monk-warriors were called to the northern territories to protect their lands.

Learning from his cousin's example and fearing being left out of important conversations, Druso worked harder on improving his speaking of the kingdom's language. Somehow, he was most interested in learning from the messengers about the plants they used for healing and cooking. Zuoz seemed to know everything about plants, and he spent a long time with Druso sharing his knowledge. As they moved through the changing landscape, Zuoz always found new plants to show to Druso and explained their uses.

Finally, they arrived at Olkam, a large village of more than twelve dozen longhouses enclosed by a palisade near a large river. Inside the wooden walls, the longhouses were arranged in rows. Totems lined the streets, and canals brought fresh water. The townspeople were gathering in the streets to see the visitors' arrival, all dressed in brightly decorated clothes. Every house around them looked freshly painted. Zuoz explained that tonight was Imbolc, the first day of spring. The villagers had been getting ready for the celebration by cleaning their homes and purifying themselves, inviting Gaia to come and bring them good harvest.

The voyagers reached a courtyard in front of a large edifice. The façade of the building was made of wood and dried mud and had an opening the size of a man—high and wide. Zuoz told the cousins that it was the village's temple. Two large extensions, looking like trees, topped the temple. Across the square from the temple was a large hall, where the village council received the travelers. In the crowd, Tesimo recognized the town elders, the astronomer, the priestess, the judge, and the other town leaders by their clothes and stances. However, there were new types of dignitaries that Tesimo had not met in the other villages along their route. There was an abbot, who, he learned, directed a nearby monastery and kept track of the village harvests. There were also other dignitaries who Zuoz later introduced as time-counters. Tesimo learned that the time-counters were charged with keeping track of different times, such as the time of the day in the town, the kingdom time, and the dates on the sun's cycle, as well as keeping record of the town history. The last group of unfamiliar notables clustered in a corner of the hall was the town's archivists, the people who recorded and maintained the town's khipus.

Without giving many details, Zuoz and Hryatan explained to the council that they were carrying messages to the high king in Sarup, and the town's welcome was appreciated. When Zuoz mentioned that they were on their way to Krpy, Tesimo noticed a change in the council members' facial expressions. One of them spit on the floor and whispered to his neighbor, something like, "I would prefer to drown in the river than go to Krpy."

Tesimo was surprised by their reaction. In a later discussion with Zuoz, he learned that before the kingdom's unification, Olkam's people used to fight against Krpy's people for land control. It was clear that feelings of animosity and mistrust had been kept alive between these people for generations. Later, Zuoz said, "Tesimo, old stories tell us that a long time ago, because of droughts, people ran out of food in many parts of the land. Earth was not fertile any longer, and people started to fight with each other—farmers against farmers, woods people against farmers, clans against clans, tribes against tribes. It was carnage.[19] Vile things were committed in those days across the land. Villages were wiped out in horrific fashion. Gaia forgave these men. Man forgot everything that was holy and good. Our people became so weak and divided that pillagers from the east ravaged our land without much resistance.

"Finally, after having gone through all these miseries, the fathers of the nations decided to meet and bury their grudge. The fathers created the unified kingdom in order to repel the invaders and restore the land of our ancestors. The new high king raised an army and booted the invaders out of our lands. Then, in collaboration with his high council and the priesthood, the high king devised ways to assist the distressed populations. Peace was restored and has been maintained in the kingdom ever since.

"Tesimo, you understand that our knowledge is embedded in our stories. Each village's life is centered around its own stories. It is sad to think that during these wars many stories of our people were lost. To prevent wars from happening again, everyone now learns the major stories of the kingdom during their year of sacrifice; these are the stories of the kingdom's foundation and the good that resulted from the unification, as well as the stories about Gaia's rules and commands."

During the meeting with the town's council, Tesimo had noticed that the town's priestess was gazing at him. At the end of the meeting, the lord invited the company to his house for respite and preparation for the evening's celebrations. As the assembly dispersed and the priestess made her way to the temple, she briefly stopped in front of Tesimo. Tesimo stiffened in front of this tall woman with beautiful, long dark hair. Looking straight into Tesimo's eyes, she told him, "Tesimo! You have the mark. Willing or not, you will change the world." And before Tesimo could ask any questions, she was gone, on her way to the temple.

In the court outside the grand hall, a great crowd was assembled around large fire pits, dancing to the beats of drums. Tesimo followed his companions toward the temple. The dimensions of the temple were impressive. Tesimo estimated that the façade was sixty feet wide by twenty-four feet tall. The whole temple, covered by a roof made of timber, was over a hundred feet long.

People slowly entered the large temple, where torches were blazing and incense was burning. Inside, people played music on curious instruments, and plates of sacred food were passed among the crowd. The sacred food consisted of loaves of bread made with dried fruits and plants. Numerous loaves were circulating between the participants, and all sampled them. Each loaf had a new and pleasing taste for Tesimo. Somehow, he felt his senses were stimulated, making him more aware of his surroundings.

Tesimo marveled at the ceremony when, by some cue he couldn't see, the worshippers began chanting the same words over and over, until finally someone blasted a horn and the chanters fell quiet all at once. A beautiful woman stood nude on a platform in the middle of the temple. She was wearing the mask of a creature with an oval face and very large, wide-open eyes. Her long dark hair looked very much like that of the priestess he'd met earlier. The woman had stunning tattoos on her sides and her thighs. Long lines and spirals made featherlike bird features on her hips and shoulders. She slowly began dancing as the crowd, in unison, started a melodious and repetitive song.

Tesimo's eye became locked on the dancer's movements, going back and forth in the lights of the multiple fires lit in the sanctuary. He felt a deep feeling of peace penetrating his body. The image of the dancer slowly became visions of the goddess mother dancing, promising blessings and plentiful harvests.

In the thick haze of incense, Tesimo sang along with the other worshippers. Like the other villagers, he fell into a deep trance. Behind his closed eyes, Tesimo saw a multitude of images he could not comprehend. His head started to spin when he suddenly felt his spirit expanding into a vast emptiness and then contracting into a small point. An uplifting feeling slowly penetrated every part of his body; his mind filled with happiness and well-being. A feeling of love that flowed between all living creatures inundated Tesimo's heart. For the first time in his life, he felt in total unity with all things.

When Tesimo opened his eyes, he was stupefied. The people around him had become egg-shaped orbs of light. In the space between them, Tesimo could see a multitude of strings of light, moving like lighting in a thundering sky. Most of the strings of fire were shiny–bright, like the sun's light, but many had other colors, from blue to red.

Most luminescent orbs were yellow, like the sun, but had spots, stripes, and veins of different colors, like red, purple, blue, green, and orange, giving each its own tint. Each had a ray of white light springing from the top. Tesimo looked up and noticed that these white rays seemed to merge together high above them. Coming back to the luminous orbs around him, Tesimo noticed that each also contained strings of light confined within their fuzzy borders

He felt he was seeing the essence of things. He wondered if he was seeing people's souls. His heart filled with love and compassion for all living beings. He intuitively knew that the bright yellow orb near him, with striated with deep-purple veins, was Zuoz's. In the crowd, he could not recognize his other companions.

As Tesimo was getting accustomed to this strange vision, he realized other orbs that had the color of the moon had joined the crowd. In his heart, Tesimo understood that these were the souls of the departed. Somehow, he felt that the souls of his dead father, mother, and all the kin of his village were here as well. He realized that his lost family and friends had never been far away from him but around him all the time. Tesimo felt overwhelmed. He kneeled and thanked the goddess mother for the gift of life and asked her to guide his life for the rest of his time on earth.

CHAPTER 9

SEPTEMBER 23, 1991
MORNING

When Sophia arrived at the Physics Institute, Erwin was in his lab, already busy tweaking the dials of a machine in a corner. Sophia found herself in a room very unlike the offices and labs of her own department. The constant whine of equipment seemed to burrow into her skull and was distracting. Huge, curved pipes dominated the large open space, and panels and equipment, the purpose of which Sophia couldn't imagine, covered every wall. Erwin, however, looked right at home with lab coat and clipboard.

"It's like a space station in here!" Sophia shouted over the mechanical hum.

Erwin laughed. "You can speak normally. I've gotten used to the buzz."

"What is all this?"

"A lot of different stuff. The only thing we need today is the AMS."

"AMS? Remember I'm an anthropologist, not a physicist."

"It's that over there," Erwin said, indicating one of the machines. "It's our AMS—acceleration mass spectrometer."

"That looks ... impressive."

"It is indeed. It's what we use for radio carbon dating organic remains from archaeological sites. Last night you said that the mummy could be between five and six thousand years old. Our equipment will give us the age of your samples with a precision of plus or minus fifty years."

"Remind me how this works," Sophia said.

"First, the sample's material is decomposed into its elementary atoms. Then the ionized atoms are accelerated to extremely high kinetic energies sent into a magnetic field that sorts them according to their masses. The special strength of the AMS is to allow separation of rare isotopes of organic materials, like those of carbon. The earth's atmosphere contains various isotopes of carbon in roughly constant proportions. The largest part is made of the stable isotope C12, with a little bit of its less stable isotope C14. The unstable C14 decomposes into nitrogen and electron at a known rate. When an organism dies, it contains the standard ratio of C14 to C12. But as time goes on, the C14 of the remains decay with no possibility of replenishment, and consequently the proportion of C14 to C12 in the organism's remains decreases over time. The measurement of the remaining proportion of C14 in organic matter thus gives an estimate of its age. We have established that over time there were small fluctuations in the ratio of C14 to C12 in the atmosphere. So a calibration curve was developed to account for these fluctuations and to calculate the historical age of the material tested," Erwin quickly explained.

Sophia understood most of it, but she did not dare ask him to repeat anything, concerned that she could appear slow. "Thank you for the explanation, Erwin. I'm ready to start the analysis when you are."

Following their protocol, they cleaned the straw samples with ultra-pure acetone in a purified airflow hood in order to remove any contemporary organic contaminations. Then they introduced the straw sample into a chamber where the sample was burned. The resulting combustion gas was injected into the AMS, where its atoms were separated and analyzed. Sophia noted all the procedural steps for her laboratory report and recorded the instrument settings Erwin was using.

They had to let the machine work for two hours before the results became available. Sophia and Erwin sat at Erwin's desk, waiting for the machine to complete its analysis.

"What did you mean last night by 'faith is greater than God'?" Sophia asked after a few minutes of quiet waiting.

After a moment of silence, Erwin answered, "Is it not written in the scriptures that faith can move mountains, or that faith saves you? What I meant to say is that faith seems to be ingrained in humankind. Faith has always been there, before there were religions. Faith is like water—some people tell you it's liquid, others tell you it's solid, and others tell you it's vapor, but at the end it's just water. I think that man had faith before he crystallized it into a god. And because it is difficult to visualize and worship an ethereal being, man gave God a physical appearance to focus and to direct his prayers. Somehow, God revealed himself in ways that made sense to people according to their understanding of the world at their time and place in history."

Sophia thought she understood what Erwin meant, but she could not reconcile it with what she had believed all her life. For her, faith appeared when man observed God's actions in nature. "I understand what you're saying, but don't buy it. I think God created the universe and everything else, including faith itself."

"I'm sorry; I was not clear. What I was trying to say is that a human's image of God is a belief. From my perspective, faith itself is the essence of God." Erwin took a pause and then added, "Don't you think that religions are like living creatures going through developmental phases? Our historical records are full of now dead religions. These religions went through birth, growth, spatial domination often accompanied by intolerance and persecutions, and then maturity and sometimes obsolescence. When the worshippers are gone, a representation of God disappears and a new one takes over. God's representations come and go, but faith remains. Faith is the only thing that makes humans' gods real. That's what I meant when I said faith is greater than God."

"I don't know, Erwin. I'll think about it."

A moment passed, and then Erwin continued. "What do you think about souls?"

"What do you mean?"

"I have always been surprised that religions want to save your soul, but they have so little to say about the nature of souls. What is the soul for you?"

"I think it's the spiritual body that we strengthen during our worldly life and that will live for eternity with our Creator after death."

"Well said. I agree with you that if there is a meaning in life, it is to prepare us for the afterlife. My curse as a physicist is the need to have a logical and complete explanation. Like, how are souls created? How can physical actions tarnish an immaterial spiritual body? What happens when we die? How can we carry over memories without any material support?"

"I don't know. These are not questions I really ask myself. What're your thoughts?"

"I have studied most religions, and I have not found any good answers to my questions in terms that modern science can understand. What I know is that our physical bodies are clouds made of trillions of trillions of particles. Each of these particles is not necessarily in our bodies and could be anywhere in the universe. These particles are bound together by the forces of positive and negative attraction. They are assembled following many layers of organization, from atomic, molecular, cellular, tissue, organ, and body. The particles keep coming and going, in and out of our bodies, but our bodies' organization—essentially, our lives—continues. There must be an assemblage point, a point of organization, a center of force that binds and holds together this cloud of particles and maintains the body structure and appearance during one's lifetime. Actually, I believe that there are multitudes of sub-assemblage points, one for each level of organization. I see these assemblage points like particles themselves, particles of organization, organizing matter as they cross our physical world. When they exit this world, the order they generated collapses and matter's particles return to the randomness of the elements. I'm not sure what my soul is, but I feel might be close to this point of assemblage deep in my own body."

"Are all your friends as crazy as you are?" asked Sophia, her head tilted to the side.

"No," he answered with a laugh. "Some are religious, but most of them are rather materialistic. Actually, I have one friend who believes that we are just brains—no soul, no overall purpose. Just brains making a world for their baby brains. Maybe it's possible, but to me, it does not answer the creation of all things and the infinite patience of the universe that built little brains out of dirt."

"So you believe but distance yourself from the 'religious.' What made you leave the church, if you believe in God?"

"I don't know. It's difficult for me to participate in organized religion. For one, other worshippers distract me. When I see some people acting with very little reverence, I get self-righteous, and that makes me upset to act like that. I have also more profound issues to reconcile—the Christian's beliefs about free will, grace, and predestination. Anyway, it's not just about faith. My real struggle is about will. When I went through my existentialist phase in high school, I became more focused on the origin of willpower than the finality of human life."

"What do you mean?"

"Here is my struggle: we all try to do what we want, but how can we want what we want?"

"Do you mean, why would people prefer coffee instead of chocolate?"

"In a way. But it's not really about our tastes, which are mostly determined by our upbringing. I'm talking about 'will' itself. We know that a lot of what we want is dictated by biological and social needs, as well as the media's power of persuasion. What I'm trying to understand is what gives someone personal motivation, the inner force that drives people to do what they do, sometimes defying the odds."

"So what do you think will is?"

"I'm not really sure. I think that 'will' and 'faith' are very close cousins, if not sisters. Faith is a lot like will. It's not clear what faith is. And you know the saying—if you have faith, you don't need proof, but if you don't have faith, there is not enough proof to make you believe. Actually, sometimes faith can be source of will or motivation. You have to have it to achieve anything, but somehow it's already in you. Nobody else can give it to you."

The AMS computer finally chimed that the results were ready. They interrupted their discussion as Erwin picked up the machine printout. Then Erwin applied the results on the calibration curve to obtain carbon dating and spent a focused ten minutes on calculations before turning back to Sophia.

"The sample is about fifty-three hundred years old," Erwin announced. "Just about right! You called it, Sophia. These results will have to be duplicated for confirmation, of course."

"Based on the mummy's flint knife and copper ax, I had no doubt that it was about that time period," said Sophia, her cheeks pink with excitement. "That's an amazing find. Otzi is going to tell us incredible things about life in Neolithic times—his nutrition, his health, his equipment, and much more."

Erwin's stomach growled. He excused himself and said he was starving. "Lunch—to celebrate?" Erwin inquired.

Sophia looked at her watch and realized it was already past two in the afternoon. They had not had lunch, and she too was hungry. "I'm sorry. I can't do lunch now. I have to report these results as soon as possible," she answered. She thought she saw disappointment on his face. She added, "What about tonight, then? Around five?"

"That will do. What about Branger Brau? It seems appropriate for a toast, don't you think?"

"That's a good idea. So okay, see you there at five."

On her way back to the Universitas Leopodino, Sophia went over her discussion with Erwin. She liked his frank speech, and his deep view of reality. She wondered if she was ready to have a relationship with him.

She finally arrived at Innrain Strasse and parked her bicycle in front of the building. She climbed the stairs two by two toward her department's offices. She stopped short at the door when she saw Gregory standing in the hall, his eyes red and his expression grim.

"Gregory? What's wrong?"

"Professor Zelinger had an accident. We just learned the news two hours ago. This is terrible. He was run over by a car last night on Freising Strasse, walking home from work."

"What happened? How is he doing?"

"It's bad. He is in critical condition. I understand that they are keeping him in an induced coma to give time for his brain swelling to subside."

"I can't believe it! That's horrible! Was it a drunk driver?"

"They don't know. It was a hit-and-run."

Sophia shook her head in stunned disbelief. "I hope he's going to be okay" was all she could think to say. She gave Gregory's arm a consoling squeeze before seeking the solitude of her office. She sat in silence for a while, thinking of the professor and wishing there was a way she could help. After a while, she realized that she still had the test results in her hand. In a daze, she rose to take them to Aton's desk down the hall. In his office, she noticed that Aton had left his key chain on one corner of his desk. Looking at the keys, she recalled the rage she saw in Aton's eyes when he was leaving the office last night and his strange reaction when she asked about his car that morning.

What are the odds? she wondered. *His car was in perfect shape yesterday. We left it for more than three hours in the cold of the mountain, and it did not appear to have a battery problem. I suppose he could have left a door open, running the battery down overnight.*

She knew that Aton parked his car in his garage, which was attached to his house. She looked at the clock, thinking, *It was about eight this morning when I bumped into him. He was on his way to extract the mummy. Riding in the refrigerated truck, the whole trip to the mummy's site would take at least four hours. Giving them at least two hours to cut the mummy free of the ice, Aton cannot be back before 6:00. It's now 2:55. That gives me at least three hours.* Sophia needed to know. On an impulse, she took the keys and left the office.

Aton's house was only a twenty-five-minute bicycle ride from the university. When she arrived, she parked her bicycle across the street from Aton's house. The house was on a small lot surrounded by an iron fence. A brick garage was built beside the house with the car entrance facing the street.

The street was deserted. It took her three long breaths to gather her courage and then cross the street to Aton's garage door. It took two tries before she found the correct key. She entered and closed the door behind her. In the darkness, she could see that Aton's gray Polo was there. She walked around the car and stopped in front of it. There were no signs that Aton had tried to jump the car battery—no charger was attached to the car. With horror, she saw that the car's front bumper was damaged, and she bent over to examine the extent of it. The bumper was all banged up. Shaking, she bent down on one knee and looked underneath. She saw a small piece of ripped fabric still attached to the car's frame, some tweed material such as one would find on a man's suit.

She stared at the piece of fabric for what seemed a long time, struggling to absorb the horror of the situation. She staggered to pick up the piece of fabric from the under the car when she heard car door noises coming from the street in front of the garage. *Could Aton be home already?* Panicked and terrified, she stayed low, listening intensely. Then she heard noises in the house, and the doorknob of the door connecting the garage to the house started to twist.

She just managed to hide behind the car when the door opened and the garage light was turned on. She heard steps from the door to the front of the car and a voice mumbling. She knew that she would be exposed if somebody went in front of the car. As quietly as possible, she lowered herself as much as she could and inched toward the back of the car and then froze. She listened intently to the intruder's movements over the noise of her fast-beating heart. She realized she had to breathe when she felt ready to faint. More steps, and she had the feeling that the intruder was coming down to inspect the back of the car. She crouched behind it and held her breath. She heard the intruder mumbling again and then more steps, indicating that the intruder had left the garage. Carefully, she raised her head and peeked at the door. Thinking that whoever was in the house could come back at any time and discover her, she quickly retreated to the street door. She cracked it open and carefully looked right and left. The street still seemed empty. She decided that the coast was clear and left in a hurry, closing but not locking the garage door. She quickly walked away for almost a block before crossing the street and coming back for her bicycle. With shaking hands, she grabbed her bike and quickly pedaled back to the university.

She sped through the streets, her mind racing, trying to wrap her head around what she had just seen and what it might mean *Oh my goodness! Aton tried to kill the professor last night. This guy is dangerous. If he finds that his keys are missing, he will immediately suspect me. Very few people have access to his office. I would be deader than dead!* Her stomach cramped as she pushed her legs to the limit.

She arrived at the university, ran up the large wooden stairs to the department offices, and stopped just before reaching Aton's office door. There was no sound, other than her heavy breathing. She dared to enter and found the office empty. She placed the keys back on Aton's desk the way she had found them and left in a hurry. Her heart was pumping from anxiety and from her breakneck bicycle ride. *Please let it be a coincidence,* she prayed. *Please let him not realize I took his keys.*

She went up to the renovated attic to see if Gregory was there. She could not find him, but another student was there, quietly reading articles.

"Did you see Aton at any point this afternoon?"

"No," he answered. "I've been up here all afternoon and haven't seen him at all. He's probably in his office."

She went back to her office and sat at her desk, wondering what to do next. *Should I go to the police? But what if I'm wrong? What if it was a coincidence? But it can't be. He lied to me.* Sophia knew she had to do something. *But how would I explain my presence in Aton's garage to the police?*

She had agonized for fifteen minutes when the ring of the office phone made her jump off her seat. Aton was on his way back and said he was calling from a gas station. He was annoyed because he had called earlier when they left the mountain ridge and wondered why she was not there to answer.

"I just came back from the Physics Institute," she told him. "I have the results."

Aton seemed pleased with the carbon dating of Otzi and hung up. She could breathe again.

If Aton has been on the ridge all day, he couldn't have discovered his keys missing. But who was at his place this afternoon? Sophia sat at her desk, staring into space and pondering what to do next. *Could Aton's car damage have been caused by something else? Let's say he hit a post last night. But why would he claim it was a battery issue this morning? Why lie about that detail?* She shook her head, confused by her own muddled thoughts. Her eyes went to the clock automatically, and she realized it was time for her dinner with Erwin. She was no longer in the celebratory mood she'd enjoyed that afternoon, but she decided to go, hoping for comfort from him.

When she arrived at the restaurant, Erwin was already there, waiting for her in a booth. He stood up when she reached the table and helped her to sit. He had heard the news about Professor Zelinger and expressed his sympathy as she sat down. "How are you?" he asked. Sophia smiled sadly. It was a sad circumstance, but she couldn't help but feel glad that Erwin cared about her and was thoughtful. Still shaking and after a moment of consideration, she decided to confide in him about what she'd found at Aton's house that afternoon.

"You shouldn't have gone there by yourself. I would have gone with you; it would have been safer."

"I know. I was not thinking clearly. But now, what do I do?"

"You have to go to the police—even if it is a coincidence. If you don't, you'll always wonder, and he might get away with murder. Something has to be done."

"But I'm going to be in trouble if I admit to breaking into Aton's garage."

"Well. You don't have to share that detail. You don't have to say that you stole Aton's keys and broke into his garage."

They decided that Sophia should tell the police about the conversation she overheard between Aton and Professor Zelinger and say that she saw the damaged car on the street in front of his house. With a lot of apprehension, Sophia agreed, and they went to the police station, which was a few blocks from the brasserie, on Innrain Strasse next to the university.

After a brief delay, Inspector Muller escorted them to his office. The inspector took her report suspiciously. She related what she'd overheard last night and said that she saw his car by the curb with its front bumper damaged. She was surprised because the damage was not on the bumper the day before. She also told him that when she'd seen Aton that morning, he'd said he took a cab because he had a dead battery. After hearing what happened to Professor Zelinger, she suspected that Aton may have tried to kill the professor. "I just wanted to let you know what I knew," she finished.

"Thank you," said the inspector. "We'll investigate Aton's car."

"If the car is not on the street," Sophia said, "it could be in the attached garage."

This raised the inspector's suspicion, and she had to further explain that she had been invited to Aton's house two years ago and remembered the layout of his house. She was becoming more and more uneasy, and she and Erwin were very relieved when they finally left the police station.

Now they just had to wait. Sophia was worried about the possibility that Aton would figure out she gave the tip and try to retaliate. Erwin comforted her, telling her that she did the right thing.

"Do you pray to your God?" inquired Sophia.

"Yes, I do pray," replied Erwin.

"Please pray for Professor Zelinger's speedy recovery, and pray for me that I did the right thing in going to the police about Aton."

"I will surely pray for you both," responded Erwin.

It was becoming late, and Sophia's body was feeling tired after this very long day. It was time to go. Erwin escorted Sophia back to her apartment, walking beside Sophia as she pushed her bicycle. When they arrived at her apartment building, she attached her bike on the communal rack. Erwin gave her an awkward hug, and he went on his way. She did not know what to think about the whole situation. She moved quickly to bed but could not find rest in her sleep. Her mind was racing with the events of the last days.

CHAPTER 10

DAY 24
KRPY

The following morning, Tesimo woke up with a splitting headache. He couldn't remember how or when he'd gone to bed. Next to him, Druso was still asleep. Zuoz's and Hryatan's belongings were stacked next to their empty beds. Tesimo assumed that they woke earlier and went outside.

Slowly his memory came back. When he regained control of his senses, the masked dancer was gone. In the temple, the feeling of happiness was palpable in the air. The cheerful and smiling crowd slowly exited the temple through the large opened doors. The flow of worshippers naturally split into groups of family members, who returned to their houses to feast together. The companions followed the Lord of Olkam to his home for the festivities. They ate a delicious meal made of spiced meat and vegetables that made Tesimo's taste buds tingle. Tesimo and Druso were given their first beers, served in fine clay cups with elongated handles. The cousins did not enjoy the taste at first, but after a few cups they started to be exultant. At the end of the meal, the assembly first listened to songs of past heroes and their accomplishments, and then joyful music was played and the assembly started to dance. After that, Tesimo did not remember a thing about the end of the evening.

He found his two traveling companions having a morning meal in the house's central hall. He returned briefly to wake Druso, who resisted rising. They went to the river for their morning bath and ablutions and then rejoined their companions in the central hall for the morning meal. Both Zuoz and Hryatan were smiling broadly at the cousins as they sat at the table.

"How do you feel, my friends?" Zuoz asked.

"I don't feel well. My head hurts," answered Druso.

"Mine too," added Tesimo, generating laughter from both messengers.

"You are good dancers," Hryatan finally said.

"Did we dance?"

"Oh yes, you did! Don't worry; you were fine," he added, observing that Tesimo was blushing. Tesimo and Druso looked at each other with the same confused expression. Tesimo could not remember what had happened last night. He only remembered having a good time during the feast following Imbolc's celebration, drinking beer and listening to ancestors' stories.

Still smiling, Zuoz stood up and told the company, "We will be leaving soon. Let's go present our thanks to the Lord of Olkam and be on our way."

It was still early morning when they left Olkam. As they walked the few miles leading to the river, they passed the remains of two large concentric circular ditches, having four entrances that Zuoz called a rondel.[20]

"This structure was made long ago by people long lost to us," he explained. Rotten wooden posts planted inside the rondel looked old indeed. The cousins felt the place was very uncomfortable, unnatural, taboo somehow. There was an awful, smoky smell in the air coming from a large fire surrounded by a few people on the side of the inner ditch.

"What are they burning?" he asked.

"That is a bustum, a death ceremony," Zuoz explained. A fire was lit in a hole, and above it a dead body was being immolated. "This is some people's belief—that the soul of the departed reaches the doors of the otherworld faster if the material body is reduced to ashes. You would see more bustum if we traveled northwest from here."

Druso and Tesimo were repulsed at the idea of burning an ancestor's body. Behind them, Hryatan chuckled. "People have different ways of treating their dead. Here, they burn their dead and store their ashes in jars having a human shape that they keep in their houses. If you travel as far as I do, you will see many other ways people take care of their dead. I understand that in Baden, your people bury their dead. In Hamoukar and the lands surrounding my city, we believe that both fire and earth are pure and holy. We don't want to pollute fire or earth with the physical impurity carried by the bodies of our dead. My people understand that the decay of a dead body is the work of a malicious spirit. To prevent the malicious spirit from staying around, they give the dead to vultures, which quickly eat flesh and bones. In a land northwest from Hamoukar, people consider the bones of the deceased as the seeds of their lifelong body. They believe that like seemingly dead seeds that come back to life when they are sown, the bones of a person contain the seeds of his or her new life. Families keep the ancestor's bones in decorated clay ossuaries in their houses. They ask them for guidance and good luck."

Pointing at the dilapidated earthwork on the side of the road, Hryatan added, "You see, this rondel was a funerary center used by ancient peoples who have now disappeared. I think they placed their dead in the center of the circle and waited for the flesh to be eaten by animals. They then collected the leftover bones and buried them in their houses. You will see more rondels north from here. Personally, I don't care about what will happen to my bones after death. I'm not worried about it."

"Are you worried about anything?"

"I'm only worried about my honor, the honor of my ancestors, and the honor of my people. Death is nothing to me."

Tesimo wondered about his own death and whether he cared what would happen to his flesh and bones. He thought about his father, murdered and left in the mountains. And then he thought about his mother, family, friends, and Elena. He was afraid to imagine what violent death had struck them at the village. Thinking about his own death, speaking mostly to himself, Tesimo said, "After all, buried, burned, or cut in pieces and eaten by wild animals, whatever happens to the body after death should not matter. In the end, we all go back to the earth, back from where we came. It is only one continuous cycle of life."

"You are getting wise, my young friend," Hryatan told him.

"My only hope for the afterlife is to be reunited with my loved ones," Tesimo added.

Later, Tesimo asked along the way, "Zuoz, last night I saw people like they were clouds of light. Did I dream it? Have you seen that too?"

"Tesimo, sometime we limit our world by what we are able to express. There are worlds out there that no words can describe and no ears can hear. What you saw last night was the world beyond its touchable appearance. The Soma you drank took you to the seer's world. You saw people and leaving beings for what they are—bundles of light. The solid aspect of our bodies is our shield, a protective shell for our bundles of light. You were able to see through those shells and see the essence of our world."

"I saw that people's orbs of light had various color shades. Why is that?"

"People live and experience different things that make them closer to different aspects of life. Each aspect of life has its own color, which gave the different tints to people's orbs of light."

"What was the bright light coming straight up from of the top of the orbs?" inquired Tesimo.

"This is our ray of faith. Our people learn to orient their faith toward the common good. Their faith was going straight up because during the celebration, we were all wrapping our faith around the ray of Orion, the ray of unity. At the end, it is through the ray of faith that our souls reach the otherworld."

"Have you seen my faith? How does it look?" Tesimo asked curiously.

"Yours waivers and fluctuates." Looking at Tesimo's saddened face, Zuoz smiled and added, "Don't worry; it usually takes one year of practice to control your ray of faith. We all learned to see by ourselves in our year of sacrifice. But most of us can't stay constantly in the state of seer. Understand that 'seeing' does not help for everyday life. We are human and have to fulfill the duties to our kin and help each other. We are all engaged in maintaining our communities and have little time to enter the world of seers. Our celebrations help us to realign our faith in a communal act of 'seeing.' Master seers reside in the kingdom's houses of knowledge. They explore the skies and enter worlds that no words can describe. I hope you will have the chance to meet some of them someday, if you decide to enter a year of sacrifice."

In the silence of a quiet pause, Tesimo continued walking, thinking about Zuoz's answers. A little time later, Zuoz resumed. "There is something we all learn, which is to respect our bodies. Your body is to your soul what an eggshell is to an egg. Our bodies, like a shell, contain and protect the lights of our souls, the light that was given to us at birth.

"We do things that affect our bodies and consequently our time on earth. Living in the faith and following Gaia's commands strengthens your shell around your vital light. Selfishness and arrogance makes your shell porous and lets your light flow out of it. Once your light is gone, you are dead on earth and in the otherworld.

"Your body is like the skin of a chrysalis, allowing the larva of your soul to become a butterfly and fly away. You know, the otherworld can be a frightening place when the time comes. Through faith, Gaia guides our flying."

Tesimo was still contemplating Zuoz's remarks when the company arrived at Olkam's river crossing. It was a very large river named the Danube. At that location, there was an island in the center of the river. Large ropes had been laid between the island and both sides of the river. Tesimo could see how locals were using the rope to move all kinds of goods across the river. The goods were placed on raft platforms built over dugout canoes, attached side by side. The raft's passengers used the ropes to pull their raft back and forth from the riverside to the middle island.

Along the way, they had already crossed small and large rivers. The first rivers they encountered were small enough to be crossed by sandbar. Where the rivers were too deep to cross on foot, locals had built bridges, either with tree trunks or ropes suspended across the expanse. Later, they faced a larger river that they crossed in canoes built from hollowed trees and propelled by the locals using wooden paddles. At first, it seemed magical and terrifying for Tesimo to be floating on water. He was always afraid that monsters under the shimmery surface would jump out and drag him down to the bottom.

They crossed the Danube River on a large rowboat, which went directly across the river and was much faster than a raft. Tesimo was frightened of the current and fought to hold on to his courage and composure. At the start of the crossing, Garkan howled, whimpered, and shook in absolute terror, struggling not to leap from the boat. In the middle of the river, she resolved to lie as flat as she could by the travelers' feet. Once across, Garkan bounded from the boat and ran from the river. The travelers thought the dog was lost, but as they loaded their packs on their backs and prepared to continue on foot, she came back, happily trotting, now safely on land.

Two days after the crossing of the river, they came to a village made of smaller individual houses instead of the longhouses of the valley. The villagers wore similar clothes, but they were decorated with different stitched patterns colored red, black, and ochre. Women wore their hair braided down their backs. The council members who welcomed them also wore belts decorated with tooth shells but with distinctive designs. In spite of these differences, the villagers were friendly, and the company was welcomed, as they had been everywhere else since they entered the kingdom.

After going north for a few more days, Tesimo noticed that the length of daylight seemed to become much shorter, instead of becoming longer as he'd experienced in his village following the winter solstice. Worried, he asked Zuoz why this was happening. "Is the sun disappearing or dying?" asked a concerned Tesimo.

"Everything is fine, Tesimo," answered Zuoz with a smile. "Your eyes are sharp to have noticed these differences. Here is how the world cycles proceed: the solar cycles have two halves. The first one is from Mabon, the fall equinox, to Ostara, the spring equinox. The farther north you go, the shorter the daylight is for a date of the solar cycle. Then, between the spring equinox and the fall equinox, it is the opposite—the farther north, the longer the daylight.

"In this time of the cycle, this part of the world is seeing the daylight increase a little bit every day, but we are moving north faster than these little bits, and as a result, it seems to us that the daylight is decreasing. If we were to stay where we are for two days, you would see that tomorrow's daylight time is longer than today's. Don't be afraid, Tesimo. All is as it should be."

Zuoz later told him that while learning the night sky, he went to an island very far to the north, where the sun never set during summer and never rose in winter. Zuoz explained, "It's a fantastic place to learn about the stars because you can see them circle the sky for many moons at a time. Our brothers have a small monastery of astronomers who learn the stars and their movements in the sky. I went there for six moons, from midsummer to midwinter. But you have to be careful when you are there because it is deadly cold during the winter."

"How can that be—nights without days, or days without nights?" Tesimo exclaimed.

Zuoz shrugged. "To see it is to believe it."

Tesimo was fascinated to hear Zuoz talk about the stars. Along the way, Tesimo learned about planets, stars, constellations, and their movements in the sky. On clear nights and early mornings, he enjoyed gazing with Zuoz at the beautiful and immense starry blackness above. Zuoz pointed at groups of stars that had names of animals or objects. He told Tesimo the stories of each constellation and their relationship with each other. These stories helped Tesimo to quickly learn the names of many of these stars.

Hryatan took on the task of teaching the cousins to count. Tesimo's clan never needed a complicated counting system. They had words for numbers from one to five on their fingers and counted the number of fistfuls if more were needed. The simple barter exchanges in their isolated village did not require counting very high. Hryatan explained that along with astronomy, counting was one of his people's oldest arts. A very long time ago, his people developed a counting system based on twelve numbers, each corresponding to one moon of the sun-cycle. Each had its own name, from one to twelve.[21]

"With each finger of the right hand representing one dozen, five fingers in your right hand is called a full and counts for sixty. Now, the fingers of the left hand each represent a full. With both hands, the maximum you can count is 360 or one large—that is five full in your left hand and five dozen in your right hand. And you keep going. Sixty larges is a gross, and so on."

At resting stops, Tesimo also learned from Zuoz how to use khipus to count and record measures. It was a complicated art with lots of features to memorize.

Zuoz also told the cousins that the ancient counters counted everything that needed to be counted. In addition to counting things for barter, the ancient counters also counted time and distance.

"I will start with time. Do you two know that there are 365 suns in the solar cycle?" Looking at the cousins' blank eyes, Zuoz added, "Yes, that's many suns, more than a large. Anyway, working with the astronomers, the first counters divided the solar cycle into four seasons timed on the solstices and equinoxes. The spiritual thanksgiving celebrations of the seasons were given at the midseason days, also called cross-days.

"I hope you know that each moon is about twenty-eight suns long. The ancient counters divided the moon in four quarters of seven days each that are called weeks.[22] The ancient counters also noticed that there were thirteen moons and one sun in one solar cycle. This added sun became special; it was named the great sun of celebration.

"The ancient counters also noticed that the length of daylight varied from day to day over the year. The first counters measured the length of daylight and night by counting the number of heartbeats it took from sunrise to sunset, or from sunset to sunrise. Using their hands to count at first, one counter could easily count measures of sixty heartbeats counted on five fingers of the right hand. They called the duration of sixty beats a minute. Working together, a second counter could count time with his hand in multiples of sixty minutes called hours.[23] The harmony of this world is such that there are twenty-four hours in a sun; that is from one sun's zenith to the next sun's zenith.

"Ancient counters started to keep records of the time in Malta, the birthplace of time counting," continued Zuoz. "They later discovered that incense sticks burned at a very precise pace. They made incense sticks marked in hours and minutes and used incense sticks to count the time. Using their discovery, it became easy to keep track of Malta time as they were traveling in the kingdom, and Malta time became the kingdom's time. All the archives kept in the royal centers are recorded using Malta time. In all these centers, a bell is always rung at noon on Malta time. However, according to where you are, it can be a little strange to hear the Malta midday bell in the morning."

"What do you mean?" asked Tesimo.

"You see, when you travel west from Malta, the sun becomes slower. It does not reach its zenith at the same time as Malta but later. The farther you travel west, the later the sun's zenith. And it is the complete opposite if you travel east—the earlier the sun's zenith. It's how you can calculate—knowing the kingdom's time and using the right khipu—how far west or east you are from Malta.

"Anyway, since all local and royal events are recorded in Malta time, time counting became an art by itself. Good time counters count time in their sleep. Time counting is a very important part of kingdom life. It is used for many key affairs of state, the ancestors' cult, astronomy, geography, and more. Nowadays, people ask time counters to keep track of much more than in the past, like notable family events and stories."

Tesimo learned later that the ancient counters also created a means to measure distances. They measured walking distance by counting the number of their steps. There were three feet in a step, a distance also called a yard. There were sixty steps in a course, and sixty courses in a league.

119

Travelers preferred to speak in half-leagues, a distance called the mile, because a healthy man could travel three miles in an hour. A mile was 1,800 steps or 5,400 feet. Through the messenger network, a messenger could travel thirty miles a day. Smaller distances were measured in thumb lengths, one foot measuring twelve thumbs. Even smaller distances were measured in fractions of a thumb.

Tesimo was very happy to learn all the knowledge of the world, even though some nights his head felt exhausted inside, aching like an overused muscle. He had learned so many stories about animals, ancestors' lives and advice, brotherhood behavior, and faraway lands. Some of the stories came together to make bigger stories. Important stories were known throughout the kingdom and were referred to by their names to make a point in a discussion or argument. From these stories, Tesimo learned the names of stars, places, peoples, plants, and animals he had never imagined before. Meanwhile, his cousin Druso was mainly interested in learning about plants and animals and playing with their faithful companion Garkan.

Tesimo was amazed at both Zuoz's and Hryatan's knowledge and drank in all of it as best he could. One evening at a relay, he asked them how they learned so many things, and they both answered that they learned their arts in houses of knowledge.

"I went to Brodgar," said Zuoz, "far away north from here. I spent two years learning the ancient arts of counting and sky reading. There, I was also taught the four major rules of my order: Be faultless, always talking for the good of all. Accept the hardships of life, and look to the east—a new sun will always rise. Doubt more than you believe, and you will access wisdom. Always be your best. Who knows, Tesimo?

Maybe Brodgar could become your house of knowledge if you decide to receive the education of a royal messenger."

Tesimo kept this thought in mind for the rest of the day. That night, he went asleep dreaming about Brodgar, imagining from Zuoz's descriptions what the house of knowledge could be.

As they got closer to Krpy, the cousins saw more and more houses painted red and black. Also, more and more people were wearing red skullcaps and clothes with striking colored decorations. From their ceramics to their dugout log canoes, everything was beautifully decorated with white, black, and red painted patterns.[24]

The path took a sharp turn, and Garkan, who led their party by a few dozen paces, disappeared from view. Suddenly, they heard a terrible noise and Garkan barking. Tesimo and the travelers hurried forward and found Garkan with a wildcat digging its claws and teeth into Garkan's back. A few feet farther, a mother wildcat was walking backward, growling and hissing loudly, standing between her two kittens and the brawling dog and cat. Druso rushed by him and hit the wildcat with his stick. The cat let go of Garkan and turned his attention to Druso, preparing to jump. Druso swung his stick back and forth in front of him, forcing the cat back a few steps. He edged forward, continuing to swing his stick in long fast arcs in front of him. Finally, the cat ran back to his mate and kittens and quickly disappeared into the brush lining both sides of the path.

Druso knelt by Garkan who was trying to recover from the commotion. Her wounds bled, and she struggled to stand, her shoulder clearly hurting. After inspecting her wounds, Druso decided to carry Garkan in his arms, and the travelers resumed their advance.

Hryatan walked beside them and smiled. He patted

Druso on the back and told him, "You are courageous for saving the dog!"

Druso was still frightened of the strange animal and hoped never to see another one again. "What was that? I never saw an animal like that before."

Hryatan smiled wider. "That was just a wildcat. You are lucky. I have seen much larger cats than that one." He used his hands to indicate size and held his hand at his hips. "These are very dangerous and can easily kill people. In Hamoukar, we also have smaller cats than the one we just met, and some can be very friendly. We like the little ones because they help us protect our grain storerooms by hunting rats and mice."

While they were hosted for the midday meal in a small village on the road, the cousins gaped in astonishment at the sight of a man holding some large wooden assemblage behind a pair of beasts bigger than they had ever seen. It took them a moment to understand that the beasts were pulling the wooden contraption, not the man pushing it on the beast. The bottom of the contraption dug a path through the dirt, churning up the darker, richer earth from underneath. Both cousins were amazed at the sight of this new and powerful way to turn the dirt over.

The cousins learned that the device was called a plow, and the animals were called oxen. These animals were neutered bulls, much easier to handle than bulls and much stronger than bulls or cows. They were ideal for performing heavy-duty tasks like plowing fields or dragging heavy loads. Tesimo was impressed by how much work could be done with such a powerful means of towing loads.

Nevertheless, these large animals looked like monsters to the cousins, who were not used to animals much bigger than goats. When a villager leading a cow crossed their path, the cousins jumped aside, much to the amusement of the crowd observing them from the corners of their eyes. Not willing to be the laughing stock of the village, they mastered their fears and walked beside the large beast.

Villagers offered them food and milk. Tesimo thought that it was goat's milk like he used to drink in his village. After the first sip, Tesimo jerked back, holding his mouth shut to keep from spitting. He saw that Druso had the same reaction.

What kind of milk is that? Tesimo wondered. *It sure isn't goat's milk. I really don't like that tang.* When he regained his composure, he asked what animal produced this milk. He was told that it was cow's milk. A woman came with honey in a jar and poured some in both of the cousins' bowls. The mixture now tasted much better, and the cousins finished their bowls. They regretted their decision when, later in the day, they felt bloated and had cramps in their stomachs. From that day on, the cousins avoided drinking cow's milk, thinking it was the source of their discomfort.[25]

They left the village on a foggy morning. Tesimo asked Zuoz to explain to him the solar cycle celebrations. Zuoz answered, "As I told you, the kingdom's calendar measures the growth and retreat of life and nature, under the control of guardian moon and guardian sun. Both rule over the life of the kingdom. We have two calendars. Guardian sun calendar rules the cycles of life. Guardian moon calendar rules family and communal lives. The guardian sun cycle is marked by four major celebrations held on the quarter days of solstices and equinoxes. There are also four major guardian moon celebrations held in the cross-quarter days, indicating the change of the seasons.

"Our first quarter day is Yule, the midwinter solstice, where we celebrate the start of a new sun cycle. We decorate our homes with evergreen, reminding us of the survival strength of life through dark time. People offer each other presents in the way Gaia offers us the gift of a new year. The next celebration is the cross-quarter day of Imbolc, the festival we celebrated at Olkam. Do you remember?"

"Oh yes, I do," Tesimo quickly responded.

"Our next celebration is Ostara, the spring equinox, marking the day of the sun cycle when daylight overcomes darkness. This is the time when herd animals are born. Families offer eggs and hares to children to mark the event. Then comes the cross-quarter day of Beltane, the first day of summer. The day is celebrated with flowers and dancing. Large bonfires are lit, and young people enjoy jumping over them. The next celebration is Litha, marking the midsummer solstice. This is the day on which the sun shines the longest. After that comes the fall's cross-quarter day of Lughnasadh, the harvest festival. After the harvests comes Mabon, celebrating the fall equinox, a time to thank earth for the bounty of the harvest.

"The last cross-quarter celebration is Samhain, the first day of winter. This is the time of the year when the veil between this world and the otherworld is at its thinnest, making it easier to communicate with those who have left this world. It is time to reflect on death and celebrate our ancestors by telling stories of their lives around the night fire."

Tesimo thought of his own people's calendar, which was much less elaborate. It was also roughly divided in four seasons, separated by solstices and equinoxes, but with much simpler celebrations.

A few days later, they finally arrived at Krpy late in the afternoon. They passed another abandoned rondel before reaching the town gates. The town was beautiful, with a tall wooden fence, massive totems, and sparkling canals keeping the town fresh and clean. Tesimo marveled at the beauty of the place, but something did not feel right. Their welcome reception was not as friendly as in previous villages. They crossed town under the scrutiny of haggard villagers. They reached a large central court between the great hall and the temple. The temple was an immense building, three stories tall.

A crowd led them to the entrance of the great hall, where they were offered water for refreshment and washed the dust of the roads from their feet. The Lord of Krpy and his officials waited for them. They were introduced to the town's notables, grouped on both sides of a large hall. Tesimo recognized the town leaders—the elders, the astrologist, the high priestess, the judge, and the abbot. Behind them were time counters and archivists.

Zuoz told the assembly that they were on their way to the high king, who would be at Sarup for Ostara. The lord offered all of his help and asked them about their journey. Zuoz told him of their encounter with the Yamna in the south. Later, Zuoz artfully turned the discussion to the report of the empty villages to the northwest of Krpy.

"Dear lord, on our way to the high king, we heard stories of abandoned villages north of your territories. Is there any truth to these stories?"

With a deep voice, the Lord of Krpy explained what had happened to the deserted villages at the base of Ore Mountain.

"These villagers were unwise. We all knew the mount was taboo, forbidden, and that a beast lived in this mountain. The villagers were tempting the beast by settling so close to the mountain. The villagers were punished, taken by the beast. We found remains of half-eaten people left in the abandoned villages. Our priestess spoke to the beast's spirit. She told us the beast has been irritated and can only be calmed if our people make a food offering every moon. Since we started to give the offerings, no more villages have been attacked."

Zuoz thanked the Lord of Krpy for the explanation of the situation and complimented him for his wisdom. After dinner, Zuoz thanked the lord and the town for their hospitality and asked for the permission for him and his companions to retire in preparation for the next day's march. They were taken to a house down the street to spend the night. On their way, they noticed a caravan being assembled beside the temple. Asking their escort what was happening, the man told them that the next food-offering caravan for the beast of the Ore Mountain was being prepared.

Once they had retired to their room, their escort brought the companions a meager dinner for the night. The man said he was sorry to have so little for their guests, but most of the food was going to feed the beast. Whispering, the man added, "I would prefer to die trying to kill that beast than starving by continuing to feed it. I don't understand the priestess's command. Why not ask for protection in our fight against the beast instead of feeding it like cowards?"

As soon as they were alone, Zuoz sat between Hryatan and the cousins and whispered, "I don't believe there is a beast in the Ore Mountain. I think the lord is lying. I am not sure what is happening here, but I plan to follow that caravan to see who the lord is really feeding. The next moon is in two days. We will leave town tomorrow for Sarup, as I told the lord. The road for Sarup is the only road going north from here, and it is also the road to the Ore Mountain. We will hide in the surrounding forests and wait for the caravan. When it comes, we will follow it and see where it goes."

Early the next morning the companions left town, heading north. As soon as they reached an isolated wooded area, they left the path and hid in the woods. As Zuoz predicted, two days later the caravan passed and the companions stealthily followed behind it.

CHAPTER 11

SEPTEMBER 24, 1991
MORNING

After parking his car in the faculty parking lot, Aton Schmidt slammed his car door and walked with a determined pace toward the university building. He gritted his teeth together so fiercely his jaw ached, but he could not stop. His entire body was shaking from anger and fury.

He could still see the professor looking at him through the windshield at the moment of impact, his body bent grotesquely before being thrown into the air. "Running him over should have done it," Aton growled to himself. "But no! The old goat survived. If he comes out of his coma, I'll likely never see the light of day again, much less finally have my name attached to something important. The mummy is mine and mine alone. I can't let that happen. The old goat has to die." Aton stopped and whipped his head back and forth, wondering if he had been speaking aloud to himself. *I mustn't be so careless*, he thought as he resumed his walk.

At daybreak, banging at the door had awakened him. The police, armed with a warrant, demanded to search his garage. They wanted to see his car. Masking his surprise as best he could, he managed a cold smile. What did it matter to him anyway? His cousin had repaired his car while he was out in the mountains recovering the mummy, and the only thing the police could do was to notice that his car was in good shape.

Luckily, before leaving Innsbruck, Aton had called his cousin Leopold. He told him that he had hit a parking post and that his car needed a replacement bumper. He explained he had to leave for the day, and he needed his car repaired for a date he had in the evening. He promised that if his cousin could fix the car while he was out of town, he would buy him a steak dinner. Leopold laughed and agreed, as Aton knew he would.

Aton and Leopold had been best friends since childhood. Leopold lived on the family farm near Innsbruck, and as children they had spent their summers together, exploring the countryside. Leopold was a good mechanic and repaired his own farm equipment. More than once, he had helped Aton with household issues, often enough that Aton had given him a key to his house. Leopold didn't ask any further questions; he only teased him about being a careless driver. Aton was later delighted by his cousin's excellent work when he saw his Polo looking like new.

That was how the police found his car in the morning.

"Has this car been in an accident recently?" an officer asked him.

"No, as you can very well see. What is the problem with my car, Officer?" Aton answered.

"We have reason to believe that your car was involved in a hit-and-run accident last night. Have you taken your car into the shop in the past forty-eight hours? Please keep in mind, sir, that we can check for ourselves."

Aton resisted a smug smile and congratulated himself on the foresight of having Leopold do the repairs rather than a shop. "Look, Officer—if I had an accident, you would see some damage. Do you see any damage on this car? I've been recovering remains of a mummy in the mountains all day. You can verify that easily. I was with the university's truck driver. I've had no time for errands or to take my car to a shop."

As the officer was recording the name of the truck driver that Aton provided, he asked, "Why did you take a cab to the university yesterday morning?"

Aton squinted at the police officer. "My battery was dead."

Aton pointed to a battery charger on the shelf of the garage. "I charged it last night. Officer, I don't know what happened last night, but my car is a popular model, and I've not been involved in any accident for years. You can easily check that. Now, if that's all, I must go to work and check on the state of a frozen mummy we stored last night in the university's laboratories. Is there anything else you want to ask me?"

Aton thought of this morning's discussion as he climbed the large internal stairs leading to the fourth floor. His mind was spinning. *Why do they suspect me? Why did they come to my house?* There was something the officer had said, but he couldn't quite remember why it was significant. He was barely under control. His mind burned with fury so he couldn't think. Suddenly, he froze, his foot on the top step to the fourth floor. *How did they know I didn't use my car the other morning? That had to be Sophia!*

Aton berated himself for leaving his keys on his desk the day before when he'd left his office in a hurry. When he came back from the mountain late at night, he had been happy to find that his keys were on his desk where he'd left them. But now he realized he had made a mistake. *How could I have been so stupid to forget my keys? She must have taken them and seen my car. She knows! That little pest knows, and she went to the police. I'm not going down for that! Now that the old goat is gone, who is in charge of the department? Me! And I'm going to fire that little bitch! She won't be around long to ask questions. She can't prove anything.* Aton smiled to himself as he started moving again. Better yet, it would be his name—and his name alone—attached to the Otzi find.

Since he had joined Professor Zelinger's team, Aton never received the success he had expected. Twice he started research projects that ended in total fiascos. For two years, he worked to understand the customs of people in Egypt's Nubian Empire. As he was wrapping up his paper for publication, an excellent paper from a German team was published on the exact same subject. The paper went into such detail that it made Aton's research look amateurish. Nobody was interested in publishing his, except for the obscure Austrian *Archaeology Bulletin*, a sleeper publication with little weight for his résumé. Last year, his eighteen-month research on Austrian medieval warfare became obsolete before he had a chance to complete the article he was preparing. Using the same line of research but on the larger geographical area of the Danube Basin, a team from Hungary published a groundbreaking paper. Once again he was left behind with unpublishable findings.

The mummy find was his dream come true, his salvation. To be fired on the same day was not acceptable. Professor Zelinger had told him that it had been a difficult choice, but there were more talented researchers in the department. *More talented researchers, my ass! I will show him ...* The professor had told him that he might not be cut out for this job. "You don't have the patience, the insight, the intuition," Zelinger had said. "You should reevaluate your career path." It had been too much.

The police visit was a close call. He did not have a solid alibi for the evening of the accident, but his car was fine. It was his good fortune that they hadn't asked him where he was on that night. Just in case, he would have to come up with an alibi. As he climbed the stairs to his office, Aton thought, *I will see what to do with Zelinger later. Right now, let's get rid of that little pest!*

Sophia had spent a very restless night, tossing and turning. She couldn't sleep; she worried whether the police would follow up on her information and what they would find. She wondered if Aton would be at work or in jail in the morning. She worried about what would happen if he saw her again. Unable to sleep, she got up and went to the office very early in the morning. Once at her desk, she tried to work on her discovery linking Malta and Newgrange, but she could not focus her thoughts.

Aton passed by Sophia's office, saw her at her desk, and barked, "You! In my office—immediately!"

Sophia almost jumped out of her skin when she heard Aton's shout. She was stunned to see him and could barely move. She had hoped the police would already have him in custody. She stood up and walked stiffly toward the door. Aton was already in his office, shuffling through paperwork. She felt a knot tighten in her stomach and struggled through the few steps it took to face him across the desk.

Aton was sitting at his desk, holding in his hand the report she had left the day before. He didn't look at her as he spoke. "The minister has asked our department to eliminate a position. Since Professor Zelinger is incapacitated, I am now in charge of the department, and that choice is left to me. It was an easy choice to terminate your position, effective immediately. There are more talented researchers in the department. Perhaps you should consider whether this is the right career for you. You lack the patience and the insight needed to become an archaeologist. Perhaps you can find a job teaching something. You will get your two-month-notice salary, but we do not want you here any longer. Please give me your keys and take your personal effects as you leave."

Sophia stood blinking, stunned. There was nothing she could do. Not only was Aton in charge with Zelinger in the hospital, but she also knew that he was dangerous man. "I understand," she said in a voice barely above a whisper.

Aton supervised as she piled up the documents and items that had accumulated on her desk and bookshelves for the last two years into a pair of cardboard boxes. She felt Aton's eyes on her back and couldn't help picturing him attacking her at any moment. With her hands shaking nervously, Sophia packed as quickly as she could. Reaching across her desk, Sophia cut herself on the surprisingly sharp edges of a Neolithic dagger that she had left there.

The dagger was part of the university's collection. Seeing it, she felt tears prick her eyes as it hit her that she would no longer have the privilege of working with such beautiful objects. The dagger was twenty-four inches long and three inches wide and was chipped out of dark flint stone, respecting the alignment of three light brown spots left in the centerline. It had been borrowed for one of Professor Zelinger's classes—Sophia was supposed to return it to the collection for him. Sophia first had procrastinated over taking it back, hating the idea of stowing something so beautiful in one of the drawers in the attic. She was fascinated by the craftsmanship and skill of the Danish man who had sculpted such a masterpiece, more art to her than weapon. The surface had multiple gleaming facets of the stone chipping work, with an astonishingly controlled geometry, as the dagger had a perfect symmetrical shape.

Later, she realized that the label indicated it had been found in Malta, twelve hundred miles away from Denmark. What was a Danish dagger doing in Malta? It might have been further evidence of long-distance contact for her research. So she delayed the return of the artifact to the collection.

After over five thousand years, the stone blade was still razor sharp—sharp enough to cut two of her fingers as she carelessly raked things into her cardboard box. Holding her injured fingers with her other hand, Sophia looked at the dagger, thinking it was from the same age as Otzi the mummy.

She blinked the tears out of her eyes. Now, she would have no chance of testing her theory or contributing to the field; she felt her career had ended.

"Come on, Miss Bruckner, get moving," said Aton. "And don't be so clumsy!" he added as he gave her a tissue. "Leave this dagger on the desk. This dagger is not your concern anymore. Let's go. I don't have all day. Take your boxes and go!"

She wrapped the tissue around her wounded fingers and left her office. Still stunned, she went downstairs, attached her boxes to the back of her bicycle, and left. Twenty minutes later, Sophia was in her apartment and collapsed in a sobbing heap on her couch. It took her a long while to pull herself back together. Lying on her bed, she stared at the ceiling and contemplated what she should do next. Above all, she wanted to see Erwin. He was the only person who could give her some comfort.

She biked to the Physics Institute, secured her bicycle, and took the elevator to the sixth floor. She walked down the sterile corridors and entered Erwin's department. Her heart fluttered for a second when she found him in the lab, busily noting readings from electronic panels.

"Hey, Sophia, is everything okay?" he asked, keeping one eye on his instruments.

"Aton fired me. I don't know what happened with the police, but Aton was in the office this morning. And he fired me, just like that," she said, snapping her fingers.

Erwin turned to her in surprise, but quickly turned back to his instruments, noting something on the tablet in his hand. "I'm so sorry. I want to hear everything, but I can't talk right now. Once this process has started"—Erwin indicated the data scrolling across a panel—"it can't be paused. It should run its course in about forty-five minutes. Why don't you get tea or coffee in the cafeteria, and I'll meet you there as soon as I can. Try not to worry too much."

Sophia waited anxiously for him, her hands wrapped around the paper coffee cup. Finally, Erwin arrived, and she told him all that Aton had said. Despite herself, she found tears returning to her eyes. "What am I going to do?"

Erwin looked grim. "Let's see if we can speak to Inspector Muller and find out what happened. I'll go with you. We have to understand what's happening."

They loaded Sophia's bicycle into Erwin's car trunk and went back to the police station. They had to wait almost an hour before the inspector would see them. The officer listened with raised eyebrows as Sophia told the story of this morning's altercation with Aton. Then he told her, "We take accusations like these very seriously, Miss Bruckner. That's why we spent the morning examining his car, which we found in good condition. I spent two hours on the phone confirming Dr. Schmidt's whereabouts all day yesterday. There was no way he could have taken his car to a garage in that time."

"Are you saying I'm a liar?"

"I don't know what to tell you, Miss Bruckner. We did not find anything. Now you are telling us that Dr. Schmidt 'fired' you. I don't know what's happening between you two, but it's not our problem. Don't waste our time on your personal affairs."

"Wait a minute," Erwin interjected.

The officer turned to him. "Did you witness any of this? Did you see the damaged car?"

"Well, no," Erwin admitted. "But I know Sophia. She's not a liar, and she's not crazy. She's intelligent, a first-class researcher, and a decent person with a sound mind. You need to look into this more seriously."

The police officer turned sour. "I took it seriously. I spent a day on it and found nothing to support the theory and plenty to dismiss it. I appreciate your standing up for your girlfriend, but don't assume you can tell me how to do my job."

It was midafternoon when they were escorted out of the police station. Sophia was demoralized but too exhausted even to cry. She had lost her job and now she had lost all credibility with the police. Suddenly, she realized that on top of everything, it could become even worse. Unless Professor Zelinger recovered quickly, Aton might become her thesis adviser, and he would probably fail her. *I'm doomed*, she thought.

Erwin suggested having coffee at Café Adikuss, a block away on Anichstraße.

"It's not fair!" said Sophia. "I saw what I saw! How am I supposed to just drop it?"

Erwin said nothing but looked pensive.

"Do you think I'm crazy? Do you think I invented a silly story just because?" Her voice was strained, nearly shouting. She wouldn't be able to stand it if she lost the only friend she had made in Innsbruck, along with everything else important to her. She turned and started down the street. He followed her and gently grabbed her by the arm.

"Calm down! I believe you; I trust you!" answered Erwin. "I'm on your side, you know. I don't understand how Aton managed to get out of it. I was just wondering how he did it. I bet Aton had someone repair his bumper while he was on the mountain, removing Otzi from the ice. It wouldn't have made any difference if you had told them the whole story. By the time they did check it out, the bumper had already been changed. And now we look like imbeciles."

"That's not right," complained Sophia. "You do the right thing, and you get punished for it. It's just not right!" For a minute, they remained silent, lost in their thoughts. Sophia's heart was troubled.

"Come on, let's get go sit somewhere." proposed Erwin. They entered a nearby cafe that was a student hangout and found an empty table in a remote corner.

Over the past three days, Sophia had felt a flame growing in her heart when she was close to Erwin. During the long discussions they had, she could not stop thinking how much she liked his company. She liked his broad smile, instilling trust and happiness in her. She also had to admit she liked his muscular arms and trim frame. He was tall enough that when they stood looking at each other, Sophia had to lift her eyes upward to meet his. He seemed thoughtful, but also active and comfortable in his skin.

Looking at Erwin across the table, Sophia tried to test her feelings for him. A great part of Sophia's social life outside her studies had always been centered on her choir practices and Sunday mass, where she mingled with her church acquaintances. Although she was beginning to have feelings for Erwin, she wondered if such a relationship could even work, in part due to their different religious ideologies.

Her faith had always been her anchor. In times of pain, her church had always been her support, and it was where she found her peace. Erwin seemed to be quite a free spirit. *Would he come with me to mass on Sundays?* she wondered. *He doesn't seem to be against my faith.* She was wondering if they could spend more time together, learning about each other's spiritual perspectives, perhaps taking steps toward something more serious. *Would we have a chance together? His ideas are a little out there, but they are rational and scientifically grounded.* Actually, she felt he was rejuvenating her faith.

"Would you go to church with me?" she heard herself ask.

"Maybe. Why do you ask?"

"I don't know," answered Sophia, blushing. "You said you didn't have a church, so I was just wondering if you would want to visit mine."

"Sure! I would love to. Fair warning—you have to be careful with me because I can drive a priest nuts."

"Why's that?"

"Well ... first, I have a tendency to rationalize and question everything. Often, every last detail. In essence, I have to get straight to the bottom of it, and sometimes it can be disturbing. Take, for instance, your current circumstances. The church teachings are that our God is all good and all powerful. Why are you, a faithful believer who always tries to do the right thing, being punished for reporting Aton who is a criminal to the police? How could this powerful and merciful God allow such a thing to happen to you?"

Sophia was dumbstruck. "I don't know. I guess … it's as they say … 'God works in mysterious ways.' God sends me obstacles to forge my personality and make me stronger. I don't know. How do you account for unfairness?"

"Randomness," answered Erwin. "You see, I have difficulty with accepting that God can be both all good and all powerful at the same time. It's hard to imagine that the horrors happening all over the world have a 'purpose,' even a mysterious one. Like a pedestrian being killed by a drunk driver on the way to church—how can that have a purpose? It's hard to believe that a God who could control the landing of every single drop of rain could also allow for deadly floods. So either God is all powerful and decides not to prevent these atrocities, or God is all good but isn't powerful enough to stop them."

"So what's your point?"

"Personally, I have accepted that our world is made of chaos and probabilities. I think that God lets nature generate infinite possibilities and waits patiently for the right conditions to interact with our world. By allowing randomness to happen in the universe, it is not surprising that bad things happen to good people along the way."

"So you don't believe in miracles?"

"On the contrary. In a random world, everything is probable. In that world, it doesn't take much energy to change the probabilities for an event to happen. With a touch of a finger, God can create any events he wants."

"I see. That's very deep, but it's not helping. If what you say is true, why doesn't God continuously produce miracles to save the innocent and prevent the evil?"

"I'm with you; I don't understand. Maybe there is reason in chaos, an invisible order that we're too small to see."

Sophia felt overwhelmed. She was very tired and wanted to go home. In addition to the homework she had to finish for tomorrow, she needed to find someone's notes to catch up on the classes she had skipped all day. She could not afford to fail a class. "Erwin, thank you for everything," she said. "I'm sorry, but I have to go. I have a ton of work due tomorrow, and it will take me all night to finish it."

They walked silently back to Erwin's car, and Sophia retrieved her bicycle.

"Call me tomorrow and let me know how you are,'" said Erwin as they parted.

Back in her apartment, Sophia took the draft of a report that was due tomorrow from her briefcase and sat at her desk to review it. In spite of all the willpower she was able to muster, she was unable to concentrate. It took her three more painful hours to complete a half decent report. She had not had lunch or dinner and thought she needed to eat something. She went to her pantry, but nothing inspired her. Her favorite cookies couldn't even tempt her; she wasn't hungry and could not force herself to eat anything. She finally went to bed to get some rest, but she kept replaying in her head the events of the past three days and couldn't sleep. She lay in the dark, her eyes wide open, until the glow of the morning sun peeked through her shutters.

CHAPTER 12

DAY 34
GOSECK

 In the forest mist, they followed the caravan for two days along a rough, unmaintained path. As they drew closer to Ore Mountain, they came to an abandoned village. The company made its way through deserted streets, haunted by the emptiness. Druso quietly cried when he saw the skeleton of a dog, still attached to its leash in front of an empty house. Garkan was at his heels as they quickly cut through the eerie ghost village.

They reached their destination a day later. From afar, they spotted the caravan stopped by an outcrop on the edge of Ore Mountain. Bull skulls mounted on poles flanked a wooden platform. They observed Krpy's men, quickly piling the food offering on the platform. They left in a hurry as soon as they completed their duties, without noticing the companions hiding in the woods. Unsure how long they would have to maintain their watch, the companions cautiously stole food from the pile and concealed it in a cave nearby. For two days, they stayed in their hiding spot, their eyes on the beast's food offering. Then, late morning, Garkan raised her hackles, growling softly at men coming down from the mountains. Druso commanded her to keep quiet, and they observed men they now recognized as Yamna, loading the food on horses. The men left with the offering table the same way they had come.

Stealthily, the companions followed the Yamna up the mountains, staying on either side of the path to avoid being detected. They struggled to keep up, traveling uphill the entire day. They came to a large plateau and reached the edge of a clearing where the bedrock was exposed.   Hiding behind bushes, the companions were shocked to see the view before them. On one side of the clearing were a few huts where the Yamna were now unloading the food offering. In the center of the clearing were several pits dug into the bedrock. Workers were climbing in and out of the pits, removing rocks by the basketful and piling them up in large piles. Among the piles, other workers were sorting through the rubble for rocks with purple tints[26] that they placed aside. The purple rocks were then loaded in baskets secured on the backs of horses arranged in a caravan. Yamna warriors guarded the pits and forced the workers with whips.

Zuoz and Hryatan examined chips of the purple-tinged rocks on the ground around their feet. "These are tin mines," Hryatan whispered to the company. "I am sure that these people are the ones taken from the deserted villages. The Yamna are our mountain beast."

They observed the Yamna camp from the cover of trees while determining a plan of action. It was terrible to see the slaves being worked to exhaustion, covered in dirt, and denied water or rest for hours. The company watched, powerless, as the ruthless warriors threw those who succumbed to exhaustion in the nearby pits. At night, when it became too dark for the slaves to work, they were placed in two pits close by. A single sentry guarded each pit, while the other warriors spent the night in two huts dug into the ground and covered with thatch roofs. In the middle of the night, the two guards called to each other and then walked to their respective huts. Soon, the forms of two sleepy warriors emerged from the huts and went to guard the slave pits.

Around midday of the following day, the horse caravan loaded with tin ore left the mines, heading east. The companions counted only ten Yamna warriors, with no horses, left in the camp to control the enslaved workers. The company waited patiently for night to fall. At the changing of the guards, Zuoz and Hryatan swiftly crawled to a hiding spot behind the abandoned guard spot. When the new sentries arrived at their posts, Zuoz and Hryatan sneaked up behind the guards and cut their throats with copper blades, while covering their mouths to prevent them from yelling for help. Zuoz and Hryatan bade Tesimo and Druso stand in the guards' places. They gave them the helmets of the dead warriors, so they would look like Yamna in the dark of the night.

While Zuoz and the cousins were holding their bows at the ready, Hryatan quietly descended into the first pit. He went down through a succession of wooden ladders and platforms. In the moonlight, he saw sleeping bodies at the bottom of the pit. He quietly woke a young man lying on the ground and whispered to him to be quiet. He explained he was there to free them and urged him not to make any noise. The young man understood and they very quietly woke the other people in the pit. Everybody understood that their escape depended on their silence, and they quietly moved up the ladders. Zuoz, on the last ladder rung, helped the villagers out of the pit and directed them to the edge of the clearing to the path that would take them down the mountain.

Then Hryatan and Zuoz moved to the second pit to free the remaining slaves. Even with their bows at the ready, the cousins were extremely afraid that a Yamna might come from one of the huts and recognize them, despite their disguises, or that Garkan would jump out of the woods and bark in the night. In total, about four dozen exhausted villagers, supporting each other, slowly made their way to the woods on the edge of the rocky plateau. After he helped the last villagers out of the pit, Hryatan watched the slow progress of the beaten, exhausted people. He whispered to Tesimo, who was still standing at the guard's place, "We will not be able to flee fast enough with all these injured people,"

"Hryatan, look!" hissed Tesimo.

Hryatan turned to see a warrior emerging from a hut. He walked groggily to the other side of the hut entrance to urinate over a small bush. His eyes must have been barely open, because he took no alarm. Hryatan leapt from his hidden spot; in a few quick steps, he reached the Yamna from behind. With a single precise movement, he cut the warrior's throat. He caught the falling body and lowered it slowly to the ground. Not a sound was made.

Hryatan returned to Tesimo and said, "We have to eliminate the three remaining Yamna in that hut. If we do not, the Yamna will recapture us before we're down the mountain. Aim your arrows at the hut entrance. Shoot anyone in the head. Do not waste arrows. This one did not have his armor, but the other ones may."

Hryatan disappeared into the hut. Tesimo heard mumbling and then a yell. Suddenly, an immense warrior surged through the door. Tesimo let his arrow fly, and the warrior fell dead. A second later, he saw Hryatan's sword emerge from the door. Hryatan waved his sword back and forth a moment, signaling to the waiting archer. Slowly, Hryatan showed his face. "Good shot," he told Tesimo, looking at the dead Yamna on the ground. Hryatan counted in a hushed voice. "With the other two I killed inside, there now are six fewer Yamna."

Tesimo tried to slow his raspy breathing, recovering from the quick but tense encounter. All was quiet. Hryatan whispered, "Watch the other hut. I'm going to get whatever Yamna weapons we can gather." A moment later, he exited the hut, holding Yamna spears and swords in his arms. "Let's go!" he said.

When they reached the place where the freed villagers had gathered, following Zuoz's instructions, Hryatan gave the stolen weapons to the strongest ones. Hryatan now felt more secure. He doubted that the four remaining Yamna would pursue them without reinforcements. That should give them enough time to reach safety.

On their way down the mountain, Zuoz told his companions that his suspicion had been confirmed. The Yamna were an imminent threat, and there was a possible conspiracy in the kingdom concealing the Yamna presence in these mountains. From now on, they should trust no one. Their journey had become more important than ever, and they needed to reach the high king in Sarup as soon as possible.

The company, now much larger and slower with the exhausted villagers, walked all night and reached the valley at the foot of the mountain late in the morning. By the time they came to the cave where they had left the stashed food offering, the whole company was wracked with hunger. While the villagers ate and rested, the companions discussed what to do with the villagers. It was probably unwise to let them go back to their villages, for the Yamna would likely come back and kill or enslave them again. Also, Zuoz suspected that somehow the Lord of Krpy might be collaborating with the Yamna. If that were the case, it would be dangerous for the villagers to go back to Krpy, where the lord would rather have them killed than have them spreading news about enslavement. Finally, the companions decided to offer the freed slaves the choice to go with them north to the town of Goseck[27].

Most of the villagers agreed to go with them, but a few decided to try reaching their extended families farther west. Zuoz prayed to the goddess mother to bless and protect the departing villagers, and the companions led the others northwest toward Goseck. For the first two days, they had to circle around the mountain range and cross a dense forest to reach a plain. They finally found a road within the messenger network. The road was well frequented with villagers, traders, and pilgrims. With the help from the other travelers on the way, the troop managed to reach Goseck the following day.

Goseck was a large village with more than twelve dozen longhouses. A monumental dolmen dominated the countryside on a nearby hilltop. The size of monument's stones was far greater than the standing stones and stone circles that had so inspired Tesimo along the road. Looking at it, he remembered how he had marvelled at structures a quarter of its size. He wondered if he would ever see something that was as awe-inspiring.

At the entrance of the settlement was a well. Women and children were using ropes to pull buckets from it filled with water. The well had a six-foot-wide square wooden frame. Tesimo was surprised by the skills of Goseck's carpenters, who had assembled and fitted the wood beams that framed the four sides of the well. The mortise-and-tenon joinery was mind-boggling to him. Using sharpened bone chisels and wooden hammers, artists had sculpted birds and animal decorations on the sides of the boards. Looking down, Tesimo saw that the water surface was at least ten feet below ground level.

After they were fed and refreshed, the company was offered changes of clothes. They were then accompanied to an assembly led by a large blond man in his twenties, wrapped in a blue cloak and surrounded by local officials. His clothing was ornamented with large disks of yellow metal. At his side, he wore a beautiful dagger made of black stone that reflected the sun on its perfectly chiseled surface. The tall man introduced himself as Alaric, the high king's son.

Tesimo was speechless as he realized that he stood in the presence of the son of the man in charge of all the territories they had traversed since he had left his mountains.

"Welcome to Goseck, Zuoz!" Alaric said. "We were made aware of your arrival by runners from the villages through which you traveled. I was not expecting to see you here, and in such a large number. You've added members to your traveling party."

"These villagers were being kept as slaves by Yamna. Once we rescued them, we had no choice but to bring them with us, lest they be recaptured or killed."

"Yamna! Here?" said Alaric with a shocked face. Looking at the crowd gathered around them, Alaric added, "You all look tired. Please come, accept our hospitality, and rest and recover in the great hall while you tell us all that has happened to you."

The group was directed to the largest house in town for rest and a welcome meal. They were given food and drink while Zuoz and Hryatan related the story of their journey. The cousins were given beer but left it untouched. Zuoz reported their encounters with the Yamna and the threat they presented to the eastern frontiers.

"It is difficult to believe that the Yamna are so close. These savages must be dealt with—and immediately. We must quickly raise an army to push them out of the kingdom."

Hryatan respectfully stood. "I'm Hryatan, monk-warrior from Hamoukar, sent by my king Akkad to meet the kingdom's high king." Hryatan unsheathed his bronze sword. held it high above his head, and told the assembly, "This sword is made of bronze. Bronze is a new metal we created in Hamoukar. It is harder than anything I know."

After a short silence, Hryatan continued, "I know you dislike copper swords because they bend and notch easily. Our people found that adding tin to melted copper makes a new metal much harder than copper alone. Tin is very rare in Hamoukar; we obtain it from the East. The Yamna have stolen the secret of bronze from us. We learned that they found a way to obtain tin from the Minoans, sea-rafter people who control the trade across the Blue Sea. With that tin, the Yamna started to make bronze weapons and are now threatening to destroy our world. At high cost, we have learned that the Minoans are getting their tin from the Green Island and the Great Island." Looking at Alaric, Hryatan added, "Those are your father's islands in the Green Sea. I was sent by King Akkad to ask your father to stop the Minoan trade and to teach your people the art of bronze making so you can protect yourself. Lord, I'm afraid that the situation is even more serious than we thought since we have learned that the Yamna have found another source of tin in the Ore Mountain." After a pause, Hryatan added, "Lord, with all due respect, allow me demonstrate its power. Please, choose a fighter, and I will spar with him."

A space in the center of the room was cleared for Hryatan and one of Alaric's men to spar. Alaric chose one of his best men, who came smiling to confront Hryatan. Facing each other, the men allowed their two swords to gently touch and feel the space between them. Then, in one swift movement, Hryatan hit his opponent's stone sword, which shattered into pieces.

The room became silent.

Hryatan thanked his opponent, who was still astonished by the shattered weapon. Hryatan then gave Alaric his sword. "Take it, Prince Alaric. Feel how my sword is thin and light." As Alaric was assessing the sword, Hryatan added, "Lord, I was selected for this mission by King Akkad because my father was a blacksmith, and when I was young, I learned the art of metals. Here are measures of tin." He took small bags from his bag saying, "If you mix one measure of tin with seven measures of copper, this makes eight measures of bronze."

"Hryatan, when can you teach us this art?"

"Tonight, if my lord requests it. Could we please be guided to a burning kiln?"

The villagers took them to an open-air shop where the villagers were firing their clay potteries. Hryatan requested that the oven be left open and fed with more wood. He also asked for a stone vessel and handfuls of the copper pebbles often found by rivers. Hryatan opened a bag and poured its contents into the stone vessel. The coarse powder had shininess that reminded Tesimo of the Ore Mountain stones.

Then Hryatan measured seven measures of copper pebbles with his bag and poured them into the vessel.

Hryatan took a large branch to make an opening in the center of the burning furnace. He then used the same branch to slide the stone vessel into the depth of the fire. He moved away from the burning heat coming from the kiln and told Alaric that they had to be patient for the transformation to happen. Meanwhile, Hryatan took a hard stone tool and asked if he could make a cut in one of the sandstone tiles at the oven entrance. With their approval, he quickly cut with his hard tool through the soft stone and created an elongated wedge-shaped cavity. He then came back to the oven and retrieved the hot stone vessel. Its contents were now a liquid that glowed like the sun.

Using long and strong sticks, Hryatan and helpers carefully slid the vessel close to the cavity he'd just made. He tipped the vessel and allowed some of the liquid to fill the cavity. The glow of the liquid slowly diminished and became the color of Hryatan's sword. When it was cool enough, the wedge-shape was removed from the cavity, and Hryatan gave what looked like a sword blade to Alaric.

For a moment, Alaric remained quiet, wearing a displeased expression. Then he spoke. "The kingdom is in grave danger. We had heard rumors without understanding the urgency of the situation. We leave tomorrow for Sarup to organize our defense."

Later that night, a runner arrived at the hall, where a meeting was held. The messenger told Alaric that the high king had left Sarup for the kingdom archives at Brodgar. Alaric told the group that the news did not change their plans. The fastest way to Brodgar was still north to Sarup and from there a boat to Brodgar. They would leave tomorrow for Sarup, as planned.

The following morning, Tesimo and Druso were already up, admiring the facades of the houses, when Alaric emerged from the great hall with two runners. He sent them away in opposite directions. He spotted the cousins and approached them.

"Zuoz has told me of your losses and your part in his journey here. Thank you for the help you have given them and the kingdom."

Tesimo and Druso bowed, amazed by the show of gratitude from such a man.

After Zuoz and Hryatan joined them, Alaric said, "Before we depart, we have to go to the temple and receive the blessing of protection from the priestess for our journey."

The temple was near the great hall. The structure was open to the sky and seemed to glow with a holy presence. As soon as the cousins entered the hallowed space, they were peaceful and ready to worship. All of the travelers entered the temple and the priestress burned incense while reciting incantations in an unknown sacred language.

When they left the temple, a cart pulled by two oxen was brought to them. The cousins were stupefied. It was the first time they had ever seen a wheeled vehicle. Alaric chuckled at the cousins' gaping mouths. "Don't worry," he said, "we are all going to walk together."

"King Akkad of Hamoukar gave this wagon to my father many sun cycles ago. My father was impressed by the ingenuity but his council did not see the need for transportation. After all, they said, the oxen do not walk faster than a man. Nevertheless, my father had a few chariots made for his lands and gave this one to me. I use it to carry my bags and provisions when I travel throughout the kingdom."

On the north side of town, they passed a very large rondel enclosure. Zuoz said that the astronomers were still using this monument because it was at a very rare place on earth where guardian sun and guardian moon had a special interaction. He explained that in this place, the directions of the sun's solstices were square with the directions of the moon's major standstills. "There is another place like this farther west, called Stonehenge," Zuoz said to the cousins. "Maybe you'll visit it one day."

As they walked, Alaric thought aloud about his strategy, making plans to raise an army to stop the Yamna as soon as possible. He had already had discussions with Hryatan about the horses the Yamna rode, as well as the manner of their armor. Since the Yamna calves were not protected, he wanted his men to be trained to fell the horses with long spears and to attack the Yamna by cutting their calves first and then killing them on the ground.

After they walked together for a few days, Alaric came to like the smart, young Tesimo. He was astonished that this shepherd from behind the White Mountains had acquired such a command of their language in less than two moons. During rest stops, Alaric gave Tesimo lessons on sword fighting. They practiced fencing each other using wooden swords. Alaric experimented, trying to determine the best move to cut the calf muscles of a mounted rider to disable him.

"I don't like metal weapons," Alaric said to Tesimo one day. "Stone swords are the only real swords. I am sad to admit that bronze is going to destroy our honorable way of fighting with our beautiful stone swords. We are living in terrible times. I will have my people collect tin and copper and bring it to Sarup. We will make our own bronze with the tin of the kingdom's islands, and we will push back the

Yamna. Much to my regret, it is our only way of driving back the enemy."""

As they traveled, Alaric explained the hierarchy of the kingdom and his place in it. The high kings of the past had divided the kingdom into five provinces, and each province was divided into sixty houses. Each house was ruled by a lord and each province by an overlord.

The three hundred lords formed the high king's General Council, and the overlords formed the high king's High Council. The role of lords and overlords was to maintain their respective territories in order to provide security and food to the people of the kingdom. Each of them had a residence on the Green Island, where they conferred with the king at least four times a year, during the mid-quarter festivities. The high king himself had a residence on a small island, called the Isle of Man, a few miles east off the coast of the Green Island.

They left the forests and entered prairies where large herds of massive animals called bison roamed the land. The multitude of these animals was stunning. At each encounter, the company was careful not to scare the herds and create a stampede that could crush them.

The villages they encountered in these new lands had the same longhouse shape that they had previously seen, but they were built with stone walls. The hair color of the villagers had changed from dark to blond. On the way, they passed other monumental dolmens near towns and villages. Tesimo understood that these dolmens were passage tombs where people placed their dead to be reduced into bones, the bones later being buried under the floors of their houses.

Over the following days, they reached the summit of a hill where the largest dolmen Tesimo had seen so far was located. Druso was the first to point north toward a silver patch glistening on the horizon.

"What is that, shining there?" he asked Zuoz.

Zuoz squinted and then smiled. "You shall see."

As they came closer, the silver patch grew into a flat horizon with no ends. Tesimo realized this was an immense expanse of water with no discernible borders. The cousins could not easily comprehend what they saw before them. They stood there for an instant, marveling at the sight.

CHAPTER 13

SEPTEMBER 27, 1991
MORNING

Sophia was in a sullen mood. Three days had passed since Aton fired her, and her wounds were still raw. As far as she knew, Professor Zelinger was still in bad shape at the hospital, with no signs of coming out of his coma. She rarely left her apartment and was trying to work on her thesis through her depression and distracted concentration. She used to love her apartment, but now it was beginning to feel like a prison. Her apartment was on the top floor of a building that bordered Burggraben Platz. The climb was long, but the view made it worth it. The building was a mix of old and new, with cobbled archways and intricate facades but renovated interiors in a modern style, with clean lines and high gabled ceilings. The view from her apartment looked on to a plaza, which was always changing, according to the seasons—Christmas decorations in winter, flowers for the spring festival, summer musical bands, and the tents of Oktoberfest. Her furniture was basic but elegant. In an alcove, she had placed a natural-wood low-framed bed and an old headboard that she had painted teal green. Dominating the main living space was a large desk she'd made with steel tube supports and plywood. She had a little kitchen and a small bathroom, both clean with new fixtures and appliances.

From her bed, Sophia watched the drops of rain trailing down the windows of her apartment. It was still dark outside, and the rain was heavy. It was turning out to be one of those cold fall showers that seemed to darken the world for days. She was dreading confronting the weather outside.

She looked at the clock and read eight fifteen. In a panic, she realized she had to get up. There was a lot of work to do. *Get out of bed, girl!* she told herself. She put her slippers on and moved slowly to her kitchen corner to put on the kettle for morning tea. She felt like she was moving aimlessly, like a zombie. She was still disheartened by her experience and was feeling betrayed by the system.

She went to the bathroom and went through her grooming rituals. Then she poured the boiling water into a large cup and added a tea sphere. She sweetened her tea with honey and set herself up to work at her makeshift desk. She could not imagine going back to the department to work with the other archaeology students in the attics of the university, even though the pleasure of seeing Gregory and other friendly faces might help mend her wounds. She could not bear the thought of seeing Aton again.

She had heard through the grapevine that Aton was working crazy hours around his mummy. He would barely leave the building, only moving from the cold room in the basement to his top floor office and back. Sophia often tried to imagine what she would say if ever they met in the university's corridors. She would do anything to avoid that.

She hated the feeling of hatred she was now carrying with her. She hated that this man had made her experience a poisonous feeling that she could not ignore. The feeling was so profound that it disturbed her faith. She was brought up to believe that she was a good person, but suddenly her heart was full of black venom. She tried over and over to pardon Aton for what he'd done to her, but it did not work. She couldn't let it go, at least not yet.

She shook her head, looking at the documents amassed on her desk, determined to make progress. She started with the mindless task of filing the articles she had found yesterday, listing each of them in her growing bibliography. Her eyes fell on a paper that she had skipped—it was titled "The Sacred Landscape of Ancient Ireland."[28] The document laid out the locations of the four Irish "royal sites" built during Neolithic times, sites that formed an eighty-mile-wide equilateral triangle. Something about this article felt familiar. Immediately, Gregory's story about the alignment of the gothic cathedrals in France came to mind. Was it possible that the Neolithic centers that she was studying created a pattern?

Sophia found a map of Europe in her files. Malta was visible, very close to the map's bottom. The top of the map showed lands north of Dublin, just where Newgrange was located. *Great!* she thought. She pinned the map on a wall and then placed two pins where Malta and Newgrange were located. She mentally listed other famous Neolithic sites.

"For sure Stonehenge, the most famous of all," Sophia told herself aloud. She scrutinized her map until she found its location and pinned it too.

Gregory said Chartres was a highly active holy center at the time, she remembered. For the moment, her burning hatred recessed as she lost herself in the possibilities. She found Chartres on the map and pinned it as well. She stepped back and stood astonished for a moment in front of the map. The four pins seemed strangely aligned.

She got a yellow string from her bedside drawer and attached one end to the Malta pin and then stretched the string all the way to the Newgrange pin. The four pins were directly aligned on the string, forming a straight line.

This is crazy. It can't be ... She could not understand how she had never read a thing about something so obvious. *Is it possible this alignment has never been reported?* She knew that these four sites were built around the same time period between 5,600 and 5,200 years ago, but she found it hard to believe their positions could have been planned like that.

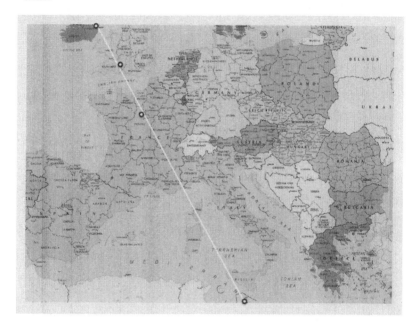

Could this alignment be a freak of nature, an accident? Is something off in the map projection? Somehow, she doubted that was the case. Looking at the straight line of this string stretching across Europe, she felt it must have been designed that way. If true, such an observation had the potential to alter the understanding of the entire European Neolithic social organization.

Sophia was conscious that the hypothesis that a Neolithic society could have planned a 1,600-mile-long alignment of their highest spiritual centers contradicted the scholarly consensus that there had never been an organized Neolithic civilization. Neolithic Europe was believed to be an assemblage of a multitude of independent egalitarian societies of farmers, each having their own individual societies and religious beliefs. She had been taught that during this time period there were not road systems, and interregional communication was extremely slow, if not nonexistent. Sophia could not understand how such primitive societies could organize an enterprise of this magnitude.

The idea that Neolithic people purposely aligned their holiest sanctuaries would mean that even though these centers are architecturally different, they were part of a unified central religion. Actually, this would mean that the spread of spirituality and sacred monument buildings in Europe was a planned and coordinated movement. Such a thing could be possible only if there was a powerful elite controlling most of Europe and the British Islands—a central force able to conceive such a plan, map the terrain, and raise local resources to build these monuments at these specific locations. This is crazy. I'm crazy.

This discovery could shine a new light on the motivations that made Neolithic Britons drag enormous stones for hundreds of miles to build Stonehenge on that very spot. They could have built it anywhere, but it was built precisely under the axis of this alignment. The giant stones used to build the monumental dolmen buried under Chartres's cathedral were dragged for many, many miles to that precise spot, possibly because it was right on this alignment. *I have to show this to Gregory*, she thought. *This is an alignment of the greatest monuments of Neolithic Europe.* These monuments were the highest places of worship at the time, for more than fifteen hundred years.

If her hypothesis was correct, the precise location of these sites seemed to show that Neolithic man had detailed knowledge of European geography and geopolitics. It would also mean that Neolithic man maintained long-range communications and traveled much longer distances, including at sea, than currently estimated. Also, Neolithic man would have had the knowledge, science, and technology to make precise spatial coordinate measurements across a distance of sixteen hundred miles. As far as she knew, these people had had only rocks and sticks. She could not imagine what their methods might have looked like or what kind of math they must have been capable of performing.

She still wondered how it was possible that nobody had ever seen this alignment. This information had been public for centuries, and nobody had noticed that the most important Neolithic sites of Europe were perfectly aligned. She couldn't help but doubt her conclusions. However, staring at the map, she could not find a flaw in her reasoning.

Sophia wanted to share her finding with someone, just to make sure she was not crazy. She guessed Erwin was in his lab by now. She called him, but he didn't answer. She called his house, but an answering machine picked up. She left a message and tried to get back to the work of thesis writing, bibliography creating, and organizing. She could not sit still, could not concentrate on the material in front of her. If her findings were true, they could completely modify several sections of her thesis. She thought that she was done with it, and now she might have a lot more to write. *But how could I propose something so radically contradictory to the established academic belief?* If only she could talk with Professor Zelinger.

She decided to go to the library to check for publications about this alignment. She couldn't continue working until she satisfied her curiosity. She packed her research materials, including the map from the wall, after having replaced the pins with colored stickers. It was still raining, so she wrapped herself in a warm, sturdy raincoat and decided to leave her bike in favor of the bus.

After hours of pouring through indexes, she could not find any paper or publication related to her discovery. She found many reports on alignment among sites relatively close to each other, but no mention of a Newgrange-Malta alignment. She wondered whether the four sites she pinned on her map were the only ones on the axis. There were thousands of Neolithic remains in Europe, but she was interested in only the greatest monuments of the period.

She noticed that Filitosa, the most sacred Neolithic high place on the island of Corsica, was also very close to the newfound alignment. She placed a pin for Filitosa on her map, exactly on the string already stretched. From all her reading, all the greatest known European Neolithic high places were pinned on her map. Then she tried to call Erwin again from the telephone booth of the library. This time he answered from the lab.

"I think I've made a discovery," Sophia told him. "Do you have time to discuss it?"

"I would be happy to hear about it," answered Erwin. "I just started an experiment that I cannot stop. Why don't you come to the lab? I'll have plenty of free time between measurements. We can talk while I keep an eye on my research."

"Great, I'm on my way. I should be there in twenty minutes," Sophia said. She packed up her materials and tried to ignore the disapproving look of an elderly man who was reading from a thick book at another table.

As she left the library, she passed in front of the open door of the archaeological department located on the same floor. She thought about that beautiful dagger she'd had to leave on her desk. Most likely Aton would have left the dagger there, since she was the only one who knew where to replace it in the collection. It wouldn't do to leave this precious artifact in an empty office in an unlocked department.

She gathered her resolve and approached the door tentatively. "Hello? Is anyone in here?" she called. No one answered. She looked around and down the hallway and stairs, but she saw no sign of Aton or anyone else. Moving as quickly as she could, she entered and dashed directly to her old office. The door was open, and there on her old desk was the dagger. She knew where the keys of the collection were and would be able to relog it very quickly.

I can't believe this door is not locked. I don't think Aton cares if the dagger gets stolen or broken. It's not going to happen under my watch. Somehow, she felt guilty that she had not stored the object sooner, as she had been asked to do. She started to grab the dagger when she heard Aton's loud voice behind her.

"Miss Bruckner, what are you doing here?"

Sophia jumped out of her skin and ended up facing Aton. When she regained her composure, she answered, "I was passing by, and I wondered if the dagger was still on my desk. It needs to be properly returned to the collection before it gets lost or broken."

"Miss Bruckner, this is not your desk any longer, and you have no business in this office. You weren't trying to steal this dagger, were you? Get out!" he yelled. "I am calling the police. Get out of my department! I am also going to call the Ethics Committee and ensure that you are expelled from this university for intended theft of a collection artifact. Out of here!"

Sophia retreated in a hurry and ran down the stairs toward the exit.

CHAPTER 14

DAY 52
BRODGAR

"This is the Gray Sea," said Zuoz. Druso went all the way to the water's edge and knelt to fill a water skin, but a fisherman, with a horrified look on his face, grabbed at his arm to prevent him. Druso still could not quite understand the language, especially when spoken so quickly with a strong new accent. So he turned to Tesimo for explanation.

"He said you can't drink that water," Tesimo translated. "It will only make you thirstier."

"What? How can that be?"

After an exchange with the fisherman, Tesimo said, "He says try a little of it and you'll understand. But don't fill any water skin with water from the sea."

Druso knelt and tasted the water and immediately spat it out, making the fisherman laugh.

They spent the night in at large seaside village Dwasieden,[29] where Alaric's boat was harbored. The cousins marveled at fish meats they were offered. Tesimo was determined to try everything, even the strange morsels of flesh the fishermen scraped with ridged rocks. Druso couldn't bear the sight of the fishermen eating what they called "shells," popping the gray flesh into their mouths without even roasting them over a flame. For his part, Tesimo laughed at Druso's disgust and insisted they teach him the method.

They left early in the morning as the sun climbed over the eastern horizon, lighting the sea like blue fire. Alaric's boat was made of planks bound together with tight leather ropes, sealed with a mixture of fibers, sap, and grease. Their boat was larger than any of the other boats in the bay. It was manned by twenty-four rowers and seemed to move with ease. As usual, Garkan started the boat ride by howling like a lost child. As the complaints of the dog diminished, Tesimo watched as the coast became a gray mass on the horizon and slowly disappeared behind them. With his mind still full of his new experience, he wondered what new marvels were waiting for them in Sarup.

Before the coast vanished completely from view, Zuoz came to him, pointing his arm north toward the open sea, and said, "On the other side of this sea, there is a land of ours. Near the cliff of its most southern coastline lays a sanctuary of Ale's Stones,[30] marking the point of harmony. You should witness this wonder some day. It's a circle of sixty stones that was established a long time ago by my brotherhood and has been used for time immemorial as a celestial observatory, ritual center, and season marker. Almost forgotten is that in its center is buried a dolmen hosting a black statue of goddess mother as the pregnant virgin of the world."

Zuoz went on explaining that there was a relationship between earth and sky. "Tesimo, have you noticed that both guardian sun and guardian moon are the same size in the sky?"

"I thought they were, but it's difficult to see because the guardian sun is so bright; it blinds you," answered Tesimo.

"We call the size one of them occupies in the sky a sliver. The ancient astronomers found that when they observed either guardian sun or guardian moon from the center of a circular ditch, or a stone circle, they counted 720 slivers on the fringe of the circle. The harmony of the world is such that that 720 is twelve times sixty. The ancient astronomers called one degree the space occupied in the sky by guardian sun and guardian moon when they cross a vertical line. Think about the face of a red guardian sun, low above a hazy horizon and passing behind the trunk of a tall tree in the distance. Do you remember what a minute of time is called, the duration of sixty heartbeats? Anyone staying still for four minutes of time could observe the right edge of this majestic guardian sun touching the thin dark line made by this staff planted far away," Zuoz said, showing his walking stick. "Then the guardian sun's face crosses behind the staff until its left edge leaves the other side of the staff. This space in the sky representing two slivers is called one degree. The ancient counters divided the circle of the horizon into 360 degrees."[31]

The cousins' heads were spinning with this new flow of knowledge.

"The ancient counters were fantastic men and women," Zuoz added. "They measured many more things than you could think." Tesimo was amazed by what he was hearing, and he gained a new understanding of the world.

Druso scoffed, shaking his head and petting Garkan's head to comfort her.

Rowing near the coast and beaching their boat at night, it took them five days to travel to a large Norse settlement on the coast of a vast island in the Gray Sea, near the sacred site of Sarup. The town was arranged similarly to Goseck, with longhouses placed in nice rows and a central courtyard. Villagers came to the coast to greet them and pulled their boat onto the beach. Tesimo followed the crowd as they went through a wide street to a great hall near the center plaza, built to host Alaric's family. The villagers happily organized a sumptuous feast. News of their arrival traveled quickly, and soon boats from all of the surrounding lands and islands arrived, bringing emissaries and gifts to Alaric and his crew.

The travelers were offered new clothing, colored with local patterns, in exchange for their worn ones. They were then introduced to an assembly in the large hall. The place was full of the heads of the village—judges, priestesses, astronomers, time counters, and traders. After a few appreciative words, Alaric introduced the companions. He asked Zuoz and Hryatan to tell of their journey and the Yamna threat as they had related it to him.

They told of Tesimo's destroyed village and his father's death, their fight with the Yamna, the empty villages near Krpy, the Ore Mountain, and the enslaved villagers. Hryatan explained that the Yamna were making bronze weapons, stronger than stone and copper weapons. He explained that he traveled from Hamoukar to reveal the secret of bronze to the high king in order to combat the intruding Yamna. Finally, Alaric summarized the news they received from the east about the invasion of Yamna tribes that destroyed everything in their path and enslaved all survivors of their raids.

"Dark times are upon the kingdom," Alaric announced to the crowd in a booming voice, "but we will fight, and we will prevail over our invaders. We will regain and preserve the peace of our kingdom. My word is my bond."

During the feast later that evening, Tesimo noticed a young princess was watching him intently, but she looked away every time he turned to look at her, avoiding his glances.

Princess Astrid thought that Tesimo was a very brave man, crisscrossing the wild world to accomplish a noble mission. She could not help but notice that Tesimo was also an attractive man, with his dark hair and dark eyes. His voice delighted her, speaking with an accent from a distant land. In her mind, he looked like a hero of legends. She slowly inched closer to him and when finally they were able to talk to each other, she asked him to recount his journey. She quickly noticed that in spite of his strength, Tesimo was kind and shy.

Tesimo blushed at the attention from a female, something he had not experienced since he fled his burning village, leaving Elena behind. Though he was pleased by her kindness, his heart was torn, as he still mourned Elena's loss. *As Zuoz said, life should go on,* he told himself. *There is no bringing Elena back.*

The pair had a long conversation, talking of all that Tesimo had recently learned and how his understanding of life had changed in such a short while. By the time they separated for the evening, the princess felt a flame had been kindled in her heart for Tesimo.

The next day was a day of rest for Tesimo and Druso, as Zuoz and Hryatan made plans with Alaric and his council. Tesimo was not needed, and when he walked through the great hall and met Princess Astrid, they had a conversation. She offered to show him the splendors of Sarup. Lightheaded, Tesimo accepted immediately, leaving Druso and Garkan on their own. Astrid guided Tesimo through the streets of Sarup and visited the main places of the town. She told him about the figures sculpted in the totems and the related accomplishments of her ancestors. They passed a large hill, the top of which was crowned by a circular wooden enclosure surrounding the high-lying terrace with ditches and palisades. Astrid told him that it was the holiest place of the North Sea. It was where her people traveled from all around the region to conduct their funeral ceremonies and communicate with their ancestors.

Tesimo wondered why people had so many different ways to treat their dead. *Dead is dead. Does it matter?* he asked himself. He thought of his burned village and his relatives and friends, with no one left alive to perform any rites at all.

Tesimo and Astrid spent most of the day together and grew to like each other more and more. When they were on their way back to the hall, they saw Druso sitting on a bench outside, with Garkan at his feet. Tesimo realized that when he'd left with Astrid, he did not think about telling Druso of his departure. Druso saw them coming and walked away, his dog following him. After dinner, Tesimo tried to talk to Druso, but Druso snapped at him, "Why are you not with Princess Astrid?" Later, Druso ignored all attempts Tesimo made to start a conversation. Druso was moody and irritable. Tesimo understood he had hurt Druso's feelings, but he did not know what to do to repair their relationship.

Fortunately, later that night Druso came to him and said, "I'm sorry that I acted the way I did. I guess I was hurt and jealous of Princess Astrid. Other than you, I've lost everything I had, and sometimes I feel alone." He sighed, looking at his boots. "I too need a loving face to rest on."

When Alaric later met with the companions, he knew they would be leaving soon to deliver their message to the high king at Brodgar. Alaric told the companions, "I wish I could accompany you to Brodgar, but I can't. Tell my father that I am arranging our eastern defenses, and there is much to be done." Both Zuoz and Hryatan thought Alaric's decision was wise.

As they were packing to leave, Princess Astrid took Tesimo by the arm and led him away from the others. "It is our custom for a woman to select a husband when she turns thirteen. My thirteenth birthday falls on Mabon, the next equinox. I will wait for you these six moons, for you would be my dearest choice. If you return by Mabon, I will know you have chosen me as well, and I will become forever your spouse." She gave him a carved figure of a bird as a good luck talisman. "Remember me when you look at this bird. Be wise, safe, and lucky. Please, come back to me!" She gave him a final farewell embrace.

Tesimo's heart was burning as he looked in her eyes. "If it is the last thing I do, I will come back to you, my dear," he promised.

Tesimo's heart was heavy when they left Sarup early the next morning, with Astrid's talisman attached around his neck. They reached the coast and climbed aboard the boat already stocked for their journey to Brodgar in the Orkney Islands. A priestess prayed to the great goddess, asking for protection for their journey, and then they left the harbor.

All members of the crew were Norse, like Alaric. The Norse people settled on these islands were explorers and long-range traders. Most of them lived peacefully, but a few became infamous marauders.

Their boat was bigger than the boat that had brought them to Sarup. It too was made of wooden planks attached front and back with tight leather strips, shaped by the central inner structures on which benches were set for the rowers. The hull was covered with animal skin and waterproofed with grease and sap. It was close to fifty feet long and six feet wide, equipped with twenty benches for the rowers. The captain's name was Trygve. He was seated on a central platform two feet above the rowers' heads. When all forty strong Norse rowers manned their oars, the ship could cross the water at amazing speed—fifty to sixty miles in a day.

As they were leaving the harbor, pointing west, Zuoz told Tesimo, "In that direction is the Thornborough Henges, where Orion rules. Further away is Newgrange, one of our most sacred places. I hope one day you will have the chance to visit these places."

The Norsemen were robust people. Most of them wore coats made of the thickest fur Tesimo had ever seen. They wore helmets made of thick animal skin topped with two tusks. One of the oarsman explained to the cousins that at the age of passage, a child had to kill a mature walrus to become a man. Then the would-be man-child earned the right to wear the tusks of the slain walrus on his helmet.

They ate raw and dried seal meat and fish that they captured along their journeys. For four days they sailed north, keeping the coast on their west side. At night, they anchored the boat in the safety of fjords the sea had dug into the rocky coasts. At one stop, Tesimo witnessed a Norseman hunt a sea lion by cornering it against a cliff and piercing its side with a spear. After killing the large animal, they ate its flesh raw. Tesimo and Druso could hardly refuse, afraid to offend these fierce warriors. The Norsemen hung what remained of the meat on the sides of the boat to dry in the sun. Around the campfire, the men told them fantastic stories of places beyond the sea and far from the kingdom, tales of frozen lands and sweltering countries. Tesimo had the impression that the sea was like a mother to them, and they loved it as much as farmers loved their lands.

The following morning, to the cousins' dismay, the Norsemen turned the boat west and entered the open sea. Tesimo looked with fear as the gray line of the coast disappeared on the horizon. The rowers pushed and pulled at the oars continuously, alternating shifts for food and short rests, until well after dusk, when they finally reached land. More than once during the crossing, Tesimo wondered if he would survive this journey. Often, he thought they might be lost, rowing for so long without land in sight to guide them. He was immensely relieved when they finally saw the coast at nightfall.

For the next five days, they continued north, keeping the coast on their east. Then one morning, the Norsemen awakened the group before sunrise, earlier than usual, and they started to row the ship west toward open sea. They reached a place where large sheets of ice were drifting on the water. As the sky turned dark, they anchored their boat on a bank of ice for the night. The following day, Tesimo looked around, blinking in the rising light, and was stunned by the spectacular sight of ice mountains slowly moving south. Avoiding the icebergs, they continued their journey as soon as the sun rose. Both cousins could not keep their eyes away from these ice monsters towering over their boat. By midday, they crossed the path of huge, gray creatures that broke the water's surface, spit streams of water high in the air, and then dove again. Once, one of these huge animals propelled itself into the sky and sent large waves rocking the boat when it fell back into the sea. Druso screamed while the sailors laughed. He and Garkan cowered together in the bow until the boat moved away from the pack of sea monsters.

The next morning, the sky turned milky, as if the clouds had descended onto the sea. A gray and wet blanket surrounded them. The Norsemen seemed unperturbed by it. Druso and Tesimo were frightened, positive that it meant doom for them all. Captain Trygve was not concerned. He could direct his boat through the fog because he had a stone that told him the position of the sun in the sky, even if they could not see it through the mist.[32] The stone changed color when directed toward the sun, even in the fog. Consequently, he knew where the sun was even though it was invisible to them. Tesimo was very impressed by the captain's stone, but he was afraid that they could still hit an ice patch and sink in the frozen sea. He was also terrified each time he heard through the fog the noises of marine animals swimming close to their boat.

Tesimo was very relieved when the fog was gone the next day. Past midday, the captain yelled at his men, pointing his finger at the western horizon. Zuoz helped the cousins see small dark dots on the horizon that were the Shetland Islands, their last stop before the Orkney Islands. As they slowly got closer to the coast, Captain Trygve shouted an order, and the sailors sprang into immediate action. The companions looked in the direction the crew was gazing and saw a ship coming from the opposite direction. Asking what was happening, they were told that they were about to cross paths with a ship that was a marauder's ship. Zuoz explained here had been a recent rash of violent attacks that had wiped out farms in the

Shetland and Orkney Islands, and the approaching boat was most likely on its way back from a raid.

"The captain is going to intercept the boat," Zuoz said, worried. "He says they are wicked, selfish men who shame the honor of the Norse people, for they pillage the hardworking farmers." Tesimo could see that Captain Trygve bore a look of hatred and fury so fierce it made his blood run cold in fear.

The companions' boat was bigger, with more rowers and fighters. The marauders' ship clearly saw this. Intimidated by the outlines of the warrior's horned helmets, it tried to evade the approaching boat. It was no use. Tesimo felt that Trygve's boat was flying at the marauders through the water. Pulling up alongside the smaller boat, several of the Norsemen threw heavy rocks attached to ropes into the bow and stern of the marauders' smaller boat. They quickly pulled on the ropes, forcing the two boats together.

Before Tesimo could fully prepare himself, he found himself drawing his bow and leaping across into battle. Hryatan charged forward with his sword, while Tesimo remained behind him to cover the advance with his bow. The Norsemen fought ferociously, bashing the marauders' skulls with their axes and using their oars to force them overboard into the freezing water and drowning them before they could even scream.

During the battle, both boats were tilting side to side, causing Tesimo to lose his balance. He fell down between the rowers' benches. As the boat rocked violently in the waters, he struggled to get back to his feet. Suddenly, a marauder jumped onto the bench in front of him. Without his bow, Tesimo was defenseless. His hands were struggling to find his small stone knife, which was without contest compared to the marauder's sword.

The marauder raised his sword and was ready to hit Tesimo when a blow stopped him in midair. The marauder fell on his knees, arms still extended with a sword high in the air. Behind the falling man stood Zuoz, his arm holding his bow, after having delivered the arrow that stopped the marauder's life.

It was over quickly, the final surviving marauders falling to the deck in surrender. Two of their own troop had been lost in the battle. Returning to the boat, Tesimo found Druso looking at him, stunned. He was still holding tightly onto Garkan's neck, who all the time had been barking and growling, as if she too had wanted to join the skirmish. Druso was very pale but said nothing.

They found six women bound in the bow of the marauders' boat, crying quietly. They freed the women and transferred them to their boat. The women seemed unsure if they were being released or merely changing captors. Norse sailors dumped the bodies of the dead marauders into the sea. They attached the marauders' boat carrying their own dead warriors. The goods pillaged from the farmers remained on the boat, along with the captured marauders who were bound the same way the women had been a moment before.

Tesimo took it upon himself to comfort the women, offering warmer cloaks and food and speaking in gentle tones, though he was not sure they understood him. Druso, finally regaining his senses, came to help, applying clean, dampened cloths to their wrists and ankles where the rope had caused painful red abrasions. Tesimo looked back at the captain, who seemed pleased with their victory. He looked out over the open sea—clearly proud and relieved that the rogues had been vanquished—like a father over his family, a chief over his village, as if that immeasurable gray-green expanse was his alone to rule and protect.

Finally, exhausted from their travel and battle, they reached the Shetland Islands before nightfall. They rested overnight and left the next morning for Brodgar to meet the high king. For two days, they hopped from small island to small island until they finally reached their destination. The rain had started to fall when they landed on the west coast of the island. They disembarked near a coastal village nestled against a hill named Skara Brae.[33] The houses were half sunk in the soil, their walls faced with light gray stones, evenly spaced. Their roofs were made of animal skins and packed straw. The houses had small doors and were connected by networks of walkways also carved into the ground with nicely faced stone walls. The walkways were covered with animal skin to protect the walking villagers from rain. Tesimo felt like he was walking inside an anthill. Peeking through open doors, Tesimo could see that the houses had a central living space with furniture made of thin stone slabs. Though it made him feel at times too closed in and confined, he marveled at the clever construction details of these homes, designed for comfort and durability. As they wandered through the corridors, Tesimo noticed that the roofs had been built to direct rainwater toward reservoirs below for the village's use and protected the structures with a simple overhanging lip.

As they continued exploring the village, they met villagers who scrutinized them and their attire. At a turn of the walkway, the companions bumped into a man dressed in a light-colored robe decorated with a band of intricate woven patterns and the sun embroidered on his chest. His face brightened when he saw Zuoz.

"Zuoz, my child! Is that you?"

"Master, it's good to see you again," Zuoz said with a reverent bow of his head. "My friends, let me introduce you to Master Taglach, my astronomy teacher."

"Welcome to you all. Zuoz, I am so pleased to see you. What has brought you here?"

"We have come to deliver important news to the king."

"The king came here a week ago, and we rejoiced to have him here for Ostara. Unfortunately, he left in a hurry. I've been told the king is sick, and he went to Tara on the Green Island for rest and healing."

Zuoz's brow furrowed at this news. "In that case, we will need to leave for Tara as soon as possible."

"Zuoz, you will not be able to find a boat leaving Brodgar until the end of the Ostara celebration the day after next."

"A two-day delay is bad news indeed," said Zuoz, clenching his jaw.

"You look tired, Zuoz. Come with me to my home and get some rest. You are all welcome in my home. Zuoz, tell me—who are these friends with you?"

After Zuoz's introduction, the four companions followed the master, who led them to his dwelling. Zuoz had already told Tesimo stories about Brodgar, where he spent two years as an apprentice. Tesimo understood that Brodgar was one of the kingdom's houses of knowledge, established in the early days of the kingdom, and Skara Brae was one of the surrounding villages where the sanctuary dignitaries resided. Nonetheless, Tesimo was not prepared to see the splendors Orkney had to offer its inhabitants. His eyes were wide as he entered the master's house. The stone walls had red-, yellow-, and ochre-painted decoration. Around a central hearth, wooden furniture was placed. Against the walls were shelves made of flat, even stone slabs that held beautiful artifacts made of all shapes and materials, many unrecognizable to Tesimo.

One shelf contained fist-sized dark stones carved with complex delicate patterns. Tesimo was particularly impressed by one stone made from a glistening material, which gave off a black glow and was engraved with intricate spirals. The master, seeing Tesimo's fascination, said, "Please pick them up. They are meant to be touched."

With hesitant obedience, Tesimo lifted the beautifully carved stone. Its surface was remarkably pleasant in his hands. It gave him a feeling of comfort and ease, as if it were made for his hands alone.

"Beautiful, isn't it? These are towie stones.[34] We use these stones for different reasons. Some are given to us for certain achievements. The one in your hand was given to me by Brodgar's grand master for service in this house of knowledge. Other stones are used to transmit elements of knowledge to the apprentices, like these," he said, pointing at a series of stones with a varied number of rounded protuberances, forming all kinds of geometrical patterns.

The master explained to the cousins that at the end of their year of passage, the most talented youth were sent to one of the kingdom's main houses of knowledge to learn the art for which they had a particular affinity. There, they were taught the wisdom and knowledge received from ancestors, such as worshipping, healing, astronomy, counting, and building. Each house of knowledge was known for its own craft. Brodgar was known for teaching astronomy and arbitration. Stonehenge was known for its teaching in astronomy, Avebury for healing, Chartres for building and worshipping, and Malta for counting, especially time counting. In their first year, all students learned general measures and the art of khipu. Men were more prone to Sky's wisdom with astronomy, building, and measures, while women usually opted for Gaia's wisdom, like worship, arbitration, and healing. However, exceptions to the rule always were of great interest.

After three to five years of apprenticeship, the apprentices became masters and then worked for at least seven years, fostering the kingdom. Astronomers, counters, builders, and priestesses were much needed as the kingdom opened new territories and settlements. New farmers needed leaders to establish their communities, prepare for the farming seasons, build temples, teach the rituals of worship, and tend to the dead.

"How do the students learn these skills?" asked Druso, showing unusual curiosity.

"The masters, like me and many others, recount the stories and tales of the great masters from the past, who learned from the masters before them, and so on and so on it has been since before the beginning of the kingdom. Masters knew thousands of stories from their own people but also from peoples from other horizons and other skies. They seek to learn all of the stories in their areas of expertise. The most brilliant masters have even created stories to teach the history of our people, our customs, our rules, and the reasons behind them. Our knowledge is also recorded in khipus, and all apprentices learn the art of the talking knots."

Zuoz said that since they could not leave the island, he wanted to go to the kingdom archives, and he invited the cousins to join him. One of the greatest surprises of Master Taglach's house was a private bathroom recessed in a corner. Waste could be flushed away with water through an ingenious drainage system. One after the other, the four companions cleaned up and dressed in plain gray robes provided by the master. Their weapons were left in the master's house, and they walked the couple of miles that separated the village from the sacred compound, located to the east of the village.

On the way, they passed an incredible stone circle, about 340 feet wide, made of sixty erected stones, eight to twelve feet tall. The stone circle was set within an immense circular ditch, thirty feet wide and ten feet deep, carved out of solid sandstone bedrock.[35] Tesimo was very impressed by the site and had a difficult time imagining the effort and time needed to complete such an achievement with stone hammers and shoulder blade shovels. To Tesimo's surprise, there was not a trace of the mountains of rock debris removed in order to dig the ditch. It was as if it had been whisked away.

The kingdom archives were located in the middle of the ness, a narrow strip of land shaped like a finger surrounded by water. A stunning wall made of beautifully faced white stones that towered high above their heads surrounded the archives. There was only one well-guarded gate to enter or exit the walled compound. Tesimo imagined that the archives must be the most precious of all the kingdom's treasures to have been placed in such a highly defended location on an island lost in the middle of nowhere in the cold Gray Sea.

The companions were allowed to enter after Zuoz showed the guards the pendant he wore around his neck. Tesimo had always thought it was a good-luck charm, but now he understood that it was a sign of his importance in the kingdom.

As they spoke with the guards, several messengers came in and out of the compound. As they entered the gate, Tesimo realized that the walls were incredibly thick, maybe thirteen feet or more.[36] Inside the walls was a large court with many rounded buildings built of beautiful stonework and painted with red, ochre, and black patterns. Zuoz explained that each building contained the vital records of a specific region of the kingdom. The strong smell of incense coming from the first oval-shaped house in front indicated it was occupied by time counters keeping track of the different kingdom times.

Throughout the bustling compound, Zuoz scanned the symbols on each building until he found the records for the region of Krpy. The guards at the entrance let them through, and they entered the strangest room Tesimo had ever seen. In the center was something that looked like a large circular table, divided by man-height vertical separations emanating from the center. Men stood in front of each section, whispering words to each other. Zuoz explained that the table was a map of the regions they had crossed and that the attendants were keeping records of each village in each region, including a region's population, harvests, and needs. The man in charge of the room introduced himself. "I am Orbac, from the house of the Overlord Bricriu. Tell me who you are and what you want!"

Zuoz introduced the company as kingdom messengers. He told him that one of his requirements was to check on the well-being of the people of Krpy. With a snort, Orbac answered that there was nothing out of the ordinary from these lands. "The people of Krpy are superstitious and lazy," he continued. "Villages are sometimes abandoned because of bad harvests, and they claim this is the result of monsters destroying their fields. These people can barely feed themselves because they waste their resources on silly old folk tales." Orbac went on, saying that he heard about stories of abandoned villages and a beast from the mountains eating villagers, but he did not believe there was any truth in these reports.

Zuoz told Orbac he was glad that he was aware of the situation and thanked him for his time. As they left the kingdom archives, Zuoz spoke quietly to Tesimo. "Orbac is lying. He would not look at me as he spoke and wanted us to leave. There is something very wrong in this region's lordship." Tesimo agreed that there was something strange about Orbac's behavior because he was not even trying to investigate the problems of Krpy's people. It was late in the day when they returned to Master Taglach's house, where they were given a small room to rest. The master also told the companions that he had arranged the boat trip for them to go to the Green Island tomorrow, following the ceremonies.

Since Zuoz would be at Brodgar for Ostara celebrations, he was to participate in the next day's rituals. He left the cousins to go prepare his mind and purify his body with his brotherhood. Before he left, they decided to meet back at the master's house following the ceremonies. The cousins then explored the village, greeting people as they continuously arrived to participate in the next day's festivities. Many had come from far distances, and Tesimo and Druso joined a group bringing offerings to the stones of Stenness,[37] another stone circle situated on the shore facing the Ness of Brodgar. The stone in the center of the circle was beautifully sculpted with a unique angled shape. The sky was dark when they finally went back to Master Taglach's house to rest for the night.

Next day started with the equinox sunrise ceremony. Hundreds of apprentices and masters, dressed in robes of different colors, according to their specialties, gathered on the avenue leading to the ceremonial buildings. Zuoz stood with his order, while the rest of the companions watched from afar with the visiting crowds of pilgrims. Under the purple sky of the early morning, men walked in silence to the Ring of Brodgar, honoring guardian sun, while women went to the Stenness stones, honoring guardian moon.

Throngs of pilgrims gathered around the holy sites with offerings. As the sun rose, the crowds chanted prayers and sang ritual music celebrating the equinox. Tesimo's heart filled with love and gratitude. As the sun continued its ascent toward midday, the master of ceremonies concluded the ritual, and the worshippers started to leave the complex. The apprentices and teachers first disappeared from public view under the pilgrims' cheers. In turn, the crowd dispersed, and shortly after midday the companions were reunited. They thanked Master Taglach for his hospitality, and they left Skara Brae for the coastal village of Stromness, where a boat to Tara was waiting for them.

CHAPTER 15

SEPTEMBER 27, 1991
LATE MORNING

As expected, Erwin was at the screens of control panels when Sophia arrived at his lab. Sophia was very distressed about her altercation with Aton. She told Erwin what had happened with Aton and his threats of punishment. "I think I'm going to throw up. I'm a total wreck. If I get expelled, I won't graduate."

Erwin did not know what to say. "I'm sorry about what's happening. I can't believe that you have to deal with that scumbag, and he is the one ruling your life. That's so unfair. What do you think you can do?"

"I don't know. I guess I'm going to wait and see what he does. Then I'll figure out my reaction," answered Sophia, pacing in the lab. She finally sat on a nearby stool and started to calm down. "Erwin, it's crazy what he is doing. The guy is a criminal, and he is going to get away with murder and prevent me from graduating."

"I would like to help, but I don't know what to do. We have to pray that in the end, you will explain what happened, and everything will be okay. You are a good person; you did nothing wrong. Things will end up working in your favor—

you'll see. When you called me, you were excited about something. What was it?"

Sophia's mood brightened as she remembered her discovery. She drew a map on a piece of paper and explained what she had found.

"That's amazing!" Erwin said, clearly impressed. "And no one has ever noticed that before. What about that!"

"I don't know what to think. I don't understand," admitted Sophia. "It makes me wonder how precise this alignment is. Maybe they aren't actually as aligned as they appear. I don't have the mathematical skills to check that."

"Oh, I can do that for you. Give me a few minutes." Erwin got on the lab computer, and while keeping an eye on his experiment, he looked up the exact coordinates of the sites and used satellite imagery to plot them on the screen. "It's funny; it looks like there is one site per land mass. Is there any site located in west Sicily?" asked Erwin. "That's the last island under the path of the axis between Newgrange and Malta."

"No, there is nothing major there. I thought about that too, and I did more research. There are many Neolithic remains in Sicily but nothing of similar scale to the other temples marked on the map. But you know, I'm not really surprised. In most cases, Neolithic temples were built in special places, away from populated settlements. I wonder if Malta could have been the most holy place of Sicily. After all, these are the people who built Malta's temples."

"Let's see what we have," said Erwin, entering the coordinates of the five sites in his computer. Using mathematical software, he then plotted the sites' locations on a graph. Erwin printed out the graph and lifted the paper close to the computer screen.

Suddenly, Erwin let out a sharp exclamation. "Look! It shows a 99.96 percent confidence level. That's nuts!"

"It means it's precise, doesn't it?" Sophia held her breath, looking at the computer screen over his shoulder.

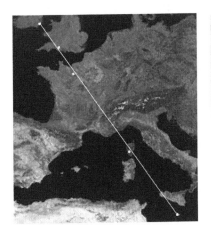 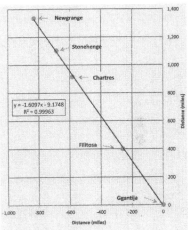

"Yes, it is. It is extremely precise. That means that the chances for this alignment to be random are 0.04 percent. The chances that it was intentionally made are 99.96 percent. You can't get a better confidence level than that. What's your bet?"

Absorbing the information, Sophia stayed quiet for a moment. Erwin said, "There is no way this alignment is random. I don't know why and how they did it, but it was definitely intentional. These sites were aligned on purpose. Hey! Would it be a discovery? You just found that the five most important European sites are aligned in a perfect line. Should that be new news in your world?"

"Hold on, hold on!" said Sophia. "Don't you think it is odd that this alignment has never been noticed before? These are the most famous Neolithic sites in the world, and they are placed in a neat line spanning 1,600 miles, separated by multiple bodies of water. How can that be?"

"It's right here in front of our eyes," answered Erwin.

"I don't know," answered Sophia, shaking her head. "This is all so confusing. The idea that these monuments were purposely aligned means that these people were able to map out Europe on an incredible scale. This is unheard of; it's insane, unbelievable. I was taught that the Neolithic religions were established independently from each other. Can you imagine the degree of knowledge, organization, and coordination the construction of an alignment of this scale would imply? How were these people able to transmit enough information from generations to generations to accumulate such knowledge, without any known writing? Tell me, Erwin, how could they have done that? It can't be."

"I don't know. There must have been other ways of passing down knowledge that we have not yet discovered. Look at the Jewish people; they were able to transmit their oral tradition for more than two thousand years before they wrote it down. All I can tell you is that the places you pinned on your map are lined up at 99.96 percent precision degree over a distance of about 1,600 miles. It's one of those things that are so large it's hard to see. Everybody has looked at these maps, but nobody saw it. You, Sophia, saw this alignment, and from now on, nobody will ever look at these maps in the same way again. You are on to something, Sophia. I'm telling you; this is a *real* discovery!"

"This is crazy. We're talking about the whole of Europe—at least everything north and west from Malta. We would be talking about an unknown ancient civilization in Europe that may have lasted more than fifteen hundred years."

"Hold on," said Erwin. "I have something to do." Erwin went to his machines in a corner of the lab, looked at some screens, and wrote numbers in his lab notebook. From there, he asked Sophia, "It's amazing that all the most holy sites of the Neolithic are aligned like that. Do we know what these people believed?"

"Again, without written records, we don't know much about their religion," answered Sophia. "Basically, it's anyone's guess. You know, I often wondered what it would have been like to live in those times. We don't know much about Neolithic man, but one thing is sure: he was very religious. Their burial rites testify to a belief in life after death. However, we understand they practiced different types of death rituals simultaneously in communal cemeteries. Body cremations were practiced where other people buried their dead with grave goods, like weapons, potteries, food, and drink. While both rituals seem to be designed to help the souls of the departed enter the otherworld, they show societies with individuals having distinct religions or philosophies of life. Since there is no sign of wars in the archaeological records for this time period, we have to conclude that these different religions might have coexisted peacefully. And it's not just about peace between each farmer clan. There are cemeteries with hunter-harvester people buried side by side with farmers."

"Huh! So do you think they had a common set of beliefs?"

"It's hard to say. We know that they used totems—you know, large standing tree trunks sculpted with images of plants and animals, probably symbolizing the spirits of their ancestors and protectors. But all over Europe we also found small statues of female figures, some of them looking pregnant, making us believe that they may have venerated a goddess mother, maybe earth, a worship associated with fertility and harvest." As Erwin returned to his desk, Sophia added, "However, it's difficult to speak of a unified religion because they left us many different types of religious monuments. At this point, there is no way to know if different religious movements used these monuments or if they were different elements of a common belief system. We have no idea. The only thing we know for sure is that European Neolithic people were deeply religious."

"How do you know that?"

"I'm saying that because they left us hundreds of thousands of religious monuments, each taking a great deal of effort and planning to build."

"What kinds of monuments were they?"

"The most common type of Neolithic monuments are the standing stones, also called menhirs in northwestern Europe. Some were up to seventy feet tall and weighed three hundred tons. They could have been used as ancestor memorials, territory markers, sacred stones, astronomical pointers, commemorative event monuments, and so forth.

"Another common type of monument was the henge enclosure found commonly in the British Islands. They consist of a circular ditch surrounded by a bank. It is believed that the function of a henge was to mark the limits of a ritual space where ceremonies were conducted separately from the outside world.

"Seemingly associated with the henges were stone circles, which could have been calendars, astrological observatories, or monuments dedicated to the veneration of stars and planets.

"Dolmens were also important monuments for the Neolithic people. We think they could have been burial chambers or portals for the souls to enter the netherworld," Sophia added in a very scholarly way. "Only in the French region of Chartres did they build dolmens of such great proportions.

"Tumuli, like Newgrange, are also called 'passage tombs,' even though there is not evidence that they were used as burial places."

"You're right. It looks like these people were busy," said Erwin.

"Yes they were," responded Sophia with a smile. "As I said, nobody truly knows why they built them all, but it's interesting to notice that most of these monuments are aligned with specific celestial events, mainly the sun's solstices and equinoxes. That's why scholars believe that the worship of these people included the sun, the moon, and probably the stars."

"Interesting," acknowledged Erwin. "Father Sun—I can totally understand that. After all, I read somewhere that there isn't one atom of your body that doesn't come originally from the sun. In many ways, you can say that the sun is the father of all matter surrounding us. I can also understand Mother Earth. Earth is not just a planet; it's a jewel in the universe. One in billions, Earth has all the right stuff—just the right distance from the sun; the right mass, temperature, and material composition to allow, after about two billion years of transformation, the emergence of organic life. Add a few billions years of evolution, and here we are. I can easily see earth as the mother goddess."

"You are crazy, you know?" Sophia leaned forward to stare at the map.

"Maybe, maybe not," replied Erwin.

"Anyway, standard academia's position is that all of these Neolithic monuments were constructs of different local religious movements, independent of each other. There may have been traveling 'preachers,' but everything was built by independent groups of local farmers. I was taught that there has never been a megalithic civilization." Sophia turned to Erwin and looked at him with raised eyebrows. "So if I write that the largest places of worship of the Neolithic Age were purposely placed along a single line across Europe, I don't think that would be well received. Nobody is ready to talk about the existence of a higher level of organization than local or even regional tribal leadership during the Neolithic Age. This alignment of the most sacred temples could only exist if an incredibly organized and powerful elite across all of Europe had planned and implemented it." After a pause, Sophia added, "The scale of this thing is unbelievable—1,600 miles."

Still looking at his instruments, Erwin said, "To me, it is hard to believe that these people had the knowledge to align these constructions in the east-west direction with such primitive tools. I'm not sure how you do that when you only have rocks and sticks. You see, it is relatively easy to know how far north or south you are by measuring the altitude of a fixed star or by determining the length of daylight at a specific date on the calendar, the easiest date being a solstice. For instance, in winter, for a specific calendar day, the farther north you are, the shorter the duration of daylight. It was tabulated in such a way that by measuring the length of daylight for a specific day, you could know your latitude.

"However, it is much more complicated to know how far you are east to west because the length of daylight on a specific calendar day is constant along a parallel. The only way we have found how to calculate the distance east-west from a starting point is to measure the difference in the altitude angle of celestial bodies at a certain time of day, using the time from the starting location measured with a timepiece. For example, if you travel west from here and don't change the time of your watch, the sun will not reach its apex when your watch says noon. It could be minutes or hours difference, according to how far east or west you have travelled. That's why we have time zones. But without a system of standard time and a means to measure it and keep it, we don't know how to calculate distances travelled in the east-west direction. In modern history, we had to wait for the invention of the mechanical clock in the fifteenth century to allow ship captains to calculate how far east or west they had travelled on the open ocean. Each degree the sun's position is off from its apex at noon, at standard time, corresponds to a specific distance travelled east-west on water. It is puzzling to me that these people were capable of such prowess with only primitive tools. Unless ... do you know if hourglass clocks existed during the Neolithic period?"

"No, as far as I know we haven't found evidence of hourglasses in the Neolithic archaeological records. If I'm correct, hourglasses came thousands of years later, around the fourth century AD," answered Sophia.

"I see. This alignment is very puzzling. Do you have any additional relevant sites?"

"Yes, I found a few," said Sophia, taking a list from her briefcase. "Would you mind plotting them?"

"Not at all. Give them to me," said Erwin, going to a desk to take a pad of paper.

"So we're talking about active sites in the late Neolithic, about the time when Otzi the mummy was living, roughly 5,300 years ago. There are not any more Neolithic sites of the caliber of those already plotted on the map. In terms of size and influence, you can count the other relevant sites on the fingers of one hand. Starting with standing stones," she said, holding out one finger of her right hand, "the greatest fields of menhirs by far are located in France, at Carnac,[38] west of Chartres. More than three thousand very large stones are still standing nowadays, aligned in many parallel rows for miles. Our assumptions are that there may have been many as ten thousand menhirs in these fields. By all means, Carnac must have been an extremely important place in Neolithic times."

"Carnac—I've got that," said Erwin, writing on his notepad. "What else do you have?"

"Regarding the stone circles, after Avebury,[39] the second largest one is Stanton Drew,[40] located in England. The next largest stone circle is the Ring of Brodgar in Scotland. Another notable stone circle is Ale's Stones in Sweden.[41] It's also called the Swedish Stonehenge. It isn't a circle anymore because in the tenth century, Vikings moved the stones to build a stone-boat monument for one of their kings. However, the remaining stone socket imprints in the ground show that they came from a large circle made about 5,300 years ago. Actually, it is not very far from Sarup on the Danish island of Funen, probably the most sacred place of the region, encompassing Scandinavia, Denmark, and northern Germany. Sarup was a large cult center surrounded by earthworks and moats."

"I see, I see," mumbled Erwin taking notes. "Anything else?"

"Regarding henge constructions, the largest one in the world is the henge built around Avebury's stone circle. Maybe the next largest one is at the site known as Knowlton Circles[42] in England. There is also another interesting site called the Thornborough Henges,[43] which is a group of three large henges aligned over a one-mile length. Talking about henges, I have to say that the henge built around the Ring of Brodgar is very impressive. It has a circular ditch of about ten feet deep, thirty feet wide, and 1,200 feet in circumference, carved out of solid sandstone bedrock. It's an incredible task, using only rudimentary tools made of stone and bone. Even more mysteriously, there is no circular bank around this ditch. The builders carried away all the rock debris, and we have no idea what they did with it. The immense mass of debris is completely gone, swept away."

"Interesting. I got all that. Any other sites?" asked Erwin.

"We have the dolmens. There are a few very large dolmens in the Chartres region, the largest one being the one that Chartres Cathedral is built on. There are also large dolmens in northern Europe. The second largest dolmen is probably the Great Dolmen of Dwasleden, in Germany." Looking down her list, Sophia added, "There is one last thing that may have some relevance. It's *La Vallée des Merveilles*,[44] the Valley of Wonders. It's a desolate rocky canyon high in the Southern French Alps that contains by far the largest European collection of early Bronze Age petroglyphs. It is certain that it was a very important place during the early Bronze Age, and perhaps its significance began in the late Neolithic period.

"Okay, I'll look into it."

A metallic sound and a beep signaled that Erwin's experiment was finished. He looked at the computer printout and, with a grunt, placed it with his binders into his backpack.

"Everything okay?" asked Sophia.

"Yes, everything is fine. It's just another data point."

Erwin looked at his watch and said, "Look at the time! It's almost one. I bet you haven't had lunch."

"You're right, I haven't. Do you want to grab some lunch?"

"Sure. I need to swing home first. Can we meet at around one, one fifteen, at a cafe downtown? How about Grintzhop, near Leopold University?"

"That's fine. I too need to go to my apartment to get my material for the afternoon classes."

She thanked Erwin for helping her compile the analysis of her discovery. Sophia unlocked her bicycle, and they both left the building heading in separate directions.

CHAPTER 16

DAY 81
NEWGRANGE

The journey from Brodgar to Newgrange was uneventful. The travelers' boat hopped from small island to small island until the exhausted voyagers finally reached the coast of the Green Island. The next day, the sunset enflamed the western sky as they passed the Isle of Man,[45] the king's residence. They knew that the suffering king was not there but resting at Tara, his encampment near Newgrange's healing center on the Green Island.

The following day they reached the coastal village that served as harbor for both Tara and Newgrange. Tara was almost a day's walk inland, so the companions rested in the village for the night. During their evening meal, Zuoz explained that the high king had four standing meetings per year with the general council. The meetings were associated with the four cross-quarter days of the solar cycle. The first meeting was the festival of Samhain, celebrated during mid-autumn, and it was held at Tara at about the same time religious ceremonies were performed in Newgrange, a few miles away. Then, during the mid-winter festival of Imbolc, the king met the general council at Ailinne, south of the Green Island. At the mid-spring festival, Beltane, the king was in Cruachan on the west side of the island. Finally, the king met the general council at Emain Macha, north of the island, for the mid-summer festival of Lughnasa.

Early the next morning, they left for Tara. Their path led them through the lush Boyne Valley, the most sacred place on the island. Both sides of the wandering Boyne River were covered with sacred monuments. It was late in the afternoon when they arrived in view of Newgrange's immense temple mound. The construction seemed to bulge naturally from the ground, but it was too perfect to be a natural formation. A large wall of shining, split quartz rock surrounded a dark opening on the southeast side of the monument. In front of the opening was a massive stone laid sideways, with engravings of linked spirals. Other enormous engraved stones circled the base of the mound.

Tesimo could see the temple was not quite finished. Lines of workers were coming and going, climbing to the top of the temple, carrying either large boulders or baskets of clay and leaving with their baskets empty. Zuoz led them through the busy workers to meet the great astrologer and great priestess. Zuoz greeted the officials warmly and reverently, as if returning home to his elder family after a long departure. After having given them the greeting due to their rank, Zuoz explained the urgency of their mission and their need to see the high king.

The priestess answered, "Zuoz, the high king left for Avebury four days ago. As I hear, his health is getting worse, and I am sad to tell you that he is no longer capable of leading. With Alaric away in the north, the high council is now in charge of the kingdom."

Zuoz turned to the cousins and saw Druso leaning heavily against a stone, his eyes closed and his head drooping, while Tesimo swayed on his feet. Zuoz motioned to a young astrologer apprentice who was in the room. "Could you please show my friends a dry place to sleep? They are exhausted and need rest."

Tesimo was about to object but found he didn't have the energy. Zuoz and Hryatan turned back to further discuss the growing threat to the kingdom, while Tesimo and Druso followed the young apprentice to a camp nearby the enormous building. Pallets were laid out for the workers to sleep in shifts, and the cousins chose two empty spots, where they fell asleep quickly.

The sun was already high in the sky when the cousins finally woke, blinking in the light. They rose and walked around to admire the sacred precinct. In its entirety, it seemed vibrant with significance. The brightness from the sun seemed to make the grass glow a brighter green than they had ever seen before, and the stones gleamed with a golden light.

A boy about their age came to them and said, "Welcome. My name is Neemar. I was asked to take care of you during your stay at Newgrange. Here are fresh clothes. Let me know if you need anything more."

Adjusting their clothes, Tesimo and Druso looked at the impressive mound of rocks workers were assembling, continually adding more rocks to the pile.

"Is this your first time visiting Newgrange?" asked Neemar, smiling. Pointing at the mound with both hands, he added, "The beauty doesn't decrease with time, but you grow accustomed to it. What're your names?"

Both cousins answered simultaneously.

"My name is Druso."

"My name is Tesimo."

"Neemar, are you a builder?" asked Druso, looking at the young man's strong arms, straight posture, and sharp eyes.

"Yes, I am. It fills my heart with love and brotherhood. And it's a joy to be building this beautiful tumulus. Our ancestors have built many temples, but Newgrange is the biggest one that has ever been built. It is dedicated to the light of the Yule, the union of guardian sun with earth, the light that gives life on earth for a new sun cycle."

"We are honored to be on your sacred grounds," Tesimo said.

"You are welcome here," responded Neemar. "We have worked on this holy place for generations. My father and his father and his father before him gave a part of their lives to this place. We are living in great times. The master builders told us that the sanctuary would be completed within six solar cycles."

"You have built a mighty sanctuary," said Tesimo.

"Yes, it is. You see, long ago, the great builders came from the South and drew a large henge on this exact spot," Neemar said, making gestures with his arms. "They instructed my people to fill the shallow henge with large rocks found on the coast, twenty miles away, laying them down on the circle. More rocks were brought to make the sacred chamber in the center of the mound." Neemar pointed at the chamber's entrance. "These boulders come from a valley many miles away." He pointed to a line of workers walking on a path that led southwest from the construction.

The cousins were in awe; they had never seen anything so monumental. There were hundreds of workers around them—some resting before going back for another load, others busy at their tasks. Though many worked in silence, they bore expressions of concentrated joy. Men carried boulders, and women helped to settle them into place and secure them evenly with grass and clay. Other women moved through the crowd, carrying vases with water and baskets of flat bread balanced on their heads.

"All these people ... they're all about our age," remarked Druso.

"Yes, we are all here for our year of service." Neemar noticed the cousin's questioning faces. "When children of the kingdom begin to stand tall and no longer require their families' constant protection, they are of an age for their year of service. They come here to offer the priesthood a year of service or, as some others call it, the year of sacrifice."

"Why don't you use oxen to carry the boulders?" asked Tesimo, looking at the line of workers painfully bringing the stones to the top of the mound.

"No animal can be used to build a temple. This would be irreverent. Building a temple is an act of worship, and they have to be built only by the hands of worshippers. The building itself is not important; what is important is the act of worship, of sacrifice. It's the sacrifice of all our generations that counts, not the size of the piles. Do you understand?"

"I think I do," Druso said.

"This holy endeavor gives physical and moral strength to the laborer. That's what's important."

"And what do you do at the end of your year of sacrifice?" asked Tesimo.

"Most of us go back to our villages, marry, and raise families. Some stay longer and join the priesthood or go on to Brodgar to learn an art," said Neemar.

"So what are you going to do, Neemar?" asked Druso.

"I would like go to Brodgar and learn astronomy ... but now that I've met Aghna, I want to go back home with her and start our family."

"It seems you like this Aghna," said Tesimo.

Neemar's eyes grew wistful, and he stared blankly over the horizon. "Aghna is a beautiful girl from my people. Her year of sacrifice started at the same time as mine. We want to get married, and we need our parents' approval to celebrate our union. That can only be done at one of the quarter-days when the families meet in the cursus,[46] north of the temples."

Druso smiled as he listened to Neemar speak. He had never found a girl he wanted to be with and wished he could feel the same hope and fire he saw in Neemar's eyes.

"You should come to the Boyne's cursus for the spring festival of Beltane, in a moon from now."

The companions had already passed Newgrange's cursus on their way to the temple mound. It was a large earth bank, surrounding a strip of flat land more than a mile long and a half-mile wide. It was large enough to hold herds on their way to or from pastures. It was a place where large families reconnected, where people met to bargain, negotiate, play, and exchange stories. At night, there were bonfires, festivals, and dances, with people holding colored ropes attached to the tops of large poles. It was a common place where young men and women found and proposed to each other.

"Each clan pitches tents, and families mingle together for several days. There are the celebrations, games, feasts, and markets. Weddings are arranged and celebrated with festivities. Most often the weddings are celebrated between youth who worked together during their year of service. That is how my parents met and their parents before them. I hope to obtain my parents' approval and marry Aghna this summer."

Neemar asked the cousins about their travels. He was fascinated by their stories and the places they had visited. "You are braver than I am," he said. As they spoke, they strolled together around the grounds and back to the worker's camp. They reached a group of women sitting together, talking and laughing as they ground flour between grinding stones and poured it in bowls on the floor. "This is my sister, Mirna. Mirna, please come meet our guests." One of the girls set her bowl aside and rose to greet them. They exchanged names, and Neemar recounted to her some of the cousins' adventures.

"What have we here?" she asked and knelt to greet Garkan, who kept close to Druso's heel. Mirna pulled a piece of jerky from a pouch at her hip and broke off a small piece. She looked up at Druso. "May I give him this?" she asked.

Her eyes were large and sparkled with good humor and intelligence. There was a sound brightness to her face, a lean strength to her shoulders and legs. Druso found he could not speak and simply nodded.

The look exchanged between them was not lost on Tesimo, and he smiled sadly for his cousin. *If I am to lose my cousin as a companion due to love, let it be in the arms of this girl*, he thought.

Back at the lodge, the cousins reunited with Zuoz and Hryatan.

"We cannot delay any longer," Zuoz said. "We must go to Avebury tomorrow to see the king."

"I thought the king was too ill to help," said Druso, a tone of protest in his voice. "The high council is here. It is they who lead now and will drive back the threat."

"So we've been told, but I am not sure we can trust all that we've been told. I need to see the king with my own eyes. The council may not be acting for the kingdom but for themselves." Zuoz stopped speaking suddenly as a messenger arrived, interrupting their conversation.

"You are invited to meet High Council Overlord Bricriu. He wants a full report on the events of your journey and the situation of his homelands in the east. He is expecting you tomorrow morning at Tara."

"You can tell Bricriu that we will come," answered Zuoz. After the messenger left, Zuoz turned toward his companion and said, "I cannot refuse the invitation. We have to go to Tara."

"I suppose that will delay our trip after all," commented Hryatan.

"I could not refuse. There is nothing I can do."

The next morning, they left Newgrange for Tara, a short walk away.

Walking ahead, Garkan rounded the bend of the path and disappeared from view. A moment later, the companions heard the dog's angry barking, but it was already too late. From the cover of the forest, an arrow was shot and hit Zuoz in the shoulder. In an instant, Tesimo and Hryatan crashed into the trees to attack the hiding aggressors. They could hear the attackers scramble through the forest, but they quickly disappeared.

They abandoned the chase through the dense wood and returned to Zuoz. Druso knelt on the ground, holding Zuoz's head in his lap. Zuoz's limbs were twitching, and Druso tried to hold him still. Zuoz seemed possessed, shuddering and vomiting in choking bursts on the road. After what seemed a long, painful time, Zuoz lost consciousness completely and grew still.

"I have seen this before," said Hryatan as he knelt. "It was a poisoned arrow. This may help." He pulled some herbs from the satchel he always kept attached to his belt and packed them tightly in the wound.

"Druso," Tesimo called, "run back to Newgrange and bring people to help us."

Hryatan lifted Zuoz on his shoulders to carry him back to camp. They struggled slowly, for Zuoz was heavy and was occasionally seized by fits of shudders and convulsions. They were met halfway by Neemar and other friends. They'd brought with them a resting pallet, supported by two wood braces, to carry Zuoz back to Newgrange. As soon as they reached the sanctuary, priest healers took Zuoz to the highest centers, where other healers were already waiting, and immediately attended to him. The healers cleaned the wound and applied more herbs. They worked over Zuoz's unconscious body for a long time, administering potions and repeating prayers. Slowly, Zuoz's face seemed calmer, but he did not regain consciousness.

Late that afternoon, Bricriu himself arrived, carried by porters. He explained that he had learned of the attack on Zuoz. Concerned for Zuoz's health, Bricriu had brought his own healer. However, Zuoz's state did not improve. For days they kept watch over Zuoz. His skin turned an ashy gray, and he seemed to shrink, his skin caving and revealing more of his skeleton with each passing day. Neemar and Mirna came to check on Zuoz twice a day, telling Tesimo and Druso the stories of the day. During the day, Druso started to leave Zuoz's tent for long walks outside, as Tesimo stayed close in case help was needed.

Tesimo learned that Druso had gone with Neemar and Mirna to carry boulders to build the temple. One night Druso told him he wanted to help build the massive tumulus. It took him a half-day to complete one trip from the boulder deposit to the temple mound. The boulders were carried in soft baskets attached to the backs of the boys. The girls distributed food supplies and water along the way to the boulder deposit. Everybody was joyful and helpful, and Druso enjoyed this time with them. The path was approximately six miles one way, and the boulder load made the return very slow through the ups and downs of the wild forest hills. To Druso's surprise, he explained, his muscle pains transformed into heartwarming feelings. Druso told Tesimo that he felt a connection with this land, a connection he had not felt since they left the majestic mountains of their childhood.

After five days, Zuoz's health had not improved. Bricriu insisted on taking Zuoz to Avebury. The main priests agreed, saying that only the great master healer would be able to save Zuoz. Bricriu inserted himself in the companions' group discussion, encouraging them to take Zuoz there. Knowing that Avebury was the major healing center, Tesimo agreed with the others that taking Zuoz to Avebury was the best thing to do for his health. They set the departure time for the next day.

Tesimo wished they could have politely refused Bricriu's assistance. Zuoz had told him not to trust anyone, and he did not feel he could trust Bricriu—he had a bad feeling about the man. Bricriu had an overly attentive demeanor and excessive adornments. Tesimo wondered if the conspiracy could have gone as high as the great council and if Bricriu somehow could be working with the Yamna. After all, Zuoz was wounded on their way to meet the overlord. Tesimo would have preferred not to attempt the long, difficult journey to Avebury while looking over his shoulder with mistrust the whole time.

Later that night, Druso took Tesimo aside. "Tesimo, we need to talk. Things have changed for me here. Since we have camped here, I have spent a lot of with Mirna, and I like her very much. I believe we have fallen in love with each other. I have promised myself to Mirna and hope to find approval to marry her on Beltane."

Tesimo listened in silence and said, "Druso, I'm happy for you, but what about our mission?"

"I don't know if we have a mission anymore, Tesimo. I don't know where we are going any longer, and I'm tired of walking day after day. This place is the first place that has felt anything like home since we left the mountains. I think I belong here, and I don't want to leave."

"I understand," said Tesimo, with a pinch in his heart.

"Tesimo, I will not let you down. I will go with you to Avebury and ensure that both you and Zuoz reach the healers safely, but after that, I want to come back here to Newgrange, where I belong now." Druso felt bad for Tesimo. "Tesimo, stay here with me. Why do you keep walking? Where are you going?"

"I don't know why I keep going, but I know in my heart that I have to," answered Tesimo. "I have seen how you and Mirna look at each other. I understand your feelings and know that I am very happy for you. If the journey goes well, you should be back here by the next moon. Who knows? I may come back and live here close to you, but now I feel there is work I must do before I am able to make another home anywhere."

After their conversation, Druso went back to Mirna, and Tesimo went for a walk around the camp, considering their discussion. *Druso is right. He knows, as I do, that at the end of Zuoz's mission, he and I will have to start lives for ourselves.* Tesimo was tormented by the promises of return he'd given to Elena, as well as by his feelings toward Astrid. He wondered if he should go to Vorep to fulfill his commitment and restore his honor before committing again.

Tesimo's thoughts shifted to Zuoz's health. It was like losing his father all over again. He was so grateful to Zuoz for showing him this wonderful new world, and sharing his wealth of knowledge over the past few moons. He also had followed Zuoz with gratitude after Zuoz saved his life in the Norse ship. He felt committed to serve him and repay his debt.

Great Mother of the World, please wrap your hands around Zuoz, and heal him from the poison, prayed Tesimo.

CHAPTER 17

SEPTEMBER 27, 1991
EARLY AFTERNOON

Sophia's discovery sent her mind reeling. On her way home, she still wondered if this alignment could be coincidental. There were thousands of Neolithic monuments in Europe, but the list she had made contained only the few most significant, most important monuments of all the monuments of this time period.

Traveling south on her mental map, Sophia thought about Carnac's alignment in France. She visualized the parallel rows of very large standing stones that spanned miles throughout the countryside. She knew that some of the rows were directed toward Chartres, and some publications assumed that both Chartres and Carnac were part of the same spiritual cult.[47] Surely Carnac was not on the Newgrange-Malta axis, but Carnac's construction and orientation made her curious. *Could Carnac be related to both Chartres and Newgrange at the same time?*

Finally home, she climbed the stairs two at a time. She went straight to her desk, reorganized the class notes, and placed them in her satchel with books for her afternoon class at four o'clock.

Sophia was delighted to have met Erwin and was excited to see him again. Probing deeper, she wondered if the heat she was feeling in her heart when she thought about him was a sign that she might want more than friendship. She put on a jacket and ran down the stairs of her apartment.

Erwin wasn't there yet when she arrived at the café, but she saw Gregory sitting at a table, reading a book and drinking a cup of hot cocoa. He spotted her too and waved her over to his table.

"I just heard that Aton fired you, but no one knows what happened. May I ask why, if it is not too personal?" asked Gregory.

Sophia explained everything, starting with her suspicions about Aton in Professor Zelinger's accident, her interactions with the police, and Aton's recent outburst.

Gregory said, "I'm sorry to hear that. Aton is a total nut. You found him unpleasant before, but now that he's found his mummy, he's unbearable. He doesn't give any time to his students, and he demands that his advisees put aside their own research to help with the mummy, with no intention of offering any publication authorship or research recognition."

"Tell me about it," Sophia said, frowning.

Erwin joined them a minute later. He was holding a letter and a computer printout. Sophia introduced Erwin to Gregory, and she asked Erwin, "So, what do you have?"

"I just received a letter from Cambridge. I've been offered a post-doc position to study the quantification of event improbabilities following Sheldrake's morphogenetic fields.[48] The proposed work is at the interface between quantum mechanics and life biology. It looks like I will be moving to Cambridge as soon as I graduate in about two months. I didn't think this would happen so fast."

It was like a clap of thunder for Sophia. She had come to like Erwin and considered being in a relationship with him. *There is no future together if he is planning to leave the country in a couple of months. What's the point? And if I get expelled, there is nothing left for me but to go back to the farm and start looking for a job.*

"Sophia, are you all right?" asked Erwin.

"Yes, yes, everything is fine. Congratulations, Erwin. I'm glad you got the job." She hoped the smile on her face didn't appear as fake as it felt.

"And now, look what I have for you." said Erwin spreading his printout on the table. "I think you are going to like this. I printed in black the first sites we discussed at the lab and the additional ones in gray. Avebury is a little farther

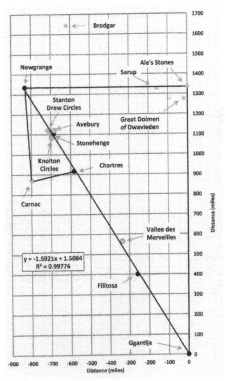

off the axis than Stonehenge, but the Santon Drew circle and Knowlton circles are right on the money, just two miles from the axis. Avebury forms a perfect right triangle aligned north and south and east and west, with Stonehenge and Santon Drew." From his notes, he read, "The distance from Avebury to Stonehenge is sixteen miles, and the distance from Avebury to Stanton Drew is thirty-two miles. I am not an expert, but it seems that these three sites are linked together and located across the path of the Newgrange-Malta axis."

"What are you talking about?" asked Gregory.

"Hold on, Gregory. Erwin is looking at Neolithic site alignments for me. I will explain in a minute," said Sophia before returning to Erwin. "That's very interesting. What about Carnac?"

"Carnac is about two hundred miles off the axis. However, I noticed that it also forms a perfect right triangle with Chartres and Newgrange. This is a larger triangle. The distance from Chartres to Carnac is 220 miles, and that from Carnac to Newgrange is 440 miles."

"Are all these distances accurate?" Gregory interjected, looking at the map.

"Yes, pretty accurate. I got them from satellite pictures. Why?"

"The ratio of the sides of both of these right triangles is one to two. The one by two ratio is important in construction. The diagonal of the double square leads to the golden number. Many sacred monuments, like the Parthenon, Solomon's temple, or most gothic cathedrals, were built using these proportions."

"What do you mean? The triangle can hold information too? Not just the alignment?"

"You see," Gregory explained, using a napkin to illustrate, "the hypotenuse of a one-by-two right triangle is the square root of one squared plus two squared—that is the square root of five."

"So what does that mean?" asked Sophia. Erwin's eyes were growing wider as he followed Gregory's notes on the napkin.

"The square root of five is what allows us to calculate the golden ratio."

"The golden ratio?"

"Yes, phi, the golden ratio. It's notated like this." He drew the φ symbol on the napkin. "It's also known as the golden number, the golden section, or the divine proportion. It's calculated like this." He wrote on the napkin:

$$\varphi = (1+\sqrt{5})/2 = 1.618$$

"What's so special about 1.618?" Sophia asked.

"The golden number has been studied for ages, all the way back to Euclid. This number has surprising properties, such as the inverse of 1.618 is 0.618, or the square of 1.618 is 2.618, but that's not all. A golden rectangle can be bisected into smaller and smaller rectangles with the same aspect ratio to infinity. You can obtain the divine proportion with a one-by-two triangle and a rope. The length of the unit plus the length of the hypotenuse is twice the golden number. Triangles or rectangles that have the golden numbers as the ratio of their sides are believed to be extremely pleasing aesthetically, and countless artists and architects, starting with the Greeks, have used them. And the golden proportion is not only pleasant, but it seems to be actually imbedded in nature. It can be observed in the arrangement of branches along plant stems, in leaf veins, or in crystal geometry, for starters. I came across it because these ratios were used by the ancient architects who designed and built the great gothic cathedrals."

"Thanks. That's interesting," said Sophia, trying to stop Gregory's usual long-winded explanation. "So what about Ale's Stones?" she asked Erwin

"As you can imagine, Ale's Stones in Sweden is far from being on the axis. But look—they too make a perfect right triangle with the whole Malta-Newgrange alignment. The right angle is even confirmed by the placement of Sarup and the Great Dolmen in Germany"

Incredulous, Sophia asked, "Is the ratio of the triangle sides also one to two?"

"No, it doesn't look like it." Looking at his papers, Erwin said, "Here are the dimensions of the triangle." He handed over a sheet for Gregory and Sophia to examine.

—Newgrange to Ale's Stones: 831 miles
—Ggantija to Ale's Stones: 1,336 miles

"Let's see what the ratio of the triangle sides is," said Gregory, excited. He bent over the napkin, making a division, and then raised his head, grinning. "The answer to 1336 divided by 831 is 1.608. That's very close to 1.618. Look. If Ale's Stones targeted location had been 1,340 miles from Malta and 828 miles from Newgrange, the ratio of the sides would be exactly the golden number 1.618. An error of only three to four miles over these vast distances is less than ..." He went back to his calculations and then said, "A 0.4 percent error. That's not bad. It would be difficult to achieve such a high degree of accuracy, even today. In a way, it seems that these people developed the one-by-two triangle into a 1-by-1.618 triangle, a gold number's triangle. But the size of the construction is incredible ..."

"But how would Neolithic people be able to calculate such a ratio?" Sophia asked.

"You don't have to do complex mathematics to get this ratio. You just take a string and make knots at even distance units. With this evenly knotted string, you can easily place on the ground markers to make a one-by-two right triangle. Now, starting from the narrow end of the triangle, you can measure the length of the hypotenuse and add the length of the small side of the triangle. The total length that you measured is twice the golden number, expressed in the length of the triangle's small side. Fold that section of string in half, and the length that you now have is 1.618 in knotted unit. That's very simple." Gregory explained.

"Are you seriously telling me that it is possible that there's a gigantic golden triangle over the whole of Western Europe, and nobody knows about it? That's crazy!" Sophia shook her head in amazement as she traced the triangle with a finger. She was mesmerized by what she was hearing. *I'm hallucinating*, she thought. *This cannot be.* She subtly pinched her arm, feeling dazed. "It must be a coincidence," she muttered.

"I don't think so," replied Gregory. "Look—the golden triangle is right here on the map with an incredible precision. Erwin plotted it, and everyone can see it now. It's undeniable—even better than the cathedral arrangement I showed you earlier."

Erwin added, "It is noticeable that most of the new sites are close to the path of the Malta-Newgrange axis. Most are less than ten miles from the true path. The Vallée des Merveilles is the most far off, at about twenty-five miles. Anyway, the addition of four new points makes it now a nine-point alignment with a confidence level of 99.8 percent. Over such a distance, it's incredible precision."

"So what does it mean? Do you think it was intentional?"

"Of course I do!"

"You don't think it's easy to line up places when they are located that far apart?" asked Sophia.

"You're joking, aren't you?" said Erwin with a chuckle. "Aligning random points, yes, it may be easier. But we are not talking about random places. You told us that they were the greatest spiritual centers of the times. To have them aligned at a 99 percent confidence level is extraordinary. A 99.8 percent confidence level is stunning!" Looking at the map, he added, "Try to align random places, like the European capitals. Let's take Dublin, London, Paris, Rome, and Athens, just because they seem to be in a line. I doubt the precision of that alignment would be more than 80 or 90 percent. If we randomly add Madrid or Berlin, the precision would drop to barely 50 percent. I'm telling you more than 99 percent is truly amazing."

While Erwin and Gregory checked the napkin's calculations in joyful disbelief, Sophia remained quiet. She wondered how in the world she could introduce these findings into her thesis without sounding like a nutcase. She wished she could talk to Professor Zelinger about her discoveries.

"Let's see ... what else did you want me to check?" asked Erwin.

Before Sophia had time to remember the remaining sites she'd identified, a couple of students entered the café, and one of them waved at Erwin, signaling for him to come to their table.

Erwin said, "Excuse me for a minute. I know that guy, and it looks like he wants to talk to me." He left their table to meet the student who had signaled him.

Erwin returned to their table with the student in tow, saying, "This is Max, a friend from Material Sciences. I told him earlier of our suspicions about Aton and what he did to

Sophia. Max told me that he saw Aton in the chemistry department in the basement, where chemicals are stored. He thought that was odd and wanted to let me know."

"I'm surprised he went to fetch anything himself," said Gregory. "He's so full of himself lately he thinks he's too good to do any legwork."

"That's the thing," said Max. "There's nothing in there he could legitimately need. His department has their own stores with the solvents they use. Most of the stuff in the chemistry lab wouldn't be helpful for archaeological work."

"I've been there before, and I know there's a lot of bad stuff in that storage area," said Erwin

"Bad stuff? Like what?" Sophia asked.

"Dangerous chemicals are stored in there. Nothing Aton should need. That's why I was surprised to see him down there," said Max.

"If there is dangerous stuff there, why isn't the door locked?" asked Sophia.

"Well, it is locked. There is a combination lock on the door, but the entire faculty and many students have the code. Anyway, Aton may have just been looking for replacement solvents for his stores. I wouldn't put it past him to steal from other departments."

Once Max left, Sophia said, "But what if Aton is afraid that Professor Zelinger could regain consciousness. If this guy is as crazy as I think he is, he may have decided to poison him."

"You may be right," agreed Erwin. "What should we do?"

"Is there a way to figure out what Aton got from the storage?"

"There may be a way," answered Erwin, thoughtful. "I've been in there to get chemicals for chemistry class lab projects. There's an inventory logbook. We could go there and see if he signed the log, or if there is any inventory discrepancy of dangerous chemicals."

"Let's do that. Let's check the storage inventory," responded Sophia. "It's a shame to miss class this afternoon, but let's go." Sophia thanked Gregory for his insight, and she left the café with Erwin.

"Let's take my car," offered Erwin. "It's parked one street over."

And they were on their way.

CHAPTER 18

DAY 88
AVEBURY

 The group left Newgrange early in the morning, with Bricriu and his escort leading the way. Young men from the temple helped carry Zuoz on a stretcher. Progress was slow, but by nightfall they reached the coastal village where a boat was waiting for them. They set off for the Great Isle early the following morning, with twenty rowers manning the large boat. For the first two days, the boat followed the coast, going south. The rowers were sculling twelve hours a day, and at night they pitched tents on land. The third day, the boat's direction changed to the open sea. The men rowed from sunrise until late at night, and they finally reached the coast of the Great Isle. Then for the next two days they kept going southeast, following the coast of the island. From the sea, the Great Isle appeared massive to Tesimo. Seeing rolling hills covered by forests and green

grass, Tesimo understood the well-deserved name of the island. They finally reached an estuary, where they landed in a large coastal village. New to Tesimo, the wooden and clay houses were round and seemed to accommodate only one family each. Affording no delays, they quickly left the village as soon as they had arranged Zuoz on a stretcher, pulled by an ox. With the slow pace of the ox, it took them another two days before they arrived at Avebury.

It was past midday when they reached the hills surrounding the Avebury site. They hiked up the large hill situated on the northwest side of the main worship center, where the healing priests and priestesses resided. Three concentric henges surrounded the hilltop. Many tents were pitched around the outer henge, but only one was built in the center of the inner henge. The center tent in the inner henge housed the high king and his healers.

At the entrance of the outer henge, Bricriu haughtily introduced the company to the guarding priests and asked to see the great priest. A priest healer came to examine Zuoz and recognized the pendant he was wearing around his neck as a mark of high status. The priest healer escorted the party across the three concentric henges and brought them to the high king's healers. The king's tent was round and wide enough to shelter a dozen people. It was made of hides sewn together and supported by timber. The tent was partitioned into six peripheral alcoves, the largest one occupied by the high king, who rested on a bed made of bear fur. Messengers had informed the healers that the companions were coming. The high king's healers came to examine Zuoz, and they immediately recognized that he was afflicted by the same fever as the king. Because Zuoz was a royal messenger, the priest healers decided to place him in an alcove a few feet from the king's bed. As this was happening, a healer told the companions that Alaric had already been informed about his father's failing health, and he was expected to arrive at Avebury very soon.

The companions and their escort were asked to leave the tent. Bricriu claimed that he needed some rest and brusquely departed. Left by themselves, the three companions walked to the edge of the inner ring and looked down at the spectacular view the location offered them. From their position overlooking Avebury's plain, the companions had a stunning view of the immense sacred place below. The size of the construction was breathtaking. Three monumental circles surrounded the main sanctuary. The first was a twenty-five-foot-tall circular bank, white like snow, and over a thousand feet in diameter. The second circle was a gigantic ditch, at least thirty feet deep and thirty feet wide, carved out of the solid chalk bedrock. The third circle was created by a multitude of standing stones at least fifteen feet tall, spaced every fifty feet, forming the largest stone circle Tesimo had seen on this long trip of wonders. For reasons unknown to Tesimo, some of these gigantic stones had been planted with their smallest point down, giving the impression of precarious balance. Within this circular enclosure stood two other stone circles, one at the north end and the other one at the south end. In the center of the northern circle was a triangle made of three even larger standing stones, and the southern circle was occupied by a row of standing stones. Two large avenues reached the sanctuary from both the east and the west sides. Each avenue was flanked on both sides by tall standing stones, also placed fifty feet apart from each other. The avenues stretched as far as the companions' eyes could see, veering off behind other hills. The view was breathtaking.

From high on the hill, they looked at a procession of men and women walking along the avenues, singing and chanting prayers in preparation of the Beltane celebration, signaling the end of spring and the beginning of summer. Tesimo stared at a hill on the horizon that seemed to be moving, confusing his eyes. He realized the hill was covered with hundreds of people working like ants, moving up and down the hill, depositing baskets of dirt on the hilltop. Curious, Tesimo asked a nearby priest the purpose of the construction.

"The Silbury Hill[49] is being raised for the worship of the guardian sun and other stellar observations," the priest answered. "For the past many solar cycles, the youth of our land have spent their years of service building this mound. With the help of our youth, the hill will be finished within five solar cycles."

Amazed by the sight, Tesimo wondered how many generations had worked to reach this point of construction.

Later that night, the companions were offered hospitality in the encampment outside the henges, but neither Hryatan nor the cousins wanted to stray far from Zuoz's tent. They paced around the henge, from time to time peeking at the king's tent for signs of news of the sick men. As night was falling, a different type of life seemed to be awaking in Avebury's circles. Campfires appeared in the sites below. Astronomers and their apprentices held torches, looking like clouds of fireflies as they stationed themselves around the stones to take measurements of the stars' positions. From his discussion with Zuoz, Tesimo knew the astronomers were measuring the heights and azimuths of the stars by sighting. They measured the angles with engraved rods, similar to Zuoz's walking stick and recorded their measurements on khipus, using kingdom time.

The companions were so entranced by what they saw that they did not notice that Bricriu had replaced the guards at the tent entrance with his own men. As an overlord, he then entered the king's tent under the pretext of checking on his health. After ensuring that no one but the two ailing men were in the king's tent section, he grabbed a small leather quiver from his pocket. He opened it and took out one poisoned dart it between his thumb and forefinger. Then he quietly walked to the king's bedside. For a moment, he stared down at the king in the weak light of torches set in tall holders in the center of the tent. He bent over the king and lifted the hair flowing over the king's shoulder.

He was preparing to jab the lethal dart into the king's neck, when suddenly Zuoz jumped on him and grabbed Bricriu's hand that held the dart. Zuoz pushed Bricriu away from the bed. They grappled, Zuoz careful to keep a firm grip on Bricriu's wrists so he could not pierce him with the dart. Zuoz squeezed Bricriu's wrist until he could no longer hold the poisonous dart, and it dropped to the floor. Bricriu kicked Zuoz's leg, dropping him to one knee. Bricriu grabbed his sword from the ground and charged Zuoz, while Zuoz defended himself clumsily with one of the large torch holders.

Garkan's barks echoed in the quietness of the night. Hryatan, Tesimo, and Druso heard the commotion in the center tent and ran toward it. Bricriu's guards prevented their entrance into the tent. Garkan barked fiercely, leaping back and forth, trying to bite the guards whenever she could. Hearing the sounds of struggle and desperate to get inside, Tesimo cut through the side of the tent with his small stone knife while Hryatan and Druso fought the guards at the entrance.

Inside, Tesimo saw Zuoz and Bricriu fighting. Zuoz was swinging a torch holder back and forth with incredible force at Bricriu, who was holding a stone sword. Timing his attack to one of Zuoz's back swings, Bricriu launched himself and stabbed Zuoz in the chest. Zuoz fell backward, and without losing a moment, Bricriu ran toward the king's bed. Tesimo charged Bricriu and shoved him aside. Bricriu spun to face the new attacker and charged at him with his sword raised over his head. Hryatan entered the tent behind him, intercepting Bricriu's swinging sword with his own. Bricriu's sword shattered into thousands of tiny shards. Left with nothing but the handle, Bricriu threw it at Hryatan, and it struck his forehead. As Hryatan reeled, Bricriu grabbed a torch holder and struck Hryatan on the head. Hryatan fell down, and Bricriu advanced on him, raising the torch holder to hit him again.

Tesimo grabbed Bricriu from behind and pinned his arms with all his strength. Finally, the last of Bricriu's men was subdued, and Druso entered the tent. The sight of his cousin struggling made Druso furious, and without thinking, he charged, swinging his walking rod, the only weapon he had. He struck Bricriu hard in the chest and then again on the head. Overlord Bricriu slumped in Tesimo's arms and slid limply to the floor.

As Druso helped Hryatan recover, Tesimo rushed to Zuoz's side. All life seemed to have vanished from Zuoz's face. It was clear to Tesimo that his friend was dying.

"Tesimo, my friend," Zuoz whispered, looking into Tesimo's eyes, "don't worry about me. I traveled to the otherworld, and I am back. I saw the guardians united as a whole in the Great Spirit. I was at the same time inside and outside their union. I was living in the present, out of time, on a point of no substance; a point going through time, shaping our destinies; a point where the extremes meet; a point of death and creation."

Zuoz coughed. In a convulsion, he grabbed Tesimo and continued with great effort. "Tesimo, promise me that you will go tell Malta's high priestess—and the high priestess only—that there are traitors in her ranks. Tell her to watch Krpy's basket." Zuoz pushed his pendant into Tesimo's hand. "Take my pendant! This pendant will open all the kingdom's gates for you. It is one of the great keys of the kingdom; it's a symbol of God. You are now the high priestess's messenger. Go to Malta." In a whisper, he added, "When you see her, you can tell her that I received my judgment from the Great Spirit, and my load is light. Tell her that all is well ..." With a final cough, he murmured, "Tell her to watch Krpy's basket. Tell her ..."

Zuoz was gone before he could finish. Tesimo was left with the pendant in his hands, looking down at his dead friend.

Alaric arrived the next morning. As soon as he heard of Zuoz's death, he came to mourn with the companions. "Zuoz saved my father twice. He found the strength to rise and stop Bricriu from murdering him. And because of Zuoz, the healers now have the poison they need to prepare a cure for my father. Not many could have accomplished the things he did."

Because Zuoz gave his life for the high king, Alaric declared a special burial. Zuoz's body was cleansed and dressed with ceremonial clothes and placed on a stretcher. Porters carried him to Durrington Henge, [50] where the ceremony was assembling. The henge, located close to the river, was enormous, close to two thousand feet wide. From its center spread concentric circles marked by twenty-foot-tall wooden posts planted straight up in the ground. The tops of some of the wooden poles had been sculpted with animal figures. There were so many poles around him Tesimo felt as if he were in a forest. A priest explained that it was the place of departure from the living. There, the procession was assembled, and they followed Zuoz's body in silence as it was carried a couple of miles along the river. This river represented the departure, the border between living and dead. Then they turned north and proceeded toward Stonehenge, following an avenue marked with two large side ditches. The avenue lined with standing stones curved west and finally arrived in view of Stonehenge.

Around Stonehenge were dozens of smaller henges, each attended and dedicated to special stars or constellations. Stonehenge itself was a much smaller version of Avebury, its dimension closer to that of the Brodgar circle. However, different from any of the other henges Tesimo had seen before, the bank of Stonehenge was situated on the inner side of the circular ditch, instead of the outer side. Inside the henge was a stone circle made of many five-foot-tall dark blue stones.

Zuoz's body was placed in the center of the circle, and a priest recited prayers for the departed. Every face was drawn and somber. They left the henge through an opening on the opposite side and went to a field where the dead were incinerated. Because Zuoz was from Malta, he was not incinerated but was buried following his customs. Tesimo placed Zuoz's bow and weapons in the tomb; other lords from the surrounding lands contributed arrowheads and food offerings to thank him for saving their king.

Two days later, the high king's fever retreated. He regained consciousness and control of his body. After Alaric related to him the happenings of the previous few days, the high king received the companions to thank them for their services. The king was still seated in his bed in the inner henge's central tent. Alaric and several lords, priests, and healers were in the company of the high king. Even though the king's face showed signs of fatigue, he radiated strength and power.

After the three companions were brought to his bedside, they bowed in respect.

"My friends," said the high king, "I understand you saved my life at a terrible cost. We too are saddened by the loss of Zuoz. But Bricriu and his band of traitors will pay for this and for his subjects he gave to the Yamna as slaves. Alaric informed me of your adventures, and we are very grateful that you uncovered Bricriu's treacheries.

"Bricriu was a fool! He thought that he could ally with these savages and take control of the kingdom. Thanks to you we have learned what the Yamna were doing in the Ore Mountain. When his messengers informed him that his plot might be discovered, he decided to kill me. Luckily for me, the poison was not as strong as he believed. Bricriu felt threatened when Zuoz went to Brodgar and inquired about Krpy's territories. When Bricriu learned you were in Newgrange, he decided to eliminate Zuoz. Luckily for us, Bricriu's poison failed to kill Zuoz, and you came here for healing. Bricriu might have accomplished his sinister plan if it had not been for Zuoz and you, my friends."

"Hryatan, tell King Akkad of Hamoukar that you made your ancestors proud. Tell him that we are extremely grateful to him for sharing with us the art of bronze making. Tell him that we will put a stop to the Yamna's tin-mining activities. We are going to use that ore to make our own bronze weapons and protect the kingdom." Looking at the cousins, he smiled and added, "Who could have predicted that two goat shepherds from behind our great White

Mountain would travel here and save the kingdom?" With a more somber face, he said, "Friends, I am grateful for what you did, and I am in your debt. Alaric told me that your village has been destroyed by the bloodthirsty Yamna. You are welcome to stay with us to help defend the kingdom."

In an unsteady voice, the cousins respectfully declined the king's invitation, explaining that they were on a mission for Malta's high priestess. The healers ended the meeting, asking the king to rest.

Alaric left the tent with the companions. He was delighted that his father was recovering. If his father's health kept improving, he was planning to return to Sarup within a week to aid and organize the defense of the eastern region.

The next day the companions prepared to leave Avebury and part ways. Alaric came to see them off. Druso and Garkan were going to join the party escorting Bricriu back to Tara to be judged by his peers. Tesimo and Hryatan were going to travel south, toward Malta. Alaric gave them a warm embrace. He especially honored Tesimo by giving him his stone dagger. "Tesimo, I enjoyed fighting with you. This dagger is yours now. May it protect you in your travels."

In Tesimo's eyes, the dagger looked like a strike of black light, shimmering under the sun. The craftsmanship of the man who chipped the stone was spectacular—perfectly symmetrical chip marks on each side of the blade; three light brown rings lined up in its center.

Addressing the remaining companions, Alaric said, "I hope to see you again, my friends. Wherever your destiny takes you, know that you will always have a place in my house. God be with you all until we see each other again."

The cousins too embraced, sad to part but understanding it was time. Druso and Garkan left with the caravan by the north road, and Tesimo and Hryatan followed the road that led south toward the sea.

They passed Stonehenge's cursus, more than mile long, indicating how populous the area was. As they walked along the cursus, Tesimo and Hryatan watched as families started to gather in preparation for the coming mid-spring celebration of Beltane.

But their mood was not bright and cheerful like these families. They walked quietly, not saying a word, grieving the loss of their friend.

CHAPTER 19

SEPTEMBER 27, 1991
LATE AFTERNOON

Having previously taken chemistry classes, Erwin knew his way around the chemistry department. He led them to the chemical storage room located in the basement. Erwin entered a code on the secured padlock, and the door answered with a metallic click.

"They should change the combination more often. This lock is still using the code from three years ago," Erwin said.

As they entered the storage space, Sophia's senses were shocked by the unusual smell of the place. For a moment, an overwhelming odor that was both acrid and sweet took the breath out of her lungs. Under the dim lights, she could see that the room was filled floor to ceiling with shelves and cabinets containing various flasks and containers of all sizes and colors.

"There is some nasty stuff in here," said Erwin, showing Sophia a vial containing a brownish liquid substance that had a faded skull-and-crossbones sticker on it. In a corner was a small desk on which a binder lay open, displaying the inventory log. "Let's see if Aton recorded anything," said Erwin as he scanned the entries. After a minute, he looked at Sophia. "As far as I can see, Aton didn't record any withdrawal in the log." Speaking more to himself than to Sophia, he said, "What chemical would have been most interesting to him?"

While Erwin went down the list, Sophia kept walking between the shelves, examining their contents. Each container was labeled with a chemical name, quantity, and receiving date and was arranged in alphabetical order by compound.

She could hear Erwin flipping sheets and mumbling. "No ... Not that ... Too obvious ... That wouldn't work ... Wow! That's bad stuff! Why would they even store that here?" Alarmed, Sophia came to look. Erwin was checking the amount of a chemical on a shelf against the amount recorded in the inventory log. "No, that's not it," he said, sounding somewhat disappointed. "It's all accounted for." He kept going down the list, checking for toxic substances. They had been in the storage room about twenty minutes when finally Erwin said, "Oh! This is bad, very bad. Look—a bottle of potassium hydroxide is missing from the shelf. The inventory listed one bottle, but it is not here."

"What is it? Is it dangerous?" asked Sophia

"Potassium hydroxide is a deadly poison if injected in the bloodstream. It would stop the heart just like that!" said Erwin, snapping his fingers. "It would be a good way to finish off Professor Zelinger or even to get rid of you, if this guy is as crazy as he seems. You see, potassium hydroxide is quickly metabolized and disappears from the body before there are any observable effects. Unless there were obvious signs of injection, I doubt potassium hydroxide analysis would be required in an autopsy, especially for a comatose patient like Professor Zelinger. It would just look like his heart gave out from the trauma."

"What should we do?" asked Sophia, visibly distressed. "I cannot go back to the police. After the last time, they'll kick me out of the station if I show up again."

"I'm not sure what to do," answered Erwin. "Maybe we should go to the hospital and check on the status of Professor Zelinger and guard him if we need to."

"Do you think it might be possible to arrange some kind of watch shifts with other students to make sure that Aton doesn't come close to the professor at the hospital?"

Erwin looked at her with a smile. "They'll definitely think we're crazy, but it's not impossible. Let's see what we can do."

***

Aton stood in his immaculate kitchen. After inheriting the house, he had stripped the entire house, and the kitchen was now white and sterile, like the rest of the house. Looking at the contents on the table, he thought about the phone call he had received that morning from a nurse at the hospital. Professor Zelinger's condition had improved, and he would soon be moving out of the intensive care unit into a recovery room. They would be waking him shortly from his drug-induced coma.

How can this get any worse? What if he recovers and comes back to the department? And what if he saw me in the car? No! No! No! This is not going to happen.

Aton started to pace back and forth in his kitchen, glancing often at the table where he had placed a small vial and two syringes. In one small corner of the vial's label was a skull and crossbones. The syringes on the table were much thinner than regular syringes used by nurses. They were chromatography syringes that he had chosen because of their small size and ultrathin needles. The poison was so strong that just a few drops would be sufficient to stop somebody's heart.

Even if they perform an autopsy, which they may never do, what will they find? Nothing! I'm home free. Dead of cardiac arrest—that's it. They probably wouldn't even do an autopsy. Nobody would be surprised if the old man's heart failed. Nobody will ever look for a tiny hole in his IV bag. And then the old goat is gone, leaving only that little pest. But she makes me nervous. I'm sure she knows something. I'm sure she is the one who went to the police. It was close. I can't take any chances. Otzi is mine ... First I get rid of Zelinger, and then I will crush Sophia like a bug.

He came to the table and removed the metallic cap wrapped around the vial's plug. Then he filled the syringes and placed them carefully in their padded case. He placed the case in his satchel under a stack of papers and left the kitchen through his garage. As he climbed into his car, he whispered, "I'm coming for you, old goat."

***

Sophia and Erwin were hardly two steps into the hospital when they saw Aton boarding a lobby elevator. Erwin and Sophia looked at each other and watched the elevator indicator until it stopped on the fourth floor.

"Where is he going?" Sophia asked. "It's not the way to the Intensive Care Unit."

Erwin pushed the button for the elevator and said, "I'll try to find what he's up to. I don't think he has ever seen

236

my face. You go check on the professor, and I'll catch up with you later."

Sophia nodded and turned down the hall, following signs for Intensive Care. "I would like to see Professor Zelinger. Could you tell me his room number, please?" Sophia asked at the nurses' station.

"Professor Zelinger isn't here anymore. He has been moved to Recovery, on the fourth floor," the nurse answered.

Now she understood where Aton was going. "Where are the stairs?" she asked.

The nurse was surprised at her urgency and blinked before pointing down the hall. Sophia turned around and ran toward the stairs and took them two at a time to the fourth floor. Out of breath, she burst into a large hallway. She looked right and left, and all seemed quiet. The nurses were calmly performing their regular tasks while patients' families were moving around or waiting here and there. Neither Erwin nor Aton was anywhere to be seen. Suddenly, there was a commotion down the hall. Male grunts and the sound of metal instruments hitting the tiles. All heads turned in the direction of the sounds. Sophia ran toward the noise, her heart in her throat.

***

When Erwin had reached the fourth floor and stepped into the lobby, he looked right and left but could not see Aton. The halls were almost empty, except for a few family members and some occupied nurses. No one paid any attention to him. He walked down the hall, passing hospital rooms, the doors of which were inlaid with narrow glass panels. He was just about to go back to find Sophia when a strange movement through the glass panel of a door caught his eye. He backtracked a few steps and, peering more closely through the glass panel, caught sight of Aton in the dimly lit room. He saw Aton pull a black case from his pocket as he approached the patient's bed. Instantly, Erwin knew that the man in the bed had to be Professor Zelinger. He was difficult to recognize, as he was so thin and covered in bandages. Aton raised his hand, holding a tiny syringe and took hold of the professor's IV bag hanging next to the bed.

Erwin barged into the room and lunged at Aton, grabbing the hand that was holding the syringe. In the struggle, Aton's syringe fell on the floor. In a surge of panic, Aton managed to shove Erwin against the far wall. Erwin's head made a sickening smack against the wall, and he slid woozily down to the floor. The IV bag's hanger and other medical instruments clattered to the floor. Aton stood still for a second, slowly absorbing what had just happened. His eyes were burning with hatred. Erwin struggled to pull himself to his feet, but staggered and fell back against the wall, dizzy from the blow.

Rattled, Aton ran for the door just as Sophia arrived, blocking his exit. Her eyes, wide with fright, quickly passed Aton's and saw Erwin slumped in the corner of the room. In that instant, Aton spotted his syringe case on the floor and jumped to grab it. He snapped the case open and pulled out the second syringe. He held it up for Sophia to see.

"Get out of the way, or I'll kill you!" he said coldly.

Brandishing the syringe, he advanced toward Sophia. In a flash, Sophia backed out of the door and slammed it shut, holding it closed with all her might. On the other side of the door, Aton's strength rather quickly began to overcome Sophia's resistance, and the door slowly opened, dragging her with it. Nurses and visitors were curiously peering down the hall, and she yelled for help.

"Help me! He's trying to kill me!"

While the visitors were confused and unsure, one of the nurses acted quickly, picking up the phone and speaking rapidly. A second one ran to the noise.

Sophia could see Aton's eyes reflecting rage through the glass panel. His mouth was half opened, blood trickling down the side of his face. Aton gave a fierce pull, and Sophia took a chance and let go. The effect was immediate. The door swung open spilling Aton onto the floor. She reached for the door again to slam it shut once more. Recovering quickly, Aton jumped back on his feet and grabbed at the door, tearing it from Sophia's hands. He took an advancing step toward her. The crowd gathered around the commotion, creating a large circle around them.

"I am going to kill you, bitch!" Aton screamed, moving forward with his syringe. "If there is one last thing I want to do, it's to see you die!" He leaped forward, brandishing his weapon with a deadly grip.

Sophia stepped backward, her back now against the opposite hall. She turned to run toward the gathering crowd for safety, but he lunged to block her path, swiping at her with the syringe as if it were a dagger.

Sophia looked at Aton like he was a rabid dog, which by now he might as well have been. He was oblivious to the others in the building, who all kept their distance, shocked at the sudden appearance of this madman with a syringe. Sophia saw a woman at the other end of the long hall, pushing a trio of children into the elevator. Sophia thought that she better to do something quickly, or Aton was going to kill her. She slowly backed away from Aton, not knowing what lay behind her—a wall, a hall, or a door.

Aton advanced toward Sophia, a mad smirk on his face. Suddenly, Erwin appeared behind Aton and threw himself at the oblivious madman stepping toward Sophia. He grabbed the hand in which Aton held the syringe and smashed it against the wall, shattering the glass and spilling the toxin onto the hospital floor.

"There! Down there!" shouted a nurse, directing security guards coming out of the elevator.

Erwin pushed Aton to the floor and pinned him as two security guards ran toward them. One man pulled Erwin up while the other secured Aton to the floor. Erwin stumbled, still dizzy from the blow to his head. As Sophia steadied him, he told her in an exhausted whisper that the professor was safe. Erwin and Sophia gave a weary sigh of relief.

"What's happening?" demanded the security guard, still grabbing Erwin.

Sophia pointed at Aton. "That man tried to kill Professor Zelinger with that syringe—there, on the floor." She pointed to the broken glass on the floor and then said, "He tried to kill me too. You can ask anybody here. They all saw what happened."

"And him?" the guard asked, looking at Erwin.

"He is the man who stopped Aton from killing the professor and me too."

The security guard looked from them to Aton and back. "You two, sit here and wait for the police." He called back to the nurses' station to make sure the police were on their way. He then instructed his partner to guard Aton in an empty patient room while he supervised the others in the hall until the police arrived.

Finally, two police officers arrived and began questioning the assembled group. Even Inspector Muller came to the hospital. Between Aton's arrest and the depositions, it took more than an hour for the police to reestablish order. After the police officer took Aton in custody, Inspector Muller told Sophia and Erwin to get some rest and to appear at the station the following day to give formal statements. Sophia and Erwin slowly walked away from the hospital and stood by the fountain that marked the hospital's entrance. They were finally alone. Now that the whole affair was over, it felt like a bad dream.

They looked at each other quietly. On an impulse, Sophia wrapped her arms around Erwin and hugged him, burying her face in his shoulder. Erwin enclosed her in his arms. Without saying a word, they stood at the fountain, quietly hugging each other.

CHAPTER 20

DAY 98
CHARTRES

 hree days after leaving Stonehenge, Hryatan and Tesimo reached the southern coast of the Great Isle. Their journey had been uneventful as they followed the well-maintained tracks crossing the land. The tracks were six feet wide, with a raised central area that drained rainwater on both sides of the track preventing the road from being flooded.

Their hearts were still heavy from the loss of Zuoz, and they spoke little during their journey. As they came closer to the harbor where a boat was to be waiting for them, Tesimo and Hryatan walked past the feet of a giant man holding a staff in each hand, carved in the side of a large hill. Lines of green grass had been scraped away, exposing the white chalk underneath, creating the silhouette of this eighty-foot-tall guardian. The runners Alaric had sent ahead of Hryatan and Tesimo had informed the village of their arrival.

Upon arriving at their destination, they found that their boat had already been stocked with the supplies that they and the crew would need for the crossing. The companions were introduced to the leader of their boat crew. He told them that if the wind continued, it would take about five days to reach their destination.

They left the village heading east the next morning, with sixteen scullers manning their boat. They remained close to the coast for the first two days, the scullers rowing about ten hours a day. At night, they landed and rested, eating the provisions they had brought with them, taking no time to fish or hunt. On the third day, they crossed into open water from the break of dawn to dusk, until they finally reached the coast on the other side of the sea. From there, they followed the coast of this new land southward until they reached a large river's estuary. They went up the estuary going east for one more day to a fisherman's village, Karnag,[51] where the travelers were to resume their journey by land. Their goal was to cross this land all the way to the coast of the Blue Sea, the sea of the south, and from the coast find a boat to Malta. Hryatan knew that Minoan boats always traded up and down the coast and that these boats passing close to Malta were willing to take pilgrims for some compensation.

Their travel would take them first through the Carnutes Forest, and from there they would go east to reach a large river flowing south to the coast. Learning from Hryatan, Tesimo understood that Karnag was twelve walking-days away from Chartres, the high place of the Carnutes.

The village council of Karnag received them warmly. They were given food and local clothing, more appropriate for the region. After a restful night at the fishermen's village, they began walking at sunrise. At first, the landscape was quiet and deserted. After climbing a broad hill, they came upon a very wide field where numerous standing stones had been aligned in parallel rows—dozens of rows, each sixty feet apart, extending as far as their eyes could see. After following the stones for thousands of feet, they arrived at the edge of the stone field where a large crowd was assembled.

Hundreds of young men were pulling and pushing these enormous stones, rolling them on three-foot-wide tree trunks. Like everywhere else in the kingdom, no animal was used to build sacred constructions. Some youth were maneuvering the loads forward using long beams inserted behind and under the stones. These were used as long levers by teams of workers, pulling ropes that activated the lever, slowly pushing the stone forward. Some teams moved trunks from the back to the front, while others provided replacement trunks from the surrounding forests when the wood splintered and weakened with each move of the stone. Looking around, the companions could see that many hillsides bore the marks left by the passage of these enormous stones. Young women, holding clay jars on their heads or shoulders, offered water to the workers. Others carried baskets of bread to the workers in the field. Here and there, groups of boys and girls seemed to be resting, seated in circles, weaving new ropes and singing songs.

Tesimo quickly realized that Karnag was a holy place, like Newgrange, where the kingdom's teenagers spent their sacrificial year. A tent village had been established around a central court off to the side of the stone field. Hryatan and Tesimo went to address the site's religious leaders. The leaders welcomed them and invited them to share bread together. During their discussion, the priests explained that this place was one of the most sacred places in these lands. It was called the Place of Transformation. During their sacrificial year, priests and priestesses who oversaw the construction of the fields of standing stones educated boys and girls. Each stone represented the collective work of a team of youth during their given year. Moving one of these stones not only required the strength of hundreds of young people pulling and pushing the enormous rock but also much help from the local population bringing food supplies, as well as the harvest's twelfth portion given to Gaia.

Tesimo understood that some of these youth came from as far away as six hundred miles, forty walking-days, to offer their year of sacrifice. At the end of the workday and after the evening meal, the youth gathered in groups around campfires, singing old songs and listening to ancient stories told by priests and priestesses. These stories spoke of heroes from the past, the forces of nature, life after death, purity and impurity, honor and dishonor, the unity of the world, the sense of personal and family honor, and the achievement and wisdom of ancestors. During their leisure time, the youth sat in groups, telling each other their own stories, discussing the work of the day, playing games, resting, and dreaming of the future.

Strong bonds of brotherhood and sisterhood were created in this communal effort. The sharing of all of these stories in this time of sacrifice and growth was the basis for the kingdom's peace and unity. As everywhere else in the kingdom, the completion of the sacrificial year marked the transition from childhood to adulthood. Soon after, they started lives on their own. Many of the youth met their spouses during the sacrificial year. Most returned to farming near their parents. The youth who possessed special gifts were sent to higher houses of knowledge like the Carnutes.

"During their year of sacrifice," the lead priest explained, "our youth learn many things, and among them they learn to see beyond the appearances of the solid world around us. At the end of their apprenticeship, they are able to see the strings of fire that hold the world. Young man, have you learned how to 'see'?" he asked, looking at Tesimo.

"Not really, dear priest. I think I saw the strings once, a few moons ago, during the Imbolc celebration at Olkam, but I can't see them now."

"I understand. Everything comes in time. When you 'see,' you understand that the world is only an expression of Gaia. You can perceive the inner fire of the living beings around you flowing in and out of earth."

Looking at the Tesimo's perplexed face, the priest added, "Gaia gives to us generously; we take her gift, and we give back gratefully. Gaia wants our faith, and we give it to her. Through faith, we can do amazing things. Through faith, Gaia allows us to penetrate the solid appearance of the world and lets us touch the truth. At the end of their apprenticeship, our youth will have learned how to align their faith with the faith of the community and the faith of the kingdom. During our celebrations, we all, young and old, align our faith together, wrapping it around the ray of Orion."

With an enigmatic smile, the priest said, "Do you know that stones become lighter when the faith of the lifters is in unity? At the end of their apprenticeship, the youth will be able carry stones with only their faith." Still grinning he added: " You will see; great acts of faith have moved stones much larger than these over great distances."

Looking at the immensity of the standing-stone fields and realizing how many people were needed to move a single stone, Tesimo felt a deep stirring of emotion. The unity and strength of community these youth had demonstrated each generation for time untold made Tesimo feel insignificant, like a grain of sand on a beach.

After the meal, Hryatan and Tesimo were told to follow the direction of the stones toward Carnutes. They passed through the long fields of Karnag's stones and entered a green and hilly countryside. For the next few days, they crossed villages of small farms that were grouped together around a main courtyard. Though the local people spoke their own dialect, many knew the kingdom language, and the companions were always able to communicate. As they went deeper into the forest, villages became farther and farther away, and the companions had to load themselves with more supplies when offered, like beef jerky and hard bread made of wild grains, which they softened in river water to eat. Their journey led them deeper and deeper into an immense forest. The vegetation got so thick that the sunlight barely penetrated the tree canopy, and the path was dark and obscure.

That night they stopped at a relay by the side of the road. The relay was not as well maintained as those they had used in the past. Hryatan started a fire in the hearth at the center of the room, and Tesimo went to replenish their water skins with fresh water. In the quiet forest, Tesimo climbed down the winding path that led to a nearby creek, in which they had previously bathed. He was on his knees, filling up the containers, when he heard growling behind him. He quickly turned around and was faced with three wolves, walking slowly toward him with teeth bared. Tesimo bit his lip; he'd carelessly left his bow and walking stick at the relay. With slow and controlled movement, his shaking hand came down to his belt and grabbed his stone dagger. If he stepped backward, he was afraid he'd fall in the creek behind him. To his left was a tree too large to climb, but he gradually moved close to it so that his back was protected from a rear attack.

Suddenly, the wolf closest to him leaped forward, and Tesimo blocked its attack by swinging his dagger at the wolf. The other two wolves immediately jumped on him, pushing him into the creek. One wolf had hold of his left leg, while the other one bit and pulled away the arm he was using to protect himself. He saw the third one coming back, hurtling toward his face, but it fell to the ground, its neck gashed by Hryatan's bronze sword. Next, Hryatan halved the wolf that was on Tesimo's chest and killed the third one with a blow to its back.

"How are you?" asked Hryatan kneeling near Tesimo.

"I'm hurt," grumbled Tesimo, using his bloody arms to push away the dead wolf from his body. "I'm hurt, but I'll be all right."

The bodies of the three dead wolves lay by the creek. Hryatan helped Tesimo to his feet and cleaned his wounds in the fresh creek water. Hryatan grabbed Tesimo by the shoulders and brought him back to the relay.

"Your wounds aren't too bad, but I need to treat them with my herbs," Hryatan said, looking into his backpack. Using two flat stones, he crushed leaves into a paste and applied it to Tesimo's wounds, which stopped the bleeding. He then ripped cloth from his tunic to wrap the plant mixture around Tesimo's arm.

"Here, my friend. Eat this; it will reduce the pain," he said, giving Tesimo dried mushrooms. In spite of the pain, Tesimo quickly went to sleep.

The next morning, severe pain in both his left arm and leg awakened Tesimo.

"How do you feel?" asked Hryatan, watching over him.

"I'm fine," lied Tesimo. However, he collapsed on the floor when he tried to stand up.

"Stay where you are. I'll be back shortly."

After a moment, Hryatan came back with thick branches. With some ropes he arranged a travois, and a harness attached the travois's small end. He then helped Tesimo to limp out of the cabin and laid him down onto the travois. Then Hryatan grabbed the harness on his shoulders and lifted his end of the stretcher.

"Let's go. There must be a village soon, and we will get help. The sooner the better," Hryatan said as he started walking, dragging the travois holding Tesimo behind him.

Hryatan was correct. Not long after they left the relay, they were joined by a group of people coming from the woods. Unlike the farmers, they were dressed in animal skins, and they had dark spirals tattooed on their skin. Some could speak the kingdom's language, and they helped carry Tesimo to a nearby village.

The villagers had round houses made of wood and woven branches, where they stored their provisions of berries and mushrooms gathered from the forest. This was also where they wove baskets, processed the meat from the animals they had hunted that day, and cooked their meals using hot stones. However, their living quarters were built high in the trees to protect them from wild animals roaming the forests at night. The villagers climbed up and down their tree houses using ladders—tree trunks having regularly spaced branch stumps.

The village healer closed Tesimo's wound with a sharp needle made of animal bone and strings from tree bark. He then applied plant ointment and told Tesimo that he would feel better in a few days. When the night came, they hoisted Tesimo in a large basket all the way up to their dwelling perched in the trees. They had to carry Tesimo over a three-foot-high threshold of one of their tree houses. They later explained to Tesimo that the thresholds were so high to prevent toddlers from escaping their houses and falling to the ground.

The villagers hosted the travelers for a few days, while Tesimo was recovering. Both companions were the center of attention since the villagers did not often receive foreigners. These people were strong, peaceful, and hospitable. For them, the forest was sacred, as the body of Gaia.

Luckily, Tesimo recovered quickly, and after a few days, he was well enough to walk again. They left the village to continue their journey south. A day later, their path reached a clearing near a river where a dolmen stood; it was built with three large, six-foot-tall standing stones, capped by a very large horizontal stone. Unlike the other dolmens made using raw stones that Tesimo had seen in his journeys, the edges of these stones had been shaped to fit each other almost squarely. The nearby towns were known by the names of dolmen their ancestors built long time ago.

As they came closer to center of the Carnutes, the dolmens became larger and larger. Tesimo was amazed by the craftsmanship and beauty of these sculptural achievements. It took them a few more days walking with groups of pilgrims through the dense forest before they reached their destination.

At the edge of the Carnutes sanctuary, Hryatan and Tesimo encountered a large gathering near a river. The place seemed to be bustling with the trade associated with the temple. It was a traditional resting place for forest inhabitants and pilgrims who were on their way to the holy place. The temple was a short walking distance through the thick forest.

They arrived at an immense circular clearing on top of the hill. The elevated location was stunning. Just above the trees' canopy, they could see trees glistening as far as the horizon. The light color of the ground showed that earth had been treated with salt to prevent vegetation from growing. In the center of this deserted space, a monumental dolmen stood alone. Three enormous capstones, each about thirty feet wide by thirty feet long and four feet thick, were resting on ten massive standing stones. The quality of the edge-to-edge alignment of the standing stones and the capstones was perfect. Even though the site overlooked a small river, a well had been dug close to the dolmen, delivering water that was said to have healing powers. In Tesimo's eyes, the monument was spectacular, and the site was shining with light and majesty.

Pilgrims were walking the site perimeter. Noticing the different clothing and hair color of the travelers, a priest paused his activities to ask them where they were from. He looked at them with more intensity after they answered that they were on their way to Malta. When he noticed Zuoz's pendant that Tesimo was wearing around his neck, the priest's expression changed, and he immediately placed himself at their service.

"My lords, it's an honor to have you here. How can I help you?"

"Thank you; we are fine," answered Tesimo. "We have everything we need."

"You are wearing the kingdom's key. Let me know if there is anything we can do for you. It would be an honor to serve you."

Tesimo realized that the hospitality they had received since they left Stonehenge could have been due, in part, to the recognition of the power of authority the pendant represented and not the natural generosity of the villagers. Tesimo understood that the cross he wore was more than just a piece of art; it was truly a key of the kingdom.

* * *

After allowing the travelers to bask in the majesty of the place, the priest offered to guide them to the sanctuary. Tesimo asked the priest why the setting of this dolmen was so different from the others they had seen in the forest.

The priest explained, "The dolmens you saw in the forest, like most other dolmens, are places for the dead. They are portals for the souls of the dead to find Gaia, the goddess mother caregiver in the afterlife, the one welcoming you to your life in the afterworld. We all know that our life on earth is finite, and it is natural for our bodies to return to dirt. Through faith, our souls will re-join Gaia for a new life in the Otherworld. A horrible death happens to the unrighteous ones, when the guardians of the otherworld throw their souls away. Only pleas for forgiveness may save the transgressor's soul from vanishing forever.

"The dolmen of the Carnutes is dedicated to Gaia as the giver of life, the pregnant virgin who birthed the world. The emptiness of the clearing around the dolmen represents the virginity of the mother of all, as she received the light of the sky and birthed the world. Pilgrims come here from far away to give praise and thanks. The sight of thousands of pilgrims at a celebration, aligning their faith with the ray of Orion, is marvelous, dazzling," said the priest with sparkling eyes. "They come here to thank Gaia for the gift of life, for the gift of prosperity, and for the gift of plentiful harvests. Pilgrims also come here to ask for Mother God's forgiveness for their transgressions."

They walked around the edifice following other pilgrims who recited prayers to the Mother God. They felt the spiritual power of the place as they passed by the holy well, where a priestess dispensed water on their heads. Shortly after, Tesimo felt his heart cheering a divine mother, creator of all, men and women, plants and animals. As they followed the crowd circling the sanctuary, Tesimo caught himself talking aloud. He did not know if what he was doing was praying or just talking to himself, but his spirit was full of peace and love for nature and humankind. Tesimo looked at the majestic dolmen and, from the top of his heart, asked Gaia to give him direction for his life.

After they left Chartres the next morning, Tesimo realized that the feelings of he had experienced were fading away as they again went deeper and deeper into the immense forest. For five days they headed southeast until their path deviated east to follow the contour of an expansive mountain formation. They kept going another six days after finally they left the forest. They entered large marshlands, walking on a skillfully designed walkway made of planks bound to each other, making a floating path across the swamps. They walked for days until they reached a large plain. That night, Tesimo thought he heard the earth shake while he was sleeping. When he woke up in the morning, he realized they were surrounded by a multitude of bison. The sheer number of beasts around them was amazing. On his side, with a finger to his lips, Hryatan made sign to pack their belongings and go. Quietly, they walked between the beasts until they cleared the herd.

At other times, they met wild horse herds. Even though the animals were not aggressive, Tesimo was terrified, remembering the blows they struck on his fellow villagers.

Hryatan explained that horses were rarely hunted. They were fast, strong, and dangerous, and there was much easier game to catch.

Finally, they were able to resume their march south, and four days later they reached a large river going south. They had been told at Carnutes that this river flowed all the way to the Blue Sea, the sea of the south, Malta's sea. They spent the night in a village near the river. The villagers were happy to help them assemble a raft for their journey down to Massalia,[52] a large harbor located where the river reached the Blue Sea. Hryatan knew that the Minoan boats stopped in Massalia for supplies and trade with the locals. Massalia was their best chance to catch a Minoan boat to Malta. Finally, they assembled a raft made of six-foot-long trunks attached together with ropes. They piled supplies onto the raft and left the next morning, letting their raft follow the current, guiding it with long thin poles to keep it close to the river's edge.

When they started their journey on the river, it was around two hundred feet wide, but the river quickly increased in width as the days passed. After a few slow-moving days, the edge of the river narrowed, and the speed of the river increased. Soon, the river grew rapid, with froth forming at the crests of waves. They could no longer control their raft— it broke apart on the rocks beneath the current, spilling them and their supplies into the river. They were able to swim to the east shore and took refuge in a nearby village called Courthezon.[53]

Courthezon's inhabitants were warm toward the travelers. The village head welcomed them at his house, where they were given replacement shoes, clothing, food, and refreshments. Only once the companions were settled and comfortable were they asked to talk about their adventures. The people who had gathered quickly understood the situation the travelers were in and organized the youth to start building a new raft.

That night, they ate with the village council and were proudly introduced to the youth, who were preparing to spend their year of service at the Valley of Wonders. It was an important time in the lives of these children, and they could not hide their excitement.

A day later, the raft was finished, and they resumed their trip downriver. The river became wide and slow again, and they came across islands in the channel that created a maze. Though the current was slow enough to steer, they were concerned they would take the wrong turn and get lost. They kept going west at each river fork, and three days later they finally reached the large coastal village of Massalia, at the confluence of the river and the sea.

Hryatan explained to Tesimo that Massalia was established a long time ago by Minoans as a trading post because it had a wide and protected bay. Nearby deep ravines created by the falling mountains made safe harbors for their boats. Massalia had a wooden dock where boats could anchor close to shore without the threat of damage.

They were hosted by the village chief, who gave them a little room in the back of his house. They waited for a boat for three days. Not knowing what to do with himself while waiting, Tesimo took long walks in the mountains by the sea. One evening, as he was on his way back from his walk, he saw a small dark shape on the horizon that grew larger and larger. He ran to the village to tell the news to Hryatan. For the first time, Tesimo saw a Minoan boat. The boat was rounder and larger than any boat Tesimo had seen on his journey. On each side were twelve rows of paddles. But most surprising was the piece of cloth attached to a standing beam erected in the center of the boat. As it came closer, the large cloth was dropped onto the ship deck, and rowers brought the boat to the docks.

The Minoan boat was stopping for food and fresh water. It was carrying goods, mainly tin, from Brittany to Kercz in the Orient. The boat captain agreed to take them to Malta for their weight in barley, which they would receive from Malta's harbormaster upon arrival.

CHAPTER 21

SEPTEMBER 27, 1991
LATE AT NIGHT

Since Erwin was still recovering from head trauma, Sophia agreed to stay with him for a few hours to make sure he was okay. It would not have been prudent for Erwin to drive in his condition, so he asked Sophia to drive him home.

Sophia drove very carefully and nervously as she maneuvered the narrow streets of Innsbruck. She had a driver's license but did not own a car and seldom drove her parents' car. They stopped by the restaurant to pick up Sophia's bicycle and somehow managed to stuff it into the trunk.

Erwin lived in a rental house that he shared with three other student roommates. Sophia parked the car on the curb in front of his door. She was relieved to see Erwin climb out of the car easily, and he seemed alert and clear-headed. He walked steadily over a stone pathway leading to the well-maintained alpine chalet.

Sophia kept a careful eye on Erwin, happily observing that his speech was clear as he showed her around. The house was empty, with the exception of one roommate who was studying in his own bedroom. They sat at the kitchen table and had tea. They spoke quietly and infrequently, resting from their ordeal. The whole craziness of the past few days was over, and they were numb from the accumulated fatigue. The two other roommates arrived, and everyone gathered in the kitchen.

Everybody wanted to ensure that Erwin was fine. The roommates brewed tea, talking about people unknown to Sophia. She thought it was time to go. She would have loved to stay there, curled up in Erwin's arms, but with everyone else around, she felt useless. She told herself that it was not time to start something and regret it later. She rose from her chair and told Erwin, "It looks like you are well attended. It's late. I'm going to go."

"I understand; it's late," agreed Erwin. "I'm glad I was there through this whole adventure, but I'm really happy it's over now. And thank you again for bringing me home. Nothing is going to happen to me now. I'm well looked after." He swept his hand toward his roommates assembled in the kitchen.

"All right. I'll come to check on you tomorrow morning before my classes," said Sophia.

Sophia's feelings toward Erwin were becoming difficult for her to ignore. But it was not a good time to get involved with Erwin, knowing that he was going to leave the country in just a couple of months. *And then what?* Her short-term prospects were bleak. If she did not find a job soon, she would have to return to her parents' farm after graduation. She could not ask her parents to keep paying her rent forever, and without their financial help, she could not afford to live in Innsbruck. She had already started to look for a job, and she quickly realized that there were not many job openings for an inexperienced archaeologist. She thought about applying for a librarian or an administrative job, but she hadn't found any open positions yet.

Her heart burned as she climbed up the stairs to her apartment. She wondered how it happened that she came to like Erwin so much. For the first time since her bad experience in Vienna, she felt like she wanted to share her life with someone. But why Erwin, who was leaving soon? She dropped her bag on the floor as she entered her apartment. It was late, and she crashed on her bed, her heart a jumble of emotions. A part of her was kicking herself for being so conservative and for the cautious nature that made her push away from new adventures.

After a sleepless night, she got up early and began her morning routine. At around seven thirty, she left her apartment and went to check on Erwin, as promised. The sky was gray, and the weather felt cold, which mirrored her mood. On the one hand, she was very relieved that Aton had been arrested, and she had high hopes that she would be vindicated of any of his accusations. But on the other hand, she was crushed because Erwin was leaving for Cambridge. *From there, who knows where his career will take him?* she wondered. For her, he was gone, no matter what.

On her way to Erwin's, she bought fresh bread and a newspaper to see if anything was reported about last night's scuffle. But nothing was there. Maybe it happened too late for the reporters to learn about it or print it. She found Erwin already up and preparing for the day. He was happy to see her. He told her that he had not slept much, but he otherwise felt fine. She placed the paper on the table and told Erwin that Aton had not made the news yet. To be helpful, she started to brew coffee.

Erwin placed slices of bread in a toaster and said, "I bet it will be in the paper tomorrow. No new news about Professor Zelinger?"

"I haven't heard anything new. So far so good."

"I'm glad to hear that. Hold on. I have something for you," Erwin said, and he left for his bedroom. He came back an instant later with a book he placed on the kitchen table. It was an atlas, opened to a page showing flags of Europe.

"I was interested in the decorative motif you showed me earlier, the one on the large stone in front of Newgrange. I'm sure you know the figure made by the union of three spirals like that is called a triskelion. It reminded me of something I'd seen before, but I couldn't put my finger on it. And then last night, it came back to me. The flag of Sicily! I went there two years ago, the summer I hitchhiked through Italy with a friend. I remembered the flag. Look," he said, pointing to the flag of Sicily on the book's page.

Incredulously, Sophia looked at Sicily's flag and

compared it to the picture of Newgrange's entrance stone that
she had in her bag.

"And as I was looking for that flag, I also found that
there was one other country in Europe with a flag based on a
triskelion. It's the Isle of Man, a small island a few dozen
miles east of Newgrange," he said, showing her another flag.

"Isn't it strange that Sicily, the country where Malta's builders originated, has the same insignia as the people living on a small island just a few miles away from Newgrange?" Erwin asked.

"How about that!" she said, laughing. "Who would have thought about something like that? Sicily, the motherland of Malta's temple builders, and the Isle of Man, that small island east of Newgrange. You're right; that is surprising. It seems to reinforce some sort of an ancestral connection between these two parts of the world. However, it isn't something I can use to support my thesis. It would not pass the scrutiny of the archaeology professors who will review my work. It's already too controversial as it is. Anyway, that's really interesting. Thank you very much for the information."

"You are welcome," said Erwin. "There's something else I've been thinking about," he added.

"What else?"

"I remember you told me that Newgrange was directed toward the winter solstice sunrise. Isn't it?"

"Yes, why?" asked Sophia.

"That means that Newgrange was built at the only place in the world where during the winter solstice the sun rises at an angle that coincides with both a golden rectangle and the direction toward Malta," responded Erwin.

"What do you mean? Please explain."

Erwin took a piece of scrap paper, making drawings to explain his point. "You see, of all the right triangles, there is only one that has the ratio of its side as the golden number. The two non-right angles of this triangle have very specific values. Let's call the larger of the two the golden angle. I'm not an astronomer, but I know that the location of the sun at sunrise during the winter solstice depends on the latitude. If you are on the equator, the sun rises always at the same place all year long, due east, or at ninety degrees from the north-south axis. It's different, north or south of the equator. Let's take the northern hemisphere. During summer the sun rises in the northeast horizon and during winter in the southeast horizon. Now let's consider where the sun rises for a specific day of winter, like the winter solstice. The farther north you are when you observe sunrise, the father south the sun will rise on the horizon. The direction of sunrise will be at an angle from the north-south axis, smaller than ninety degrees.

"There is only one latitude where the angle of the rising sun at winter solstice is the golden angle, and it's the latitude at both Newgrange and Ale's Stones. So you can learn about the location starting from Malta and going north to Ale's Stones. Then you have to slide the location 831 miles west, to Newgrange's location, to make the sunrise direction coincide with the direction facing Malta. It is very impressive. Malta is such a small island that if Newgrange had been built fifty miles east or west, it never would have intercepted Malta, 1,600 miles away."

Sophia was flabbergasted. They looked at the map for a few minutes. Sophia wished she could talk to Professor Zelinger about her discoveries.

"You know where I would like to be right now?" she asked.

"No. Where?"

"Right now, there is nowhere else I would be than at Newgrange. One day, I will make a pilgrimage to see for myself this place that seems to be the center of so much. One day I will be in the center of Newgrange's chamber, with its 250,000 tons of boulders overhead, and I will face the entrance corridor. I will lower my body to the ground, with an ear nearly touching the floor. I will look for that little piece of sky visible at the end of the corridor, this small opening that allows seventeen minutes of sunlight on the chamber floor only at the winter solstice sunrise. From the pictures I've seen, the piece of sky at the end of the sloped corridor is much smaller than the triangle formed by my joined thumbs and first fingers when my arms are fully extended." She used her arms and fingers in demonstration. "And I will know that whatever people might say, I will have, before my eyes, in that very sharp and narrow direction in front of me, Europe's most holy places—Stonehenge, Chartres, the Valley of Wonders, Filitosa, and Malta. All there in that tiny spot of skylight, in a perfect row, stretching over sixteen hundred miles. I'll probably be the first person in the world who truly knows what I'm looking at from that spot. I don't know when this will happen, but I promise you—I'm going to do it!"

"Awesome! Is it easy to go there?"

"No, it is not! First, it's far away, and I can't afford it right now. But in addition, only a limited number of people per day are granted a guided visit in the innermost sanctuary. Anyway, I know that whatever it takes, one day I will go there."

"I may come with you. Who knows?" added Erwin with a smile.

Sophia was overwhelmed by the feeling that somehow her discovery might change the common understanding of Europe during the late Neolithic Age, potentially more than fifteen hundred years of human prehistory. This alignment just could not be the product of random groups of farmers each worshipping their own idols. It had to have been conceived and implemented by an organized group coordinated across the whole of Europe. Her findings provided the first clear proof that all of Western Europe, an incredibly vast territory, was unified for at least fifteen hundred years by an unknown group of leaders. That meant a Neolithic civilization must have existed across Europe at that time, a hypothesis going against what she was taught in college for that time period. Holding her head in her hands, elbows on the table, she mumbled, "I can't believe it."

"I think you're on to something big," said Erwin, grinning, bringing Sophia back from her thoughts. "They may call it the Sophia alignment or the Sophia triangle."

She smiled back at him. Her eyes caught the kitchen clock, and she realized that she needed to leave to get to her first class on time. She stood up and gave Erwin a hug. She thanked him again for his interest and help. "I'll check on you later this afternoon. Get some rest."

"Thanks. I'm fine. Don't worry, and thanks for breakfast. Have a good day, and good luck with your classes. Let me know if you learn anything about Aton or Professor Zelinger."

She hurried to her bicycle, parked outside Erwin's door, and pedaled hard all the way to arrive in time for class. She sat in the back row, wanting some quiet time to absorb the scale of her discovery.

During the lecture, she was distracted by her recollections of last night's events. As she thought over all that happened, she remembered the last question Erwin had asked yesterday, before they left for the hospital to check on Professor Zelinger: *"What else did you want me to check?"*

It hit her: *Brodgar! We forgot Brodgar. Where does it fit in the picture?* The site of Brodgar was on the small remote island of Orkney, north of Scotland. It included two stone rings, one large and one small, located on each side of a very narrow strip of land surrounded by water. Very recently, the remains of beautiful Neolithic buildings had been found about halfway between the two circles. The Brodgar complex dated from 5,300 years ago. The archaeological dig had just begun, but due to the size and quality of the constructions, archaeologists had started calling them the "cathedrals" of the Neolithic.

Brodgar seemed to have been a major European center at the time. It was quite possible that Brodgar was for Scotland and the northern islands what Stonehenge was for southern England. Sophia remembered that Brodgar was hundreds of miles north of the triangle, and it might contradict her theory.

As soon as class was over, she went to the library computer and accessed satellite imagery. Using her notes, she carefully pinned the large triangle formed by Gozo Island, Newgrange, and Ale's Stones. She then pinned Brodgar, and—as on Erwin's graph—Brodgar was way outside the triangle. It did not seem to belong. In a few click of her mouse, she traced a line from Newgrange to Brodgar. She noticed that the new line was making the same angle with Ale's Stones as the angle of the triangle. *Could that be another coincidence?* she wondered.

Curious, Sophia extended the line past Brodgar, wondering where it was going. She ended up in the middle of the Arctic Ocean. Nothing significant was noticeable. She then decided to extend the line from Malta to Ale's Stones north and see where it intercepted with her new line. The result was a new triangle over northern Europe, a new triangle mirror image of the first triangle.

Unfortunately, the intersection point seemed to be lost in the middle of the ocean north of Norway, well above the polar circle. Looking closer where the lines intersected, she noticed a tiny dot. She zoomed closer and saw that it was a minuscule island, shaped as a triangle, about seven miles wide. For a few moments, she was fascinated by the rough textures of the island's surface. She reached the maximum resolution of the satellite picture and scanned the surface for any rock formations that could be of human origin. However, the resolution was too poor, and she could not see details precisely. She was looking for traces of large constructions, but the rocky surface of the island had gone though many glacial periods and seemed sterile. She came to the southern tip of the island and gasped.

There, on the tip of the island, was a large circle, three or four hundred feet in diameter. The circle could be a natural occurrence, but the picture resolution did not reveal much detail. She thought that whatever the provenance of this circle, it would be perfectly usable for astronomical observations, like any other stone circles. Actually, being so far north inside the Arctic Circle, one could observe the stars dancing in circles in the night sky without interruption for months at a time during the winter season.

Could it be true? How could it have been planned that way? Nobody is going to believe me, she thought. *How is that possible? I'm going crazy.*

Her eyes went back to the screen. Here were two golden triangles projected over all of Western Europe, forming a large isosceles triangle with a base 2,650 miles long, and sides 1,600 miles long.

And then there is an island right there, just where it is supposed to be. Anybody can do what I'm doing and see it. And then what? Nobody will believe my interpretation. They're all going to call me a fool and say my alignments are chimeras or coincidences. This can't be good.

Sophia made a printout of the computer screen and ran out for her afternoon classes. However, it was wasted time because her mind could not stop thinking about this island. As soon as her classes were over, she went to the geographical section of the library and, after some digging, found that the island's name was Bear Island.[54] Actually, it was the most southern island of the Norwegian archipelago of

Svalbard, two hundred miles farther north. She looked for everything she could find that had been published about the island, but she could not uncover any archaeological survey. Accidently, she gleaned that Bear Island was one of the seven most inaccessible islands in the world. *Charming!* In past centuries, it had been used for whaling and, briefly, coal mining. She did not find mention of prehistoric activities on Bear Island proper, but Neolithic remains had been found on Svalbard's main island.

It was getting late in the afternoon, and Sophia started to feel tired, her mind numb. She returned to her apartment where she got a snack to make up for the missed lunch. She opened her briefcase and laid the printout on her desk. She remained emotionless as she looked at the immense triangles she had traced. The two right triangles joined together formed a large isosceles triangle. It reminded her of the small King's Sites triangle of Ireland—a small triangle compared to the gigantic size of the triangle she was looking at. *What could possibly be the purpose of creating these incredibly large figures that nobody on earth could see?*

Sophia wanted to share her new discovery with Erwin, but she was conflicted about seeing him again so soon. Her heart ached. Deep inside, she thought that something could have been possible. But now, with the news of his departure, there was no point in starting something that would go nowhere. *Been there, done that,* she thought. Sophia decided it would be better to stay away from Erwin, at least for a while. She thought that it could be much worse later if she followed the feelings she was developing for him.

However, a few minutes later, Sophia could not resist calling him and checking how he was. Erwin was fine. He said he wished he could see her, but because of deadlines he had to work until late that night. Before she knew it, Sophia agreed to meet with him tomorrow afternoon. Troubled, she wished him good night. Sitting at her desk, she decided that she too should spend the evening working on her dissertation.

CHAPTER 22

DAY 129
FILITOSA

atching the men repair his ship, Afrym was in a foul mood. The storm almost had sunk his boat, and he knew he'd been lucky to reach Filitosa in Corsica. He had seen violent storms in his life, but this one had been the most frightening. Even though his boat was made of the best cedar wood available, large breakers slamming off the bridge had severely damaged the mast attachment and opened leaks in the hull.

Because this side of the island was dry and rocky, the only vegetation was brush and short twisted trees. Consequently, he had sent men away to fetch wood appropriate for the repairs. They had found pine trees far inland that they had brought back to repair the ship. He was not pleased with this wood, which was far weaker than cedar.

It would have to do, at least until they could return home. Carpenters used bronze tools to perfectly cut and shape pieces of pine to fit the other boards of the hull. Others assembled new oars to replace those broken by the ferocious breakers. Based on their progress so far, he judged it would take another day at least to complete the ship reparations.

He had stopped in Filitosa on a few occasions. The tall cliffs that protected its bay created a safe harbor against storms. A fishermen's village was at the end of the bay where Minoan boats came to trade goods in exchange for fresh supplies. Since Filitosa was close to the most sacred place of the island, there were occasional pilgrims who needed a boat crossing that the Minoans were pleased to offer for a charge. The islanders were fierce, but so far, he had always had friendly encounters with them.

Afrym was an experienced sailor and had sailed past the sea gates many times, all the way to the Green Islands, in search of tin. From time to time, on his way from their home island of Crete, he had stopped at Malta to trade the myrrh and frankincense the monks needed to make their incense sticks.

Afrym was annoyed because in addition to the days wasted in repairing the damage from the storm, his two passengers had left the ship to visit the priesthood of the sanctuary a few hours away from the coast, on the other side of the mountains in front of him.

He did not know what to think about his two passengers. Even before leaving Massalia, he wondered who these two passengers really were. He was now wondering if he could make a better deal by trading them as slaves in Kercz instead of the few bags of grains bargained for their passage to Malta.

Afrym barked some orders to the men working on his boat, still heavy with the tin he'd acquired from Brittany. *The Yamna from Kercz are going to give me gold for that tin. These idiots have a lot of copper and gold, but they can't find tin in their lands.* Afrym knew that the Yamna learned from the people of Hamoukar that when tin was added to molten copper, it made a metal harder than copper alone. This new metal, bronze, was ideal for making weapons. Hamoukar wasn't providing them with the tin they wanted. There was very little tin in the neighboring lands, and Hamoukar received their tin from a secret location, far in the East. *And I know where to find tin,* thought Afrym with a grin. He chuckled, thinking about how Minoans had managed to keep the source of their tin supply secret by giving the remote islands far northwest in the Green Sea the name "Tin Islands," though no tin could be found there. Consequently, nobody but a Minoan knew where the real tin islands were.

After the Yamna stole the secret of taming horses from the people of the grasslands and learned how to make wheels from the farmers of the East, they built their homes on carts pulled by oxen. They moved their villages to wherever the grass was greener. It was difficult to travel east because the mountain terrain was difficult to traverse, and the Macedonian warriors prevented passage. The farmland of the west was by far easier to take over for the Yamna, and they destroyed everything in the way that could stop their herds and chariots, killing native men and enslaving women and children. Afrym knew their population was growing fast and that at some point they could rule all of the land.

I don't care if these marauders slaughter every last farmer in the West with the bronze weapons they make with my tin. Thankfully, the Blue Sea buffers us from these butchers. I hate those stinking savages, but they have gold—

and lots of it. They also give away these exquisite jewels made of crafted gold for lumps of tin. That's the only thing that matters. I don't care if they kill thousands of these dirty peasants, as long as I get my gold.

Afrym's only concern was earning enough to procure two more boats, one for each of his sons, so they could travel with him and join his trade business along the coast. His mind returned to his passengers. From the start, he wondered if these two passengers were more than mere monks.

They look stronger and more experienced than the monks I know. I think it's odd that both carry weapons for protection, as they said. They look tough in their nice outfits, but my crew and I can have them subdued in an instant. I wonder how much gold I could get from the Yamna for those two idiots.

He looked to the harbor for signs of his passengers. "Where are they?" he said loudly. He was angry because his passengers had been invited by Filitosa's high priest and had left his sight. He was angry because there was nothing he could have done to prevent them from going to the monastery. He wondered if his plans to make his two passengers disappear could be in jeopardy, now that they had made contact with the Filitosa priesthood. Afrym did not want to create a problem with anyone in Filitosa because it was a well-located safe harbor.

I'm sure they told them they are on the way to Malta. How would the Corsicans react if they learned that the travelers never reached their destination? I could lose their trust—or worse, lose the safe harbor of Filitosa. Are these stupid monks worth the trouble? My agreement with them does not say to wait for them. I'm leaving when we are ready to go, whether they are on board or not.

* * *

Tesimo was awakened when Hryatan shook his shoulder. He looked around and recognized the fisherman's house where they had taken refuge after they moored in the harbor. It took him a moment to recover his senses and remember what had happened during the crossing.

He recalled that the Minoan boat did not waste time in Massalia. The sailors quickly loaded fresh water and supplies, and they left the harbor the next morning. They started their journey following the coast heading east. The Minoan ship sailed with the gentle wind and clear weather, and Tesimo had a pleasant time with the sailors who shared their food and red liquor, which made them laugh late into the night. On the third day, the boat went south into the open sea toward the island of Corsica on their way to Malta. At first, the traverse of the vast Blue Sea was uneventful. Tesimo enjoyed watching dolphins play in front of the ship. They had arrived in view of the island of Corsica when he noticed the captain looking behind him. His blood froze at the sight of the captain's frightened face. He turned around and saw that the eastern horizon had become as black as night.

The captain started to bark orders to his crew to drop the sail and drive the oars in a retreat to the coast. Tesimo recalled the sudden wind that pushed the waves into higher and higher crests, pushing the boat away from the coast. The thunder roared and rain started to fall in sheets.

Waves crashed over the deck, sweeping sailors away like leaves in the wind, ripping away pieces of the ship, rocking it back and forth like a feather in torrential waters.

The mast was ripped from the deck and fell overboard, pulling two sailors with it. Most men tried desperately to bail water off the boat, while the rest of the men attempted to control the vessel's bearing by rowing hopelessly against the surging currents. Both Hryatan and

Tesimo helped as they could. Tesimo thought he was going to die each time a monstrous wave bashed the boat.

The storm finally relented in the middle of the night. The wind strength weakened to levels manageable enough for the rowers to make progress. The sea gradually became calmer. The crew kept rowing west, scooping out the water that flowed in from the cracks. At sunrise, they were in view of the coast. Based on coastal landmarks, the captain led them to the harbor of Filitosa. The harbor entrance was wedged between two large rocky cliffs more than a hundred feet high, leading to a protected harbor. A large beach village was situated at the end of this wide, rocky canyon. The effect against the wind was stunning. Suddenly, everything became quiet; the only noise heard was the splashing of paddles. They reached the harbor, wet and weary. Afrym moored the boat to the other boats already docked in the harbor with the help of some fisherman. They were under the attentive stares of the villagers, who paused during their morning chores to watch the wretched crew coming off the battered boat.

On the dock, Gritulu, the village chief, welcomed them. The population, who offered resting places and hospitality in various homes of the village, hosted the exhausted men. As distinguished travelers, the village leader hosted Hryatan and Tesimo, granting them their own small room. Tesimo recalled he immediately fell asleep.

Standing in front of Tesimo, Hryatan said, "Yes, we are alive! I really thought we were lost. How do you feel, my friend?"

"Fine, I think, although I hurt everywhere. How long have I slept?"

"More than a half-day. It is past midday. I've already been to the harbor and checked on the boat. Afrym said it would take at least two days to repair the ship. Come on, let's get something to eat."

Hryatan showed Tesimo a pair of shoes and clothes left for him by their Corsican hosts. They entered a larger central room where three women and three children were busy shelling chestnuts at a large table, dropping the shelled nuts into large wooden bowls. The children stood up and made places for them to sit at the table. A woman welcomed the travelers and offered them fresh water, dried fish, and flat bread. One of the two other women left the room to inform the village leader that the visitors were awake.

Hryatan and Tesimo were just finishing their meal when a man stepped inside the room, He was wearing a black headband and a goat skin vest and pants, secured by a large belt adorned by small copper disks. Tesimo recognized the man from their early morning arrival. Gritulu checked on his guests' health and told them that they were welcome to stay in his house until the boat was repaired. Sitting at the table, Gritulu asked about their journey. The companions just had started describing the storm when they were interrupted by a young man dressed in a robe made of fabric as white as snow. The man's name was Marato. He was a monk from the holy center of Filitosa,[55] a few miles from the coast. He told them that the monastery heard about their arrival. The high priest sent him to the village to check on the health of the messengers. Everyone appreciated the monastery's interest, and both Hryatan and Tesimo thanked the monk for the attention. The monk was pleased to hear that the travelers were healthy, and, in this case, he was to convey an invitation from the high priest to visit him at the monastery. They were invited to spend the night there as they pleased.

Gritulu told Tesimo and Hryatan that it was a great honor to be in the presence of the high priest, and they should proceed immediately. Not having any reason to refuse, they accepted the invitation. After informing the boat captain, Hryatan and Tesimo left the village with the monk to go to Filitosa's sacred grounds.

Following the monk on ancient and winding paths through a rugged countryside, it took them the entire afternoon to reach the monastery. At the end of a rocky canyon, they reached a small valley with a hill in the center. As they traveled, Tesimo realized that the very large rocks surrounding the hilltop looked like enormous solid drops of mud with extraordinary shapes. Some looked like nightmarish faces of hideous humans or animals. Others seemed to have been cleaved, leaving large cavities as if a giant had gutted them. It was one of the strangest places Tesimo had ever seen.

They reached the top of a hill in the center of a circular valley surrounded by larger hills. The top of the hill was encircled by a large stone wall. Tall, carved standing stones had been erected on top of the wall. Somehow, these stones reminded Tesimo of the stones he had seen bordering Stonehenge. The monk asked them to wait at the entrance of the sacred place while he went to tell the high priest that the visitors had arrived. After a short time, he came back and led them to the place of worship. They climbed a few stairs that took them to a circular platform in the center of the small stone ring. Attendants stood at the periphery of the platform. In the center was a flat, circular stone.

The high priest stepped on the stone and turned around to face Hryatan and Tesimo. Tesimo felt the priest's penetrating eyes look deep into his own soul. In an instant, his body felt like it was made of warm pulsing points, light like snowflakes but warm and pulsating. He felt surrounded by a halo of peace, and his heart filled with what Tesimo believed to be the goddess mother's love. A part of his mind was in fusion with the stars, the sun, and the moon, and at the same time, he was here, facing the priest. The verdant hills around them looked like shining waves under the bright sun.

The priest raised his hand and pronounced words incomprehensible to Tesimo, even though he understood that it was a blessing. His body started to move at the rhythm of the priest's words, like rolling waves. He commanded them to stay still and let their minds feel the flow of life coming from the depth of the hill. "Be still. Let the ray of harmony purify your souls."

Tesimo could not speak but knew he didn't have to say anything to be understood. He felt that his mind had expanded to the fabric of the world. He was humbled by the experience and knelt on the ground. Tesimo couldn't say how long he had been still, but after a while he regained control of himself. He noticed that Hryatan was kneeling beside him, entranced.

The high priest asked them to rise and, smiling at them, said, "Messengers, I can tell you have pure hearts. Only pure hearts can feel the ray, and you felt it. I saw it. You are great receptacles of the ray. I'm happy that your mission has left your souls unmarked."

Marato came and signaled them to follow him toward the outer edge of the platform, close to the entrance. Tesimo's clarity slowly returned. In fact, he felt clearer than he had ever before. As they walked toward the sanctuary's gate, he could feel his body in ways he had never imagined. He could feel currents of a soft fire flowing inside and revitalizing his tired body.

Outside the sanctuary, Marato told the voyagers that he was going to guide them to the monastery, where the high priest would meet them that night. There were no dwellings around the holy center. In fact, there were no dwellings in an area even larger than the circle of hills surrounding the holy site. They had to walk another few miles of rocky terrain to reach the large housing community where the priesthood lived. The monastery was a two-story building next to a large farm. First, they were allowed to wash their hands and feet. Then they were served a simple meal and showed a small room with bunks where they could rest. However, the companions were not sleepy. They spent the rest of the day helping the monks with their daily chores.

The sun drew closer to the horizon as the high priest and the other attendants arrived at the monastery. Later that evening, both companions were taken to a round room where the high priest was waiting for them.

"Tesimo, Hryatan. I'm glad you came. You're welcome among us. We are on a small island, but we have heard about you and your quest. We heard from the runners that you saved the high king and that you have lost a dear friend. We have heard about your journey, but I was not expecting you to land on our shores. When we heard that a Minoan ship came ashore with two passengers corresponding to your description, I sent Marato to invite you here. I am pleased you came."

The high priest asked the travelers to join him at the table placed in the center of the room. Marato appeared shortly, carrying a bowl of water and dry cloths for washing and ablutions. Another monk entered the room with food and water on a tray. They pronounced the incantations to purify their meal, and once they were alone again, the high priest asked them questions about the health of the high king, their impressions of Alaric, their thoughts about the Yamna, and their travels before their arrival in Filitosa. When Tesimo asked about the place where the sanctuary was built, the high priest didn't answer directly.

"You should know that today you were granted a great honor. Not many pilgrims have been allowed to enter the inner center of Filitosa. And I think you know why, don't you?" Hryatan and Tesimo looked at each other with questioning eyes. "Filitosa is special," continued the priest. "You may not know, but Filitosa was built on a resonance point of the ray. Yes indeed, it is one of the two points where the ray resonates. The other one is in the Carnutes, as you may have guessed. I know you went there. Did you feel the ray in the Carnutes?" he asked, looking at Tesimo.

"No, High Priest. I did not feel it there," answered Tesimo. "High Priest, with all due respect, what is the ray?"

"The ray is the force generated by the prayers of all the faithful. Earth gathers them from the whole kingdom and sends them here to sanctify this land."

After their meal, the high priest granted them hospitality for the night. The high priest told them that tomorrow he was to conduct a closed ceremony and that he would not be able to bid them farewell. He hoped their boat would be repaired and that they would have a safe journey to Malta. The companions retreated to their room for the night.

***

It was just past midday when Afrym saw his passengers walking from the fishermen's village. He'd been irritated all day, concerned about his passengers and the clouds on the horizon. His boat repairs had been faster than expected, and he was almost ready to leave. *These bastards are going to regret this,* he thought. *They're going to be sold to the Yamna. I'm done with them.*

As they embarked, Afrym was already counting the Yamna gold. Then he heard Marato running on the dock, yelling for them to wait. The young monk jumped on to the ship and asked the captain to take him to Malta. He was an envoy from Filitosa's high place. Since the high priest learned that the Minoan boat was on its way to Malta, he requested that Afrym take Marato to Malta as well. The captain protested, arguing that they did not have the room for another passenger. The envoy remarked that the captain had the room for the two sailors he had lost during the storm. Marato told him this would cover his returned duties to the village after the welcome he received after the storm and the assistance he had received to repair his ship. Afrym did not know how to counter this argument. He wanted to stay on good terms with Filitosa, and refusing to ferry the kid could be bad for future visits. He finally agreed to take the monk as well.

Fuming, the captain gave orders to leave the harbor. He swore, thinking how lucky these two bastards had been. *If it weren't for that monk, those two travelers would've been my slaves by nightfall.* He certainly couldn't afford problems with Malta. It was, after all, the increased Maltese trade that had caused his family to relocate from the Red Sea to the Blue Sea on the island of Crete. Incense trade was still big and profitable, and he did not want to damage this source of income by creating an incident. *I'm not going to take a chance for these two idiots. They are not worth it. They can rot in the underworld. I don't care!*

CHAPTER 23

DAY 135
GGANTIJA

The boat's repairs held, and five days after leaving Filitosa, Tesimo finally saw Malta's islands on the horizon. The swell was heavy, and the captain shouted orders to lower the sail.

As they came closer, Tesimo could clearly see that Malta was made of several islands, the first one hiding a much larger one. Tesimo learned that the small island in front of them was called Gozo. It was the most holy island of the Malta archipelago. Gozo was the residence of the high priestess, and no boats other than the monk's boats could land at the Gozo harbor.

Afrym already knew this, and he ignored the small island, pointing his boat toward the larger island beyond. He commanded the rowers with a booming voice as the boat negotiated the reefs dotting the islands' coasts. While Tesimo was observing the steep cliffs surrounding Gozo, he noticed people watching them from the top of the bluff. He informed the captain, who sharply responded that they were monks, guardians of the sacred island.

It was past midday when they moored at Kalkara, the main harbor on the large island of Malta. Other boats were already in the harbor, ferrying pilgrims on and off the island. Many pilgrims came from long distances to worship at this place. In addition to the food offerings in grain or cattle that the pilgrims brought the island's temples, ships also brought lumber, cloth, incense, earthenware, and other necessities of life. The captain and his passengers went to a large building where the monks who oversaw the harbor's activities were located. After some negotiation, they were led to the senior monk. The senior monk quickly realized that Tesimo was wearing the kingdom key, and Afrym was given the prearranged dues for his services.

Left to themselves, Tesimo, Hryatan, and Marato started to make their way through town toward the small port of Marr, on the east side of the island, to take a boat to Gozo. Leaving the harbor area, they crossed a market where people traded all kind of things, including vegetables, meat, seashells, pottery, tools, clothes, and incense. In the center of town, they came to a beautiful large stone construction, different from anything else Tesimo had seen. The building was round with an entrance centered on a large, tall façade that had a concave curvature. In front of it was a court where priests and priestesses officiated in the worship of the mother goddess, and the guardians burned incense and offered sacrifices.

The sun was already low in the sky when they finally exited town. They came to a large monastery, where the worshippers happily offered them hospitality for the night. In the center of the monastery was a court, where a large statue of Gaia stood regally in the center. The beautiful statue showed the goddess reclined instead of standing. In Tesimo's eyes, the quality of the carving and detail expressed in the statue surpassed all others in the kingdom. The goddess representation was larger than the ones Tesimo had previously seen. A priest next to him invited him to venerate Gaia for her generosity, her exuberance in giving. On a side of the courtyard many young people were assembled, singing melodious songs as they wove strings and others assembled new khipus. At the other side of the courtyard, another group of youth prepared a thick paste in cauldrons.

The monks explained that those youth were there for their year of sacrifice. They were spending the day learning the art of counting and the art of making portable timepiece. Malta's incense sticks were the most precise timepieces in the kingdom and were needed everywhere. Many monks spent most workdays learning the art of making incense sticks used for time measurements. The sticks were put together to measure specific time length, such as minutes, hours, or even days. At other times, they were giving spiritual instructions to the youth as they worked on religious constructions across the island.

As the kingdom's timekeeper, Malta was the repository of the time counters' khipus. The whole kingdom history was archived in Malta's large khipu libraries. Tesimo had learned that it was the eighteenth solar cycle of the high king's accession, as well as the 1,367th solar cycle since high kingdom unification.

In addition to counting time for the living, the monks also counted time for the dead. Long ago, members of the royal family started to honor the departed high kings by having monks keep records of the time elapsed since the death of each high king. This honorary custom became more and more popular, and leaders and other noteworthy townsfolk started to similarly mark the events of their personal lives: births, deaths, marriages, weddings, treaties, and any other events of historical or familial interest. Consequently, more time counters were required to count the times for both the living and the dead, and more donations were necessary to support this monastery population. In many cases, benefactors gave Malta control of farmlands in their district instead of bringing yearly grain donations to the temples. Consequently, Malta controlled large tracts of lands in faraway places spread throughout the kingdom. These lands were overseen by Brodgar, which directed the harvest surpluses to Malta. As the keeper of the kingdom's time and history, Malta became a vital part of the kingdom's administration.

Through the discussions Tesimo had with monks and townsfolk, he understood that time counting had become a very important element of Malta's life, to a point that some people were concerned that the kingdom would fall if they stopped counting time. Tesimo doubted that could be the case. He could not imagine guardians sun and moon standing still in the sky because these monks stopped counting time. However, he did not choose to argue the point since he was only an outsider in foreign lands.

After their evening ablutions and rituals, the travelers were offered a meal and a place to sleep. They woke up early the next morning and continued their walk through the dry countryside to Marr. They reached the little port by late morning and caught one of the boats that frequently crossed the small channel to take priests and supplies to Gozo, where the high priestess had a residence. Noticing Zuoz's pendant on Tesimo's neck, the monks of the harbor organized their passage to Gozo. They had to leave their weapons with the monk before embarking on the boat. Tesimo deposited his dagger, Alaric's gift, on the table of the harbormaster as Hryatan removed his sheathed sword. Memories of Sarup came to Tesimo's mind.

At Gozo, they were received by monks wearing a brown fabric wrap, armed with a wooden pole similar to Zuoz's. After explaining the purpose for their visit, they were escorted to the great temple of Ggantija. Tesimo was speechless at the size of the stones that made up the temple walls and the craftsmanship required to fit these enormous stones together. As the holder of Zuoz's pendant, Tesimo made his way through the guards to the high priestess's residence. There, Tesimo had to give his pendant to an official, who took it the high priestess while the companions waited at the entrance. Some time elapsed, and then the official came back and asked that only Tesimo follow him, while Hryatan and Marato were to wait in a temple chamber. Tesimo was led through a short corridor with side rooms where the monks were occupied, arranging khipus on racks.

Tesimo was brought into a large chamber where the high priestess was reclining like the statue he had seen. Spirals like those of Newgrange swirled up the stones on the wall behind her. Tesimo bowed respectfully and waited for the priestess to address him. As he dared to glance at her with his head still lowered, he saw that she was looking at him with piercing dark eyes. Her black hair created ringlets framing her face and falling on her shoulders. She wore a knee-length gown accentuated with intricate stitching and colorful appliques and pleats at the hem. In her right hand was Zuoz's pendant. She made a gesture and her two attendants left the room. She sat up on her couch and signaled for him to come closer.

"Tesimo, I was waiting for you. Please come and sit," she said, pointing to one of the stools placed near her lounger.

Tesimo came closer to her and sat down as instructed.

"I was told of your coming. I understand that you were a friend and apprentice of Zuoz. Is it true?"

"Yes, great priestess. I have walked in Zuoz's path across the kingdom for many moons. He saved my life, and I dare to say he was my friend." After a pause, he added, "He asked me to tell you that after being poisoned, his spirit traveled to the afterworld and reached unity with God. He said that God had already judged him, and his life's burden on his soul was light. He came back to our world and sacrificed his life to save the high king. He gave me the pendant you hold in your hand. In his last breath he asked me to come here to tell you that there are traitors within the leaders of the kingdom. His last message for you was to watch the Krpy's basket."

The great priestess was quiet a moment. "I am sorry that his life had to be sacrificed in this way, but his death saved the kingdom. My heart aches with Zuoz's loss. I will miss him, but I am happy that his soul is now resting in God's unity. I understand Zuoz's message, and we will act immediately."

An attendant walked to the great priestess and bent close to her. The great priestess ushered quick words to the attendant's ears. The attendant then retreated. Holding Zuoz's pendant, the great priestess asked Tesimo, "Do you know what this pendant means?" Tesimo was not sure how to answer this question. He knew that the pendant was a mark of status and importance, but he had never thought that it had a meaning. "Zuoz told me it was a key of the kingdom," he answered.

"You are correct, Tesimo. This pendant is a key. It is true that it will open many doors, but this is mainly because it is a symbol of God."

Quietly, Tesimo waited for more explanation. The high priestess continued. "The divided circle represents the Great Spirit, union of Gaia and Sky. The straight line crossing its center is the border between light and darkness, right and wrong, honor and shame. The crossbar is the soul given to us, the reflection of the world, the boundary between life and death. The straight section underneath represents the Great Spirit entering our world through our souls, being the foundation and pillar for us all."

Tesimo listened respectfully, physically feeling each word he was told, taking it all with clarity and peace.

"Tesimo, we all have a destiny, but nobody knows what it is until it is fulfilled. Zuoz's life was not lost in vain. He changed the course of your life, of my life, and the lives of countless kingdom subjects. You too, willing or not, knowingly or in ignorance, have already changed the destiny of multitudes of people, saving them from death or enslavement.

"Tesimo, you must know that people, animals, plants, rivers, and mountains all came from the union of goddess mother and sky. Their child is the ever-present Great Spirit. Tesimo, in this world, the Great Spirit is everywhere. Break a stick, lift a stone—the Great Spirit is here and there.

"Man's spirit takes its essence from the stars, from the constellation of Orion. Man's spirit is in unity with the living spirit of the world that we sometime call God. We are all God's manifestations, and our conducts should always be intended to glorify it. Hurting a neighbor would only be hurting the divinity, closing our own door to the afterworld, the land of our ancestors. That's why we all take care of each other and receive an equal share of everything.

"Unfortunately, some of us became corrupted, and now, faithless barbarians are devastating our lands. On such occasions, we have to stand up and fight for survival. It is contrary to our beliefs to kill other humans, but when we have to do so, we do it with respect and pray for the souls of all those who are slain."

Tesimo was quietly listening.

"Tesimo," the great priestess continued, "we all know that we are born with our own death lurking within us, and this truth guides our steps. We don't know when our end will come, but we know that by doing the right things, Gaia will let us keep our vital fire in the afterlife. We have seen what happens to the wrongdoers' souls when they pass away—their life fire is ripped apart, absorbed by the infinity of the night."

After a pause the great priestess told him, "We are sad about the destruction of your village. It is difficult to understand how the Great Spirit acts on us, for your tragedy ended up being a blessing for the kingdom. God's hands have many fingers, and we are all one of them. Your sad story has saved many lives.

"Tesimo, you have already accomplished a lot for being so young. But your destiny is not over yet. You still have a lot of things to do in the future. Is your destiny to stay here, and pray in communion with our ancestors? Is your destiny to fight the war against the Yamna? Is your destiny to take you places still unknown to us? Only you can find an answer."

All was quiet in the room. The words of the great priestess were still resonating in Tesimo's head.

With equal voice, the great priestess continued. "God's words are often silent, but you can hear them in your heart. Be still, empty your mind, reach your inner silence, and listen to God's words—you can feel them. Listen to them, and they will guide you in your steps."

Then the great priestess stood up and beckoned. "Come with me, Tesimo. There is someone who wants to meet you." They left her chamber and walked through a corridor leading to the temple's great hall. As they walked slowly, she told him, "During your journey, you saw how people expressed their faith in different ways. But it is not an issue because we are all united in faith. Faith is beauty, love, intelligence, compassion, and much more, and all of that is in you. There is only one God, the Great Spirit, creator of all things, of Gaia and Sky, of the guardians and us all. God is alive. Through our eyes, he can see creation. He can hear it though our ears and feel it through our skin. We are all in God. You have already realized all these truths yourself, haven't you?"

"I am not sure, Great Priestess. My soul is still confused and disturbed by the horrors I have seen."

"Your confusion is normal, Tesimo. You have been through a lot of hardship. Eventually, your soul will calm down, and you will see reflected in it your true nature and destiny. Always try not to harm living beings, and love, respect, and help your brothers and sisters."

Through a large door they entered a cavernous egg-shaped room, walled with massive fitted stone slabs. Across the room was another large door that opened into another large room. A group of men wearing long robes were debating among themselves on the side of the room. As they came closer to them, the men stopped their discussion, and one came toward Tesimo.

The high priestess introduced him as Zebbug, the great astronomer. Zebbug placed one hand on Tesimo's shoulder and said to him, "Tesimo, I have heard stories about you. I understand you have traveled very far and visited many of the most sacred places of the kingdom. You know, very few people have made such a journey. Tesimo, have you heard of the ray?"

"Yes, Great Astronomer. The High Priest of Filitosa told me that we were under the ray. I think I felt it, but I am not sure I understood what it was."

"I see. Tesimo, of all the places you have been, have you visited Ale's Stones?"

"No, Great Astronomer. While we were on our way to Sarup, Zuoz pointed the way to me, but we hurried, as our message was urgent, and we did not cross the sea to go there. Zuoz told me that Ale's Stones was known as the point of harmony."

"That is correct, Tesimo. You are a smart young man. Ale's Stone circle is also known as the point of harmony. And do you know why it is called the point of harmony?"

"No, Great Astronomer, I don't."

"I am going to tell you, Tesimo. But first, I have to tell you about Malta's ancient astronomers. They believed that the basis of our world's harmony was in the divine proportion given by Orion. Many of our constructions are built using the celestial ratios. I'm sure you know by now that Yule, the celebration of the winter solstice, is the most important holiday of the sun cycle. It is the time when the sun and earth join to start the new cycle. This is also a time when we interlace our faith across the kingdom. Many of our sacred places were oriented to receive the light of the rising sun on that holy day. The ancient astronomers realized that much farther north from here, the solstice sun rises at the perfect orientation. They called this place the point of Harmony, and there they erected Ale's Stones.

"Thinking further, the ancient astronomers decided that these rays of the purest light should be reflected all over our lands. To do so, they decided to build the point of reflection, located as far north as the point of harmony but farther west, in order to face Ggantija. At the point of reflection, they built this magnificent construction called Newgrange, which reflects the divine ray back and forth toward here, Ggantija."

Tesimo remembered Newgrange's sparkling façade, and everything started to make sense to him.

"The kingdom's high priests and high priestesses of the time were pleased with the astronomers' constructions, and they united all the religions of the kingdom by aligning their most holy sanctuaries along the path of the ray of Orion, the ray of unification.

"What you felt in Filitosa, Tesimo, was the strength of our people's faith, channeled across the kingdom through our sanctuaries. What you felt that day was the kingdom faith."

Shortly after this revelation, another astronomer came and interrupted Zebbug, whispering something in his ear. Then Zebbug said to Tesimo, "I am sorry, but I have to go. We are debating tonight's stellar observations with the other priests. We are expecting a moon eclipse that coincides exceptionally with Litha, the midsummer solstice, and time is running out to prepare our observations. Once again, thank you for your service. I would like to meet with you during your stay at Gozo. Rest. We will talk later."

"It was an honor to meet you, Great Astronomer. I am at your service," said Tesimo, bowing to the man before Zebbug left the party.

The great priestess then told Tesimo that it was time to receive Hryatan and Marato. They met in the temple room where Tesimo had left them earlier. She said to them all, "We thank God to have guided your paths to us. You, Marato, please go back to Filitosa's high priest. Tell him that he was inspired by the highest wisdom when he sent you here with the two messengers. You ensured their safe passage.

"Hryatan, your mission was a success. We know that your people need you and that you will soon be on your way back to your lands. Tell King Akkad of Hamoukar that we are forever thankful to have received the art of bronze making. This may save our kingdom.

"Tesimo, you have demonstrated moral strength, courage, and loyalty. The kingdom needs people like you. Let us be your new family, and know that you will always have a place among us. If you choose to stay with us, you could spend your year of sacrifice here in Malta and learn our arts and wisdom. If you prefer, you can go to any of our other houses of knowledge. Take as long as you need to think about what you want do next. You are welcome to stay here as long as you want. When you are ready, come back to me and tell me your decision.

"Now, you can all go and rest. Sleeping arrangements have been made for all of you. These brothers will take you to your quarters," the great priestess said, pointing at two monks standing by the room entrance.

The monks took the travelers to a monastery away from the Ggantija temple. On their way, they passed a 120-foot stone circle surrounding a gaping hole, flanked by tall statues, the entrance to an underground sanctuary. The stones of this circle were large slabs placed side by side, forming a continuous fence. The statues in the center were similar to the other statues on the island. Their guides explained that it was Xagħra circle,[56] the place where Malta's high priesthood and Astronomers of the past were buried.

At the monastery, they were each offered a small room with a bed where they unloaded their bags and took some rest. They were also offered a meal, which they ate in exhausted silence. After dinner, Tesimo walked alone to the edge of a cliff facing the sea. It was the same cliff he had seen as they passed Gozo Island on Afrym's boat. He sat down and looked at the waves crashing on the rocks below.

Now that his mission was complete, Tesimo felt empty and without purpose. He wondered if he had fulfilled the prediction of the Olkam priestess, or if Gaia or the Great Spirit had more plans for him. *How could I have imagined, five moons ago, that I would be standing here on this cliff today? It all happened so fast. Just yesterday I was hunting wild goats with Druso. I was to wed Elena, become the chieftain and live in my mountains forever, like my father and all my ancestors. Now, I've lost my family and my world. What's next for me?*

His memories took him back to a time when he could not imagine a kingdom behind the mountains. His thoughts wandered from the unexpected brotherhood he found in Zuoz, Hryatan, and Alaric to the frightening fights with the Yamna riders; the entrancing dances of orbs of light in Olkam; the tin mines of the Ore Mountain; his feelings for Princess Astrid.

He looked at the surf, his mind reflecting on his adventures. He had traveled in the company of Norsemen, of forest people, of Minoan sailors. He had visited the most sacred places of the world, rescued the high king from death, found and lost a brother in Zuoz, and become himself a royal messenger. He could never have imagined a world so vast, with its infinite plains, forests, seas, and peoples from so many different horizons. He had learned a new language, the art of counting, and astronomy, and in the space of a few months, he'd become one of the most learned subjects in the kingdom.

Now, his mission was over. He did not have anywhere to go. He was free to do whatever he wanted to do, go wherever he wanted to go.

As he looked at the sea, thoughts swarmed in his head. Tesimo was wondering what he would do with his life now. Was his destiny fulfilled? Did he have anything left to do with his time on earth?

He'd been invited to stay here in Malta to complete his apprenticeship and become a messenger of the great priestess, or an astronomer, or a counter …

But what about my village? What about Elena? Should I go back there to see if anyone survived? Whether or not everyone is dead, should I go back just because I promised her that I would return? Does honor dictate that I must go back no matter what? But what is the point? Assuming that I could find my way through the mountains, what am I going to find there? Dried bones; burned-down houses? And if there were any survivors, how could I live with them—I, who betrayed them by being away when they were attacked? And if Elena survived, she must have started a new life with somebody else by now. Is there any reason to go back?

His thoughts circled back to the pure and sweet Astrid. His heart wanted to go back to Sarup, where he was awaited and where Alaric would lead him to fight the Yamna. *Mabon is about four moons away. It should not take much more than two or three moons to go to Sarup.*

And what about Hryatan? Am I not bound to him because he saved my life? Should I not try to repay my debt by helping him return to Hamoukar? Images of the exotic place Hryatan had described came to his mind. *Can I accomplish both at the same time? Less than two moons to go to Hamoukar. That gives me two moons to reach Sarup.*

That's tight but possible. Can I make it back to Sarup in time for Princess Astrid's passage?

Contemplating the waves, Tesimo hoped for the sea to whisper an answer to his questions.

CHAPTER 24

APRIL 3, 1992
EARLY MORNING

It was a glorious, crisp spring morning that helped Sophia shake off her gloomy disposition. She was getting ready to leave her apartment, headed to the printing shop where the final bound copies of her thesis were ready for pickup. It was a few weeks until her dissertation defense, and even though the members of the jury had read her final draft, the bound copies needed to be in their hands soon.

Six months had passed since Aton Schmidt was arraigned after the fight at the hospital. He was denied bail and awaited trial. If convicted, he could get twenty-five years in prison. The day following his arrest, Professor Zelinger was awakened from a medically induced coma. He did not remember the accident and was surprised to learn what had happened to him. He asked to have both Sophia and Erwin visit him so he could express his gratitude for their actions and saving his life.

Professor Zelinger recovered quickly, considering the extent of his injuries. However, he could not walk and quickly grew bored in his hospital bed. From his recovery bed, the professor quickly regained control of the archaeological department, and he reinstated Sophia's job. He invited students to come to visit him to discuss archaeological topics and their research findings. While he was still in the hospital, he received a visit from Professor Astrid Trømso, an archaeologist friend from Norway. Professor Zelinger had been reading the draft of Sophia's thesis, and he asked Professor Trømso if she knew anything about Neolithic settlements on Bear Island. She personally didn't know of any and asked why he was interested in such a tiny island, lost in the middle of North Sea. He showed her the chapter of Sophia's thesis about the site alignments and the predicted triangle with Bear Island.

Interested, Professor Trømso said that she would check on it as soon as she returned to Norway, but unfortunately, she had not returned any information to them yet.

While still at the hospital, Professor Zelinger advised Sophia to present her alignments objectively for what they were and to steer clear of excessive interpretation. He agreed with her thesis that the 99.9 percent precision pointed toward the idea that the locations of these places were purposefully chosen to be on a common axis. However, the archaeological establishment believed that each temple was built independently, based on local religious motivations. He recommended that she refrain from interpreting them as proof of a common megalithic religion across Europe. That could create too much controversy and jeopardize her professional future.

Sitting up in his bed, Professor Zelinger told Sophia, "The alignments are undeniably there. It is a wonderful discovery that has the capacity to change our understanding of the Neolithic world. But it takes time—a very long time—before an established philosophy can change. Now it's too early. You have to be patient. You should know that alignments are toxic in the academic world. To most scholars, they look like hocus-pocus, and it could hurt your career. I understand your excitement, but don't go too far out on a limb. Be very careful of how you present your results. My opinion is that your first paper should only be about your findings for Malta. Don't waste a minute trying to publish something about your alignments at this point. No journal would ever touch such a paper. Anyway, don't be worried about your project. You did a nice piece of work. You'll be fine; you're a great seeker." He looked in her eyes as she sat beside him in the visitor chair.

She understood what Professor Zelinger meant. Mentioning that these alignments were established on purpose would be too controversial. The scholars who had made their names establishing the opposite idea would probably burn her at the stake. *That can't be good a way to start a career. I cannot just come straight out with guns blazing. An aspiring archaeologist, not yet published, telling all these scholars that they have been wrong their entire careers—that won't go over very well,* Sophia told herself.

A couple of weeks later, Professor Zelinger became entangled in a legal dispute over Otzi's ownership with the Italian government. Indeed, a few weeks after Otzi's discovery, the Italian government conducted a survey and established that Otzi's body was found 101 yards inside the Italian border. Italy claimed the body was theirs and wanted it returned, while the Austrian government fought to keep the mummy at Innsbruck University for complete scientific analysis. The mummy was kept in a freezer at the university, untouched until the dispute was resolved.

Because of her unique situation, Sophia had to testify in both Aton's and Otzi's trials that were still ongoing. Between the frequent depositions, her thesis work, and

Erwin's graduation workload, Sophia and Erwin were not able to spare much time to spend together during Erwin's last two months in Innsbruck. She was almost glad not to see him because it was troubling for her heart every time they got together.

In a way, it was easier to communicate with him after he left for Cambridge. They were good pen pals, and Erwin helped Sophia with some statistical analyses for her dissertation.

She was very happy for Erwin that he got a job in that prestigious university. At least he had somewhere to go after graduation. Her job prospects had not changed, and she began making arrangements to move back to the family's farm.

She had put on her coat and grabbed her purse when the telephone rang. To her surprise, Professor Trømso was on the line.

"I called Professor Zelinger, and he gave me your phone number. I hope I am not intruding," said Professor Trømso.

"It's not a problem," Sophia answered. "Is there anything I can do for you, Professor Trømso?"

"Professor Zelinger shared your intriguing discovery with me during our visit at the hospital. I did some research back in Oslo, and I found an archaeological survey that was conducted on Bear Island in the 1960s. No Neolithic remains were identified, but it is possible that the surveyors could have missed possible remains because, at the time, they were more interested in the remains of Bear Island's recent commercial history, including coal mining and whaling. However, you may know that Neolithic remains were found on Svalbard, a larger island about one hundred miles north of Bear Island, as well as Iceland and Greenland, hundreds of miles west of it. So it's conceivable that Neolithic people have visited Bear Island, and we missed the traces of their settlement.

"I think your findings are very interesting because they predict Neolithic remains where nothing has yet been found. I now want to know for sure whether or not there are Neolithic vestiges on Bear Island. Listen, it just so happens that a project was canceled, and I ended up with a surplus of money in my department budget for this coming year. I asked for the funds to be reallocated for a new archaeological survey of Bear Island, and it was approved yesterday. The study is slated to start late this summer.

"I have to tell you that I was impressed by the quality of your work, and you have been highly recommended by Professor Zelinger. I would like to offer you the job of research assistant to conduct that survey for the University of Oslo. There is also an opportunity to pursue a PhD within two years. The offer comes with a full scholarship as well as a stipend for living expenses."

Sophia was stunned and speechless.

"You don't have to give me an answer right away, but I would appreciate knowing your decision within a week or so."

Sophia slowly regained control. "Professor Trømso, this is an honor. I am very interested in the offer."

"Excellent!" Professor Trømso said, clearly pleased. "Our administrator will call you soon to discuss the conditions of employment. There is a congress in Vienna I need to attend next month at about the same time you are presenting your dissertation, if I understood Alexander correctly. Since I'll be in Austria, I'm planning to attend your presentation, if you don't mind."

"Oh yes, please do. I would be honored."

"All right then. If you are still on board after discussing with our administrator, we should have a contract by then."

"Great!"

"Good. We can discuss the details after your defense. I'm looking forward to working with you."

After hanging up the phone, Sophia felt like she was in a dream, dizzy with her sudden change of fortune.

What about that? A field work job offer! And a full scholarship for a PhD. How can you beat that? And what if I find something on Bear Island? That could be what's needed to convince the archaeological community to change their thinking about Neolithic societies. In any case, it would still be a great work experience, and any published report can only help my career.

As she walked the streets of Innsbruck, she pondered the job offer. It was a unique opportunity that she could not refuse. A minute ago, she was imagining herself going back home to the farm, and now she had a dream job for the next two years.

When she picked up her dissertation copies, she was glad she had ordered a few extra copies. She was pleased to know she would be able to give a copy to Professor Trømso. With a box full of copies strapped to her bicycle rack, she went back to the university to distribute her thesis to the jury.

She was excited to share the news with Professor Zelinger. For the past few weeks, he had partially resumed his work at the university. He was using a wheelchair, even though he could now walk with the assistance of crutches. She went to his office, but Professor Zelinger was not there, so she left a copy on his desk and dropped the leftover copies in her office.

As she sat at her desk, she recalled how happy she was when she returned to her office after the business with Aton to find the beautiful Danish stone dagger exactly where she'd left it the day Aton had thrown her out. She had been concerned that it could have been lost or broken. She looked at the masterpiece for an instant and wondered how this dagger ended up in Malta. With melancholy, she finally returned the dagger to the department's collection for safekeeping.

* * *

The next few weeks passed in the blink of an eye. She and Erwin had long discussions on the phone about their respective job prospects. They knew that it was not easy to make a living in either of their academic fields. Both knew they had to take the opportunities they had in front of them, and that meant they would have to go their separate ways.

A few days before her dissertation defense, Erwin called and told her that he would be in Innsbruck to attend her presentation. Sophia was touched by Erwin's announcement, and she was excited to see him again.

Sophia's parents also came to Innsbruck on the morning of her dissertation presentation. It was a four-hour drive, and they arrived in time for lunch. They met in a restaurant a block away from the university, and they talked about Sophia's new job, life at the farm, and family gossip. After lunch, she left her parents with directions to the room where she was going to defend her thesis, while she went to have a last check on her slides in the audio-video room.

Sophia was shocked when, at a quarter to two o'clock, she went to her presentation room and found it jam-packed with a crowd of students. She and Erwin had been the talk of

Innsbruck University when their roles in Aton's arrest became public. The news of her provocative findings had spread through the Humanities departments, and everybody was interested in hearing more about it. People were lined up along the walls, and those who could not find room inside were hanging by the door.

She tried to breathe slowly as she gathered her thoughts while walking purposefully toward the podium. She discreetly waved at her parents, seated on the front row, and opened her notes.

Her presentation went smoothly. She went over the purpose of her research and the methodology of her investigation. She presented her literature analysis and concluded that section by stating, "Overall, my literature search did not reveal any new facts suggesting that Malta had a significant influence on the surrounding populations of late Neolithic Europe from six thousand and four thousand years before present. Malta's architectural, artistic, and pottery styles are unique to the islands and have not been repeated anywhere else in the world. An only possible artistic links could be the similar decorative or religious spirals engraved at both Malta and Newgrange, as well as similar stone cabinets found at both Malta and Brodgar. If religions and cultures are associated with architectural elements, only based on temple construction layout and building techniques it does not seem that Malta's religion ever expanded outside of the boundary of the archipelago, since Malta's temples are unique to these islands.

"However, my research led to the discovery that Malta is part of an alignment that includes the most important Neolithic sites of the time, stretching across the entire western European continent," she announced, projecting the map of Europe with the Malta-Newgrange alignment on the back wall of the room.

She gave the detailed locations of the sites and showed that they were aligned with a 99.9 percent degree of precision. She also presented a golden triangle formed with Ale's Stones. She decided not to mention the possible triangle made with Bear Island, since it was very speculative. In her conclusion, she added, "The alignment from Malta to Newgrange is there, measurable by all, and cannot be ignored. The question is, is this alignment coincidental or intentional?

"We know that there are innumerable Neolithic monuments across Europe. The most common monuments include henges, stone circles, tumuli, and dolmens. These people have aligned sacred places in geometric patterns over large distances, like the Royal Sites in Ireland, which spans eighty miles wide, or the Saint Michael's Ley Line,[57] which stretches over three hundred miles across England. Even after thousands of years of systematic destruction, either for religious motives or for stone quarries, thousands of monuments still stand. Consequently, if one draws a line on a map of the continent of Europe, that line will very likely connect a number of Neolithic monuments. Given the large number of Neolithic sites, the number of possible site alignments is uncountable. Therefore without any additional clues, it is nearly impossible to determine if one specific alignment is coincidental or intentional, especially over large distances.

"However, the alignment we are investigating is not an alignment of random sites but the alignment of the most important sites of Neolithic Europe at a very precise angle from the north/south direction. It is possible to calculate the probability that this alignment occurred randomly.

"Let's start by drawing a line from Malta, going north at an angle of 31.7 degrees from north to south, the smaller angle of the golden triangle we just presented. As discussed earlier, it would not be surprising if several Neolithic sites lie in the path of that line. Considering the multitude of Neolithic monuments in Europe, we can even assume that there are multiple tumuli, henges, stone circles, or dolmens statistically underneath any given line drawn on the map.

"Assuming that at least one thousand relevant tumuli were built during that time period, the probability of a specific tumulus like Newgrange, the largest of all tumuli, to be on this line is one out of a thousand. It's safe to assume that at least ten thousand henges of varying dimensions were built across Europe. Consequently, the probability for any henge on the line of Malta-Newgrange to be Stonehenge is one out of ten thousand. We can also safely assume that at least ten thousand stone circles were built during that time period. The probability of a stone circle found on this line being Stanton Drew is one out of ten thousand.

"Similarly, we can assume that at least ten thousand dolmens were built across Europe during that time period. The probability for a dolmen on the line to be the Chartres dolmen is one out of ten thousand. Therefore, we can calculate that the probability of having all of these world-renowned sites on this line drawn on this map is, at most ..."

Sophia moved to the next slide, showing the equation:

$$1/1,000 \times 1/10,000 \times 1/10,000 \times 1/10,000 = 1/1,000,000,000,000,000 = 1/10^{15}.$$

"One in one thousand trillion, or one in one quadrillion."

Sophia let her words sink in for an instant and then added, "One in one thousand trillion is a very small chance. This seems to indicate that the probability of these specific monuments being aligned randomly is almost zero. There is another way to see the problem. Let's take the twelve top Neolithic European monuments we discussed earlier. Statistically, if one randomly distributes these twelve sites over 1.2 million square miles, approximately three million square kilometers, it is possible to have random alignments of three or four monuments. With these odds, it's possible that some of these random alignments form a geometric figure. However, it is very improbable for these alignments to form a right triangle with golden number proportions just by chance. It defies probabilities. It could only make sense if the sites were intentionally built where they are by people for whom these proportions were significant."

Sophia paused before continuing, taking a deep breath. "It is currently believed that there has never been a megalithic civilization in Neolithic times. Neolithic people were sedentary farmers. Communication of ideas was slow, and cultures spread slowly by migration. The differences in architectural elements between each of these monument types reflect a diversity of rituals and traditions, seemingly developed independently from each other by local populations, each having its own styles and beliefs.

"The current scholarly consensus is that tribes having independent identity and culture populated the European landscape at the time. Different styles of decorated potteries reflect separate and independent traditions, so we established the territories of these independent populations by grouping the different pottery styles together. The spread of religious ideas are assumed to have been slow, moving with population growth and migration, over a poor and disjointed network of communication, with no clear roads between communities.

"As presented before you, the greatest Neolithic sacred places are aligned at 99.9 percent precision level. So what would these alignments mean to the scholarly consensus? Would it mean that we might have to reconsider our vision of the Neolithic man as disparate groups of simple independent farmers? The conception and implementation of such an unbelievably large project would only have been possible if our Neolithic ancestors were far more organized than we currently believe. An intentional alignment of this magnitude could only have been possible if there was a very powerful elite, capable of conceiving such a plan and mobilizing the enormous resources necessary to implement it. Recognition of this alignment's intention would imply that Neolithic man, using only rocks, sticks, and basic tools, had a surprisingly sophisticated understanding of his geographical environment. It would suggest that they used record-keeping systems to preserve and share information over hundreds of generations. Also, there may have been use of portable timepieces for location measurements."

Sophia paused and exhaled slowly. She had said her piece and was nearly done. "In conclusion, I leave it to you, respected members of the jury and all my peers, to answer these questions for yourselves: What does the recognition these alignments mean for our understanding of the late Neolithic societies? Could the placement and alignment of these monumental sanctuaries over such vast distances be due not to randomness but human design? Could these alignments be the testament of a lost, forgotten civilization, covering all Occidental Europe for more than 1,500 years, at the end of the Neolithic Age?"

As she thanked the jury, the student-packed room erupted in applause. It wasn't common to have such commotion for an archaeological thesis presentation. The reaction from her jury was far more tempered.

"Miss Bruckner," said Professor Doppler, a jury member from the University of Salzburg, "we know that Neolithic man purposely aligned sacred places, like the Royal Sites or the Saint Michael Ley Line. The alignments you described at the end of your presentation are thousands of miles long and would require knowledge and technology that seem out of reach of Neolithic societies. Miss Bruckner, how would you explain the accumulation and transmission of the enormous amount of knowledge necessary to plot such figures across these immense distances without any known written records?"

"Professor Doppler, thank you very much for asking this question," answered Sophia. "I asked myself that same question. We have examples of societies, like the Inca Empire, which reached an extreme level of sophistication in astronomy, engineering, and empire organization without any known written language. The Inca Empire had a complex network of messenger pathways that connected all of its towns and villages, informing its central administration of the state of each province, as well as communicating the emperor's commands. We also know that the Inca Empire kept records of everything by using khipus. As you know, khipus are made of llama or cotton cords attached around a central ring and were colored to signify their purpose, such as tax obligations, property histories, census records, calendar information, military organization, and so forth. It is possible that the Neolithic man possessed a similar information storage system that allowed society to store large amounts of information."

"So how do you explain that none of these devices has ever been found?" asked Professor Doppler.

"I thought of several possible reasons. The first one would be that organic fibers disintegrate within a few hundred years under natural conditions in European climate. It is unlikely that they would have resisted the thousands of years separating us from the Neolithic Age. Consequently, it's not because we have not yet found such prewriting information storage devices that they might not have been in use during these times."

"I agree that Neolithic devices would have most likely disintegrated over the past five thousand years. But would the knowledge of these peoples have been transmitted to the Bronze Age societies and have continued to be in use for the following centuries?" asked Professor Doppler.

"Not necessarily, Professor Doppler. As you know, the end of the European Neolithic Age is marked with many important social changes. Starting from around 5200 BCE in southeastern Europe to 2800 BCE in central and northern Europe, long-occupied sites were abandoned, while other sites became strongly fortified; communal burial disappeared and new burial practices were introduced; rituals associated with female figurines ended; and the old decorated potteries were replaced by plainer ones. Analysis of grave goods indicates the appearance of a more organized hierarchal society—sites with central authority. These changes have been attributed to invasions of eastern populations who wiped out these first European farmers.[58] Based on population genetic studies, the last descendants of the ancient European farmers are found in Sardinia and the Basque regions.

"We know from history that these types of invasions can create tremendous devastation to civilizations. Let's take the northern invasions that destroyed the Roman Empire and brought Europe into the Dark Ages for a millennium. Or the conquistadors who brought down the Mesoamerican civilizations and almost erased their past and history. To come back to the example of the khipus used earlier, the Inca elites who could write and read khipus were exterminated by the conquistadors and their khipu libraries burned to the ground. In a few years, the records of thousands of years of knowledge and history vanished in flames. The Inca knowledge was lost and the few khipus that survived to our day are impossible to decrypt.

"In a way, it's like what could happen if we were to lose electricity, and all the information that we are storing in our computers suddenly disappeared. Whole slices of personal and collective history would completely disappear forever."

After a few more well-answered questions, the jury complimented Sophia for the quality of her work and wished her good luck in her career.

It took almost twenty minutes for the room to empty. Colleagues and complete strangers approached Sophia to both congratulate her and ask her questions about follow-up studies. Finally, she was able to attend the customary reception in the department office. There, Sophia introduced Erwin to her parents. From Sophia they knew about Erwin's role in the arrest of Aton, and they thanked him profusely for his help. She also introduced her parents to Professor Trømso, and they all discussed life in Oslo, the beauties of Denmark, and the opportunities for archaeologists in that country. Shortly thereafter, Sophia's parents left because they did not want to drive back to Linz too late in the evening.

To celebrate, Erwin and Sophia met at their usual haunt, the Branger Brau restaurant. During the meal, Erwin congratulated her on her dissertation defense; he was happy for her. "Sophia, what are the chances that somebody like you, a humble student at Innsbruck, could find something that could potentially transform the worldwide accepted vision of the Neolithic peoples?" he asked her.

"I don't know. I think it's over my head."

"Don't you think you were the chosen one?"

"The chosen one?"

"Yes, you know—the chosen one. How do you explain that out of six billion people, you are the first one to have found these alignments? They have been in plain sight for centuries, and nobody saw it."

"You are crazy. Maybe no one has seen it earlier because distances on most maps are distorted from south to north. You know, like the North Pole having the same length as the equator. So these alignments can't be plotted appropriately on regular maps. Satellite imagery gives us a more accurate visualization of their layouts. It was just a random discovery. It was just a matter of time before somebody discovered it."

"Maybe it was your destiny to find them."

"I was just lucky. People win the lottery all the time. It's random. It's not because it was their destiny."

"I'm not sure about that. You still have to buy a ticket, and even after that, many other things can happen with the tickets. Anyway Sophia, I think it was more than luck." With an enigmatic smile, Erwin added, "I'm surprised that a person of faith like you does not take this as a personal revelation."

"Revelation?"

"Yes, revelation! It was given to you to discover an ancient secret hidden in plain view. I hope that somehow it will change the world."

"A small academic world, maybe," she said with a laugh. "I'm not sure the real world cares much about old stones."

"Sophia, the alignments are there; it is indisputable. Thanks to you, now we will never be able to look at a map of

Europe without also seeing your triangles. I'm telling you, Sophia—you already changed something in our world. You cracked the code with the golden number, and now you are the golden girl. Cheers!" Erwin said, raising his glass.

They toasted to her success and smiled at each other. After a pause, Erwin renewed the conversation. "Anyway, your discovery makes me more optimistic for the future."

"How so?" asked Sophia.

"Do you remember when you pictured yourself as being in the Newgrange chamber, low down to the ground, looking to that tiny section of sky through the entrance corridor?"

"Yes. I still dream about it. Why?"

"I've been dreaming about it too. I was thinking of looking through this small opening, facing all these sacred places. In a way, it would be like looking through the eyes of God, looking at all religions at once. It seems to me that by aligning their holiest places under one axis, these people showed that all their different expressions of worship were united in a singular higher entity or supreme order, overarching them all, demonstrated by the axis."

"I know. It seems irrefutable that Neolithic societies must have been more sophisticated than we thought. To organize such a project over millions of square miles is unprecedented. It's still mind boggling," commented Sophia. "It is amazing that so many different peoples, with so many different ways of worshipping, coexisted and cohabited so peacefully for so long."

"And that's my point," Erwin said. "Who knows? By this new awareness, the faith of these people may resurge from these old stones. I'm afraid that we may need it soon. Maybe knowing it once happened, humanity could be more inclined to accept it could happen again. In the end, all religions believe in a God who created earth. On this earth, it means that all religions must be worshipping the same creator, whatever name, shape, or form was revealed to us in different times and regions of the world. We can all live together. Anyone with true faith knows this and practices tolerance."

"And how do you see that happening?"

"I guess I have faith in faith. At its rate of growth, humanity is going to soon face enormous and unprecedented challenges. From overpopulation, exhaustion of natural resources, and so on, humanity needs to quickly find a common purpose to unite the necessary forces to change the course of its destiny. Don't you think it would be great if the leaders of all religions on earth decided to build aligned sanctuaries to symbolize their commitment to coexistence, respect, and acceptation of all religious differences and furthermore condemn all wars waged in the name of their religion?"

"And you think that would change something?" Sophia asked.

"It could. At the rate we are destroying the planet, we are going to a point where only humanity, acting as a whole, will be able to change the trajectory of our planet's ultimate demise. It's going to become very apparent that the survival of the human species is a short-term problem, and it concerns the future of our children. I hope our religious leaders will take humanity on a cooperative path, looking for common grounds, and stop religious-based oppression."

"I hope your dream comes true."

"Anyway, at the end it's all about faith. It seems that what humanity needs the most is a common faith, rather than a new religion. Simply, a new faith could emerge from the true faith already ingrained in all religions, starting with commands such as 'treat your neighbor as thy brother.'"

"You are crazy," Sophia interjected with a half smile.

"I don't think so. Look—scientific advancements have given man great tools to comprehend our situation and design plans to correct it. With the recent progress in telephone technology, fax, cable, and telecommunication satellites, people are now connected to each other everywhere in the world like never before. Ideas can be exchanged and shared in a snap. The French philosopher Teilhard de Chardin[59] offered the hypothesis that through this new sphere of communication, humanity as a whole will get together and earth's consciousness, earth's soul, will awaken. I hope he's right. After all, we just need a common goal, a common faith. Who knows what can happen? I hope that reason will prevail and a new humanity will find a way out of the death spiral of consumption-driven societies."

"I see. Nothing is simple with you," she said, smiling. "I am glad to hear you're an optimist."

"You are right," responded Erwin, returning her smile. "I'm sorry if my optimism always has hints of doom and gloom."

"That's fine," she added with a laugh. "You have some interesting ideas, but I don't have to agree with everything you say. Sometimes you are out there, you know?"

"Yeah! Just like you and your triangles ... Anyway, I apologize. We're here to celebrate your success. So once again, congratulations. You made it."

"Thanks," answered Sophia. "Soon I will be on Bear Island. I can't wait. I'm so excited."

"I'm so glad for you. I hope you will find conclusive evidence."

"We will see. You know, one of the things that impressed me the most in that story is that these people went all the way to Iceland in canoes. Paddling for hundreds of miles, heading west in the frigid waters of the North Sea. It's crazy. I can't imagine the guts it takes to paddle so far away from the coast, going straight ahead in this endlessly empty ocean, braving storms and elements. I cannot imagine the strength of their motivation."

"I agree. These people had a lot of courage," Erwin commented. "Luckily, I hope you're not going to paddle all the way to Bear Island. By the way, the season on the island is still planned for July the third, I think."

"Yes, that's the plan. I'm very excited to go to Oslo and start the preparation," Sophia said enthusiastically.

"Good! Look—I have a gift for you!" Erwin took a wrapped box from under the table and gave it to Sophia, who happily unwrapped it.

In the box was a fur hat. Sophia was a little surprised but pleased by the gift. "Thank you, Erwin. It's lovely. I'm sure I can use something like this next winter."

"Actually, it's not for next winter but for this summer."

"This summer?"

"Yes, this summer. I read that the highest summer temperature on Bear Island is seventeen degrees Fahrenheit. I thought you might need a fur hat to be comfortable while you explore Bear Island. And by the way, I bought one for myself as well."

"You did? Why?"

"I was thinking about volunteering my summer vacation with the archaeological department at the University of Oslo and offer my help with the survey of Bear Island. What do you think?"

Sophia was overwhelmed. She did not know what to say. She had wanted so much to be closer to Erwin. She knew that he could be trying at times with all his craziness, but he also could be a lot of fun. In her heart, she was ready to try.

"What makes you think you are qualified to search for Neolithic remains?" asked Sophia, beaming.

EPILOGUE

The alignments of Neolithic monuments described in this story are real. They can easily be recreated referencing computer software such as Wikipedia and GoogleEarth. If the locations of these monuments were purposely selected to mark geometric patterns across Europe, these gigantic figures are an enormous feat of engineering and they can be viewed as monuments unto themselves. The triangle formed by drawing lines from Newgrange to Ggantija to Ale's Stones could potentially be the largest monument humanity has ever built.

And if deliberately constructed, it is a complete mystery as to why and how "primitive" peoples were able to build these gigantic figures. When visiting these places, it is truly awe-inspiring to see demonstrated the strength of these people's faith that literally made them move mountains. In the novel, the kingdom people had intellect and technological means to realize such an accomplishment. However, Prehistoric Man had a much deeper connection with nature than we currently experience in our industrialized societies and in their world, they may have had other means now difficult to conceive. Since no traces remain to explain their aims and methods to construct these monuments, like the title of the novel, these may truly be *lost secrets*.

ENDNOTES

[1] Ggantija temple on Gozo Island, Malta. For more information start with (FMISW) https://en.wikipedia.org/wiki/Ġgantija, location 36°02′50″N 14°16′09″E.

[2] Confirmed by Eric Powel, "The Temple Builders of Malta," *Archaeology,* vol. 69-6, Nov/Dec 2016.

[3] Stonehenge, England. FMISW https://en.wikipedia.org/wiki/Stonehenge, location 51°10′43.84″N 1°49′34.28″W.

[4] Brodgar, Scotland. FMISW https://en.wikipedia.org/wiki/Ring_of_Brodgar, location 59.0020°N 3.2287°W.

[5] Newgrange, Ireland. FMISW https://en.wikipedia.org/wiki/Newgrange location 53°41′39.73″N 6°28′30.11″W.

[6] Ötzi the Iceman is the most well-known mummy of these ages. As an author liberty, I placed a broken arrow shaft, as in reality, only the head of the lethal arrow was embedded in the left shoulder, found later by x-ray analysis. FMISW https://en.wikipedia.org/wiki/Ötzi, discovery location 46°46′45.8″N 10°50′25.1″E.

[7] All names of places in Tesimo's journey have the names they currently have to ease cross-reference with Wikipedia and Google Earth.

[8] Baden, Austria. FMISW https://en.wikipedia.org/wiki/Baden_culture.

[9] Yamna culture, FMISW https://en.wikipedia.org/wiki/Yamna_culture; Tom Higham, "Genes, Journeys and the Dangers of Vodka," *Current World Archaeology*, 72:14–15, Sep 2015.

[10] Krpy, Czech Republic. FMISW https://en.wikipedia.org/wiki/Neolithic_circular_enclosures_in_Central_Europe.

[11] Sarup, Denmark. FMISW Sarup Causewayed enclosures placed in a Neolithic ritual landscape on Funen, Denmark, Niels H. Andersen, Journal of Nordic Archaeological Science 14, pp. 11–17 (2004), http://www.archaeology.su.se/polopoly_fs/1.138763.1371479131!/menu/standard/file/Niels%20H.%20Andersen.pdf.

[12] Pierre Pétrequin et al., Neolithic Alpine Axeheads, From the Continent to Great Britain, The Isle of Man and Ireland, Analecta Praehistorica Leidensia 40, 261–279, 2008.

[13] Olkam, Austria, FMISW https://en.wikipedia.org/wiki/Neolithic_circular_enclosures_in_Central_Europe.

[14] Chartres Cathedral, France. FMISW https://en.wikipedia.org/wiki/Chartres_Cathedral, location 48° 26′ 50″ N, 1° 29′ 16″ E.

[15] Louis Charpentier, Les Mysteres de la Cathedrale de Chartres, Robert Laffont, 1966.

[16] Carnutes, France. FMISW https://en.wikipedia.org/wiki/Carnutes.

[17] Black virgins were: as I was finishing editing this book, it came to my attention that a desecration had been committed in Chartres. Apparently some well-intentioned religious authorities and government bureaucrats have decided to spend $18.5 million renovating Chartres Cathedrals planned to be completed in 2017. They decided to repaint the cathedral interior with light colors, including pilasters of faux marble. Looking at the stained glass windows is now like watching a movie with the theater's lights on. In their ignorant zeal, the renovators accomplished the worst, repainting the enshrined black virgin with flesh colors. http://www.nybooks.com/daily/2014/12/14/scandalous-makeover-chartres/

[18] Hamoukar, Syria. FMISW https://en.wikipedia.org/wiki/Hamoukar.

[19] Neolithic Massacres, FMISW http://news.sciencemag.org/archaeology/2015/08/archaeologists-uncover-neolithic-massacre-early-europe, Aug 17, 2015.

[20] Rondels, roughly 49th to 47th centuries BC, 1,600 years before this story. Nobody knows about the beliefs and funeral rites of these people. FMISW https://en.wikipedia.org/wiki/Neolithic_circular_enclosures_in_Central_Europe.

[21] There seems to have been a time when man counted in twelves, and that system left a deep impression in human consciousness so that

most languages have twelve distinct and unique names for the twelve first numbers. I am proposing that this could be coming from the fact that there are only twelve lunar months in a year (+ 11 days). Counting dozens with the five fingers of one hand could explain why the twelve-number system is always associated with a 60-base accounting system.

[22] It would make sense that the weeks were established in relationship with length of moons.

[23] 12x5=60 full hand.

[24] Lengyel culture, FMISW http://www.anthropark.wz.cz/mmk.htm.

[25] To learn more about lactose intolerance in the Neolithic Age, see Andrew Curry, "The milk revolution," *Nature* 500, 20–22 (01 August 2013) or http://www.nature.com/news/archaeology-the-milk-revolution-1.13471.

[26] "Europe has very few sources of tin. It was therefore of extreme importance throughout ancient times to import it long distances from known tin mining districts of antiquity, namely Erzgebirge [also called Ore Mountain] along the modern border between Germany and Czech Republic, the Iberian Peninsula, Brittany in modern France, and Devon and Cornwall in southwestern Britain (Benvenuti et al. 2003, p. 56; Valera & Valera 2003, p. 11)" https://en.wikipedia.org/wiki/Tin_sources_and_trade_in_ancient_time s.

[27] Goseck, Germany. FMISW https://en.wikipedia.org/wiki/Goseck_circle.

[28] The Sacred Landscape of Ancient Ireland, Ronald Hicks, *Archaeology* Magazine, May/June 2011, 64(3), pp 40–45.

[29] Great Dolmen of Dwasieden, Germany. FMISW https://en.wikipedia.org/wiki/Great_Dolmen_of_Dwasieden.

[30] Ale's Stones, Sweden. FMISW https://en.wikipedia.org/wiki/Ale%27s_Stones, 55° 22′ 51″ N, 14° 3′ 28″E.

[31] It would make sense.

[32] Sunstone is a plagioclase feldspar, which when viewed from certain directions exhibits a brilliant spangled appearance; this led to its use by the Vikings to locate the sun for navigational purposes. It has been found in southern Norway, Sweden, and in various United States localities. https://en.wikipedia.org/wiki/Sunstone_(medieval).

[33] Skara Brae, Orkney Island, Scotland. FMISW https://en.wikipedia.org/wiki/Skara_Brae.

[34] Towie stones, beautiful specimens were found at Orkney Island, Scotland. FMISW https://en.wikipedia.org/wiki/Carved_Stone_Balls.
[35] Ring of Brodgar, Orkney Island, Scotland. FMISW with https://en.wikipedia.org/wiki/Ring_of_Brodgar.
[36] Ness of Brodgar, Orkney Island, Scotland .FMISW https://en.wikipedia.org/wiki/Ness_of_Brodgar.
[37] Standing Stones of Stenness, Orkney Island, Scotland. FMISW https://en.wikipedia.org/wiki/Standing_Stones_of_Stenness.
[38] Carnac, France. FMISW https://en.wikipedia.org/wiki/Carnac, location 47°35′05″N 3°04′46″W.
[39] Avebury, England. FMISW https://en.wikipedia.org/wiki/Avebury.
[40] Stanton Drew Circles, England. FMISW https://en.wikipedia.org/wiki/Stanton_Drew_stone_circles.
[41] A Swedish Stonehenge? Stone Age Tomb May Predate English Site, Tia Ghose, http://www.livescience.com/24157-ancient-tomb-ales-swedish-stonehenge.html.
[42] Knowlton Circles, England. FMISW https://en.wikipedia.org/wiki/Knowlton_Circles.
[43] Thornborough Henges, England. FMISW https://en.wikipedia.org/wiki/Thornborough_Henges.
[44] Vallée des Merveilles, France. FMISW https://en.wikipedia.org/wiki/Vallée_des_merveilles, location 44 4′ 34″ N, 7°26′18″ E.
[45] Isle of Man, England. FMISW https://en.wikipedia.org/wiki/Isle_of_Man.
[46] Cursus monuments are now understood to be Neolithic structures and represent some of the oldest prehistoric monumental structures of the British Isles. Relics found within them show that they were built between 3400 and 3000 BC. FMISW https://en.wikipedia.org/wiki/Cursus.
[47] Carnac was a very important spiritual center of these times. Near Carnac stands Gavrinis, a large tumulus similar to that of Newgrange, smaller in size, but with some of the most beautiful examples of Neolithic stone engraving, similar to those of Newgrange. FMISW https://en.wikipedia.org/wiki/Gavrinis, Very closely also stand the large stone circles of Er Lannic FMISW http://www.ancient-wisdom.com/franceerlannic.htm.
[48] Rupert Sheldrake, NEW SCIENCE OF LIFE: Hypothesis of Formative Causation, 1981.

[49] Silbury Hill, England. FMISW
https://en.wikipedia.org/wiki/Silbury_Hill.
[50] Durrington Walls, England. FMISW
https://en.wikipedia.org/wiki/Durrington_Walls.
[51] Karnag is the ancient Breton name of Carnac. For the flow of the Tesimo's story, I placed Carnac north of Chartres when in fact it is west of it. Carnac stones alignments are really directed toward Chartres.
[52] Ancient name of Marseille, France. FMISW
https://en.wikipedia.org/wiki/Marseille.
[53] Courthézon, 4650 BC: Oldest Neolithic village in France, Courthézon in the Vaucluse,
https://en.wikipedia.org/wiki/Prehistory_of_France.
[54] Bear Island, Norway. FMISW
https://en.wikipedia.org/wiki/Bear_Island_(Norway).
[55] Filitosa, Corsica Island, France. FMISW
https://en.wikipedia.org/wiki/Filitosa.
[56] Xagħra Stone Circle, Gozo Island, Malta. FMISW
https://en.wikipedia.org/wiki/Xagħra_Stone_Circle.
[57] Saint Michael Ley Line, England. FMISW http://www.ancient-wisdom.com/stmichael.htm.
[58] FMISW Neolithic section of
https://en.wikipedia.org/wiki/Prehistoric_Europe.
[59] Pierre Teilhard de Chardin, French idealist philosopher. FMISW
https://en.wikipedia.org/wiki/Pierre_Teilhard_de_Chardin.

Made in the USA
San Bernardino, CA
22 February 2019